£1·50

AMNESIA-SCOPE

By the same author

Arc d'X
Days Between Stations
Rubicon Beach

STEVE ERICKSON

AMNESIA-SCOPE

Quartet Books

q

First published in Great Britain by
Quartet Books Limited in 1997
A member of the Namara Group
27 Goodge Street
London W1P 2LD

First published in the United States
of America by Henry Holt and
Company, Inc., in 1996

A catalogue record for this book is
available from the British Library

ISBN 0 7043 8053 6

Printed and bound in Finland by WSOY

Trivial or impure dreaming literally
rots the fabric of the future

Lawrence Durrell

I wish I never wanted then
what I want now twice as much

Mott the Hoople

AMNESIA-

I'm moving up to the suite at the front of the hotel. Ever since the Quake I've been living in one of the single units, but now I'm making the move up to the suite. Abdul the manager is giving me a deal, sort of hush-hush between us, assuming his bosses don't fire him first and scotch the whole thing. The other day I heard the landlord chewing him out, as he surveyed Abdul's grand plans for upgrading the building. "You're throwing away money, it makes me sick!" I was standing at the top of the stairs, on the third floor, and I could hear the argument down on the first, and I thought, Well, there goes my suite. They're going to fire Abdul.

They're all Palestinian terrorists, the guys who own this building, but Abdul is a *smooth* Palestinian terrorist. He imagines himself a worldly man, and for all I know he is. He reads books. He's dapper. He harasses the female tenants but he thinks he does it so smoothly no one notices it's harassment, dropping by in the morning in his bathrobe with his cup of coffee in one hand and his cigarette in the other, complaining back at them that they complain too much. He finds their complaints—about the cracks in the walls, the plumbing that gushes through the ceiling—petulant and unreasonable, but it isn't that he says he won't do anything about them, he's too smooth for that. Rather he says he'll take care of it and then gets around to it when he damned well feels like—weeks later, months, never. . . . He makes the rest of the world feel as though it's mired in the impatience and pettiness that he has transcended through a disciplined self-education, faith in Allah, and sheer dapperness.

He saw a picture of me in a magazine, I guess, some review or another of my last book. It impressed him. The fact that it was years ago and a lousy review to boot couldn't mean less to him. He doesn't want me dissatisfied, he wants to keep me happy; he considers me a prestige item, as tenants go. He lets his bosses know I had a picture in a magazine once and now they call me to write résumés for them, business proposals, in terrorist code no doubt because I've seen, in Abdul's closet, the portraits of various Middle Eastern dictators and strongmen he keeps hidden. "There you are," he said triumphantly, when we signed the lease on the suite, "you now have a contract signed by a Palestinian." Well, he's cut me a deal, which is the only way I can afford it, and I waited until I got all moved in before I thought I should let him know I'm not likely to be getting my picture in any more magazines. I let him know his investment in my "fame" maybe wasn't the smoothest move he ever made. He wouldn't hear of it. The smirk on his face in response said, I'm a smooth Palestinian of the world. You can't terrify a terrorist.

Station 3 on the radio. So far to the far end of the dial it's barely on the radio at all. Broadcast from somewhere in the desert, way beyond the farthest backfires. . . .

Station 3 only comes in at a certain time of the evening, and when it does it collides with another signal, a channel in Algiers that's broadcasting to an asteroid hurtling out beyond the moon. The Algerian station is owned by a Moroccan religious sect that believes the asteroid is heading straight for earth and carrying with it a message from God, so the station is sending a message back, only to have it bounce off the asteroid and land here in L.A.—if I understand it right. And mixing with *that* signal is yet another that was originally broadcast in 1951, from just outside of Las Vegas when they first started testing nuclear bombs; that broadcast was vaporized by the explosion and apparently only now, fifty years later, has reassembled itself in the stratosphere. So jajouka music from northern Africa floats through Station 3 along with the death-rock anthems of young metallurgic huns from the inner valleys, and Max Steiner conducting the theme of *Now, Voyager*, all as dreamlike and beautiful as the twilight, which turns a very particular shade of blue outside my windows.

I live in an old art deco hotel on Jacob Hamblin Road, a small concrete avenue that winds and twists so much on its short two-block journey from Sunset to Santa Monica Boulevard that at the beginning you can't see the end. Even in L.A., city of great non-sequitur streets like National Boulevard and San Vicente, streets of absolutely no linear logic whatsoever that disappear on one side of the city only to suddenly reappear on the other, Jacob Hamblin Road has some crazy turns in its short life. Back in the

Thirties the Hotel Hamblin was built by the studios to put up young studs and starlets shipped in from all over America for screen tests, which is to say it became a sort of private brothel for producers and casting agents; Abdul's apartment on the ground floor was the lobby, marble and spacious. Now, along with the telephonic punctuation of in- and outgoing communiqués to and from the hotel's single women, the rooms and nights groan with the sounds of vicious homosexual exchanges. In the mornings I wake to someone somewhere in the building crying out "I'm tired of this life!" with so much force it's hard to believe he's really dying, but so much anguish it's harder to believe he's kidding.

Over the years the hotel has succumbed from its earlier, slightly debauched elegance to Caligari dilapidation. Plaster buckles around archways carved in lightning-bolt zigzags, and a coat of white paint covers doors originally patterned after the portals of Austrian chalets. A gloom has overtaken the Hamblin's dark halls, where images of huge water lilies wave in shades of brown. In front of the hotel, hovering right above Jean Harlow's name scrawled in the sidewalk, is L.A.'s last remaining fire escape, something I took note of not long ago when one of the city's backfires jumped its demarcation line and threatened to slip south of Sunset. My new suite is on the top floor in the southwest corner of the building, with eight huge windows that run to the ceiling, facing every direction but north. At one place in the apartment I can see east, west and south all at the same time. The mists of Santa Monica fill the third window, the first and second contain the looming Hollywood Hills, near the base of which the Hamblin stands; along the upper ridge of the hills tiny barren palms sway in silhouette, and the Strip is visible below them, with the passing figures of amazon Japanese waitresses drifting in and out of the sushi bars. A clandestine helicopter lands at four o'clock every morning on top of the towering silver-and-glass old St. James Club, at which time the tower's lights go out. . . .

In windows number four, five and six is the constant glint of the backfires. In windows seven and eight is the rain of their ash.

I love the ashes. I love the endless smoky twilight of Los Angeles. I love walking along Sunset Boulevard past the bistros where the Hollywood trash have to brush the black soot off their salmon linguini in white wine sauce before they can eat it. I love driving across one black ring after another all the way to the sea, through the charred palisades past abandoned houses, listening through the open windows to the phone machines clicking on and off with messages from somewhere east of the Mojave, out of the American blue. I've been in a state of giddiness ever since the riots of ten years ago, when I would take a break from finishing my last book and go up onto the rooftop, watching surround me the first ring of fire from the looting. I still go up there, and the fires still burn. They burn a dead swath between me and my memories. They burn a swath between me and the future, stranding me in the present, reducing definitions of love to my continuing gaze across the smoldering panorama as Viv, my little carnal ferret, devours me on her knees. I love having nothing to hope for but the cremation of my dreams; when my dreams are dead the rest of me is alive, all cinder and appetite. Don't expect me to feel bad about this. Don't expect my social conscience to be stricken. My conscience may be touched by my personal betrayals but not my social ones: the fires burn swathes between me and guilt as well. In this particular epoch, when sex is the last subversive act, I'm a guerrilla, spending my conscience in a white stream that douses no fires but its own.

Halfway through Sahara's routine, Viv cooks up the kidnap plan. She maps it out for me on the cocktail napkin under my shot glass of Cuervo Gold, a tangle of lines and arrows that bleed into the tequila smudges. She explains it in the din of the music: "Now we'll grab her here," pointing at the napkin, "you throw her in the back seat—" Sahara has dropped her dress at the end of the second part of her act; true to form, once the third song begins she emerges naked from behind the curtain. The third song is the naked part, every dancer, every act. It's clear right away that Sahara's mystique doesn't lie in her body. It's good enough as a body but it's not out of the ordinary: it's Sahara's face I love, and Viv too. Neither of us can get over it. She's some mysterious blend of Persia and Icelandic, perfect and remote; her face says, If you are seduced by me, it's your choice. I don't care. The other people in the Cathode Flower, all men except Viv and the dancers, have no idea what to make of Sahara, that's obvious. But Viv wants her as much as I do, maybe more. . . .

"The last time we did this—" I start to say.

"This isn't going to be like the last time," Viv shouts, over the music.

"I'm not throwing anybody in the back seat," I explain. "I'm not good at that part. Besides, I'm driving."

Viv looks at me in total exasperation. She's five foot two, a hundred and six pounds; tonight she's wearing a little white dress with nothing under it but a white garter belt that holds up her white stockings. She's a wicked little angel, and suddenly I can't help myself. I pull her up from the table and into the back of the club, around the corner into the hallway where the bathrooms are, and I pull up her dress. She opens my pants and puts me inside her. Fucking her against the wall I can see Sahara in her eyes like they're little mirrors; she has a perfectly good view of her. Oh ooh, she says, those little sounds she makes when she's not sure whether it feels good or hurts her, a confusion she finds particularly exciting. I stop when I know I'm going to come because I hold back until the evening's over, our little agreement. "The plan!" she suddenly shouts, having left it on the table with our tequila, so we beat it back to our seats. Viv watches the rest of Sahara's act transfixed.

Now all we can do is wait. Sahara won't come out into the club for fifteen or twenty minutes, doing whatever the girls do backstage after they're done. When she finally appears she glides along the back wall. She sits with the other girls in one of the booths, and Viv goes over to ask if she wants to have a drink. Viv is a lot less shy about it than I am and, since she's a woman, less threatening; the dancers always talk to her and usually after a while they come to our table. Sahara strikes me as less approachable, but after she and Viv exchange a few words she joins us, shaking my hand perfunctorily and then the rest of the time talking to Viv.

She orders a Kahlúa. In the music I can't hear a thing either of them says to each other, which is exactly the way I like it. Neither of them particularly wants me in the conversation anyway, which is also the way I like it; I just sit and check out the other dancers and drink my tequila and wait for Viv to fill me in later. From what I can tell in the dark Sahara isn't the wildly animated type, as passively remote as she appears on stage, hiding the same secret damage all of these women hide. But Viv is undaunted. She has that kind of personality people instinctively trust, and as far as I know that includes Sahara. I just want to run my wet finger around the contour of Sahara's mouth like I would around the rim of a wine glass trying to make a sound. For a moment I look away, and turn back to the two of them in time to see Viv lowering the top of her dress, and Sahara placing that mouth on her nipple. . . .

Outside the club the night sky is red from the backfires. "I didn't know they were burning tonight," I mumble half drunkenly in the car, behind the wheel. Viv is in the back seat like always and says something about how it was scheduled for next week, but the long-range forecast was for high winds so they moved it up. From what I can tell it's either the second ring or third, starting at Beverly Hills to the west and circling around to Silverlake in the east, which means we're pretty much confined to Hollywood unless one of the Black Passages is open on Sunset. Sahara has told Viv she gets off at one-thirty and we're waiting in back of the Cathode Flower for her to show, assuming she does, which would make the abduction unnecessary; I don't know that I'm really up to tossing strippers in the trunk tonight. For a while Viv is content to listen to the sky glow. "Maybe we should go watch the fire," she murmurs dreamily.

It becomes obvious Sahara has stood us up. I circle the car around to the front of the club and the sign is off, the lights are off; and so we just start cruising east on the Strip, me behind the wheel and Viv in the back seat where she always rides. A block from the Cathode Flower below the Chateau Marmont, at the corner of Jacob Hamblin Road are the hookers sitting on the low white wall that runs along the parking lot on the north side and hanging out on the south side around the bus stop in front of the deserted sushi palace. We head toward Hollywood until we can see the faint red shine of the eastern backfire, and then turn around and go back.

All the little clubs and bars along Sunset are just about to close when who do we see stumble out of one of them, shaking herself loose of some guy in the process, but Sahara! I pull over and both Viv and I hop out of the car and grab her. It's hard to know with Sahara whether she's just a little blotto or so remote that nothing registers very quickly, but either way she looks at us with more confusion than concern. In the back seat the only thing she says is, They're burning tonight; and then she slips into unconsciousness, right in Viv's arms. Viv whispers sweet nothings to her, trying to get her attention as I head west past the hookers, past the now dark Cathode Flower, down the Strip out the other end into the woods of Beverly Hills. I can distinctly see the flames of what must be the second ring, and sure enough we hit it around Benedict Canyon where the old resort used to be. The Black Passage is open so I drive on through, walls of fire lining our way. The heat of the flames revives Sahara somewhat; she stares at them in a daze. In the rearview mirror of my car I can see both her face and Viv's, the bright red firelight flashing across their eyes, Sahara's dull and Viv's alive with anticipation. Viv's got that slightly crazy look like she wouldn't particularly mind if I turned the car the fire's direction and just headed right into it.

With the fire at our back everything feels open to us, everything is possible.... Crossing into the Mulholland Time Zone from Zed Time I reset the clock of the car ahead eight minutes. On the radio I can still get the tail-end of Station 3's broadcast, a ghostly Indonesian voice drifting into the car. Sahara, who Viv has now undressed, is in a stupor—alabaster embodiment of all possibilities—and I'm inspired to turn off Sunset and head south past Black Clock Park through the rafters of the old freeway that used to run down the spine of California, from the age-blasted Spanish missions of the north to the Mexican border. As we drive, the frontiers of the west side are dark. In the rearview mirror Sahara's head lies against the back seat, her eyes half closed, staring at the roof of the car while Viv sucks her breast.

Viv's still at it by the time I hit Century Boulevard and the dark abandoned LAX. I steer the car off the boulevard and through a hole in one of the terminals where the sliding glass doors used to be. I drive through the black gutted airline terminal past the darkened ticket counters and dead metal detectors, along the hallways where passengers used to stream back and forth to and from their flights, and every once in a while the high beam on my headlights slashes across the darting figure of someone who lives here. Sahara surfaces just long enough to regard her breast in Viv's mouth and then pass out again. Over by the arrival gates I see small fires burning and a line of naked women parading up and down the empty motionless baggage carousels. Drive out through the gate toward the runway and I'm following the runway to the ocean where the planes used to fly out over the beach when, in the quiet of the night, under the smoky moon with the fading flare of the backfire to the northeast of me, I hear the sound of both women asleep.

At the end of the runway there's nothing to do but stop the car awhile, unless I want to drive into the sea. I roll down the window and listen to the waves. I push back my seat and forget about the two naked women behind me, watching and listening to the ocean, until Sahara comes to. What is this? she slurs, less fazed by her nakedness than sitting out on the end of an airplane runway with the ocean in front of her. The look on her face says she hasn't the faintest idea how she got here or who I am. Nothing quite registers until she inspects Viv more closely, whose own nakedness throws her until she gets a better look at Viv's face. Let me out of here, she demands, so I get out of the car and go around to the passenger side and open the door for her; she staggers nude onto the runway under the ashen moon. I get back in the car and watch the ocean some more while Sahara runs off into the dark. . . .

Soon I start the car and turn north. I pass Sahara, stumbling down the airfield naked, and soon I'm leaving the airport behind me and heading up the coast, surprised to see lights in some of the Marina high-rises, since I didn't think there had been any electricity in this part of town for years, when I'm ambushed, as usual, by my arch nemesis, My Conscience. I turn the car around and drive back to LAX, cruising slowly onto the landing field. Soon she's in my headlights. She's crawling around on the ground now in a haze of alcohol and panic; let's just say she's not as ethereal as she was in the footlights of the Cathode Flower. I stop the car. You coming? I call to her, and the bracing ocean breeze at four-thirty in the morning has apparently sobered her enough to convince her it might be a good idea. She scurries back into the car, first into the front seat then changing her mind and climbing into the back, next to Viv who just goes on sleeping through it all like a little white bird.

Slipping from Ocean Time Zone into Oblivion Time, I reset the car's clock back eleven minutes. Sahara grumbles about the situation all the way up Pacific Coast Highway; when her hostility toward me is finally exhausted, she goes into a monologue about her life in general—all the usual stuff about her mother who committed suicide, her homosexual brother who died last year, the rock band she's trying to start in Los Angeles.... Soon Sahara's mystique lies all over the car in tatters. Viv, in her fashion, entirely misses the depressing part of the evening and wakes silently with the first light of sun; one minute I look and she's asleep and the next minute she's awake, sitting up in the seat quietly watching the ocean out the window, still perfectly naked and content to remain that way for a while. "Stop and get some juice" are her first words of greeting, and I pull over to a little market. I get out and peer at them together in the back seat. Would you like something to eat? I ask Sahara.

"Bastard," she mumbles in response, under her breath.

"She'll be OK," Viv coolly explains. "I've assured her that when the time comes, she and I will have our revenge."

They'll have their revenge! In their eyes I'm responsible for the whole plot. I could point out it was Viv who defiled Sahara all night in the back of the car while I was just the chauffeur; but what's the use? There's no use being reasonable here: "What's reason got to do with it?" Viv would say. It's as useful as arguing about the shape of a circle. "What's round got to do with it?" The thing for me now is to just get them their food, get back in the car, and take them somewhere I can leave them to their unholy alliance. The thing for me now is to just quietly spend the rest of my life watching over my shoulder or out the corner of my eye, on my guard for the inevitable coming vengeance, and not waste two seconds trying to be reasonable about it, since I've finally learned, halfway or so through this life of mine, that with women there's no percentage at all in reasonableness. And ever since I got this through my thick head I've gotten along with them a lot better.

Right now Viv can see all these thoughts flashing behind my

eyes and, smiling, she reaches up through the car window and kisses me on the cheek. . . . So I'm not so surprised to get back to the car three minutes later, with their juice and an armful of those little processed sweet rolls in plastic packs, and find the back seat empty, and the two of them nowhere to be seen, their clothes still in a pile on the seat as they have been all night. I turn looking up and down the coast highway for a glimpse of them— but nothing; you tell me where a naked stripper and a sculptor dressed only in white garters and white stockings could disappear to, because I'll never know. Later when I find Viv I'll ask her and she'll just give me the same little smile she gave me when she kissed me through the car window. I suppose, all things considered, it was pretty shrewd of me when I went in the market to take along the car keys.

Couple of years ago, the newspaper I work for asked me to write a piece on the city's "spiritual center." I begged them not to make me. But, unavoidably coerced, I finally turned in an essay on another strip joint not far from the Cathode Flower, down on La Cienega Boulevard in the barren stretch where all the little art galleries used to be along with stores that sold Dutch clogs and designer hot dogs. It was across from the theater where Bertolt Brecht wrote plays for Charles Laughton before Brecht was run out of Hollywood in the early Fifties; last time I was there all I saw were the remains of the lingerie shop, lingerie of all colors and configurations blowing along the sidewalk like old newspapers. At this strip joint I had befriended a forlorn blonde stripper named Mona. "Befriended" is a misnomer, of course, since our friendship never existed outside a five-minute conversation now and then in the dark, and of course Mona was not her real name; I never knew her real name. She was from Stockholm and never seemed very happy. I always thought she was beautiful and sweet, but it was dark, after all. One night, as I knew would eventually happen, Mona was gone, as all these girls are eventually gone—and they don't leave forwarding addresses, a rule that used to apply to strippers in particular but has recently come to apply to everyone in Los Angeles. . . . Now about an hour past dawn, after Viv has disappeared with Sahara, I turn off Sunset and head east through the Palisades thinking about Mona. The ocean is behind me and I take another turnoff toward this bluff I know where there's a view of the whole bay, from the smoking ruins of Malibu to the paramilitary outposts of Palos Verdes. The sky is filled with the smoke of last night's backfire along the second ring, and from the bluff looking east I can see two or three of the wide scorched concentric gashes that circle Los Angeles, with old Hollywood in the bull's-eye.

With the car parked I run the radio up and down the dial one last time before finally shutting it off. In the distance below me, a last few tiny fire engines make their way back to the fire stations from the charred ring of earth. Out at sea the hundreds of Chinese junks that sail in about this time each month approach the shore with their mystery cargo. My article identifying the spiritual center of Los Angeles, incidentally, was never published, the only story I've written in a long time that was flatly rejected and which I flatly refused to rewrite. The sun has risen just high enough to come crashing through my front windshield when I'm still thinking of Mona who, for all I know, is hanging out at this very moment with Viv and Sahara, or was abducted according to the plan scribbled on a cocktail napkin and is now held captive in the Scandinavian fjords, near the top of the world.

I started talking to myself again the other day. I don't think I even realized I was doing it, until I noticed the woman in the next car looking over at me in horror. . . . Since the Quake I haven't talked to myself like I used to—in the shower, pacing my apartment, in the car or walking down the street, yakking up a storm in broad daylight and never thinking twice about it. The plain truth is I've never known anyone else I was so confident would be as understanding of what I had to say, or as patient to let me say it; if nothing else I could always be sure I would at least let me finish my sentence, before interrupting. Some years ago I mentioned it to a woman I was seeing at the time. It wasn't so much a confession, since I didn't think it was anything to confess; it just sort of came up in passing: "Well, yes, now and then I talk to myself. No, I don't mean in my head, I mean right out loud." We were at the beach, lying on the sand. She grew increasingly sullen the rest of the day and evening, until finally she admitted it seemed to her a pretty distinct sign of instability. In fact she had to admit it seemed to her a pretty distinct sign I was flat-out cracked; and she was right, of course, I've never denied it. I've never denied the deep fault line running from my psyche through my brain out my door and down Jacob Hamblin Road, straight to Melrose Avenue and the feet of Justine.

Actually it was Justine who got me talking in the car in the first place, though I don't remember exactly what I was saying to her. I was driving east on Melrose when I saw her rise before me on the other side of Fairfax, having just appeared a block or two behind me and altogether likely to manifest herself again on some other street several miles from here, some time in the next hour or two, if not sooner. She hovered high above the avenue as she always does.... Justine is a billboard. She's everywhere lately, an eruption of flesh, sprawled across a silk sheet in barely existent red panties and tassels that match her red hair, under a scrawl in red lipstick that reads *Justine*. Her breasts, pink luscious bubbles floating over the cityscape, cannot be called merely spectacular, they are supernatural, eternal like the woman herself, who was first revealed some twenty years ago on billboards just like the ones she's on now, in a similar pose, her body slightly less pneumatic as though she was ripening at the speed of her own legend. Ten years later she reappeared up and down the Sunset Strip, Hollywood Boulevard, La Cienega Boulevard . . . and now she's reappeared yet again. No one knows exactly what Justine *does*, or what she's advertising *for*; I assume she doesn't actually do anything, though there's a phone number at the bottom of the billboard for anyone interested in finding out. But as the years have gone by, with Justine bursting forth new and better each decade, ever more perfect and ubiquitous, it becomes less and less imperative that she do anything at all but watch over the city as the Red Angel of Los Angeles, from block to block and street to street and billboard to billboard and year to year. Nonetheless, I make note of the phone number anyway.

I don't have to write it down, because in the L.A. of Numbers I am Memory Central, just as in the L.A. of Names I am Memory Void. I seem not to be able to remember any thing or any one anymore, and I guess I've insulted a few people in the process; I run into somebody here or there and he starts jabbering at me and pretty soon I realize I'm supposed to know this person, I've met him before, maybe ten or twenty times, maybe a hundred. And after he goes on awhile I can finally only look him straight in the eye and say, "Excuse me, but who are you?" and then he's not too happy about it. But at the same time that I've cut myself loose of memories of people and events, the memories of dates and times and phone numbers attach themselves to my brain like gnats to fly paper. At the same time that I'm the deep well into which one can drop a bad love affair, a death, a childhood trauma and never see it again, never even hearing it hit bottom, assuming there is a bottom, I remember not only my own dates and times and phone numbers, but yours too. I'm a walking Filofax for everyone's appointments and vital statistics. I remind Viv of her lunch date at this gallery or that studio, I let my friend Ventura know when it's time to pick up his laundry. I'm the man of deadlines and itineraries and bank account codes; even Carl in New York calls in to check his schedule for the afternoon. So remembering Justine's phone number, written so inconspicuously at the bottom of the billboard that I have to figure she would really rather not hear from me at all, is a snap. I don't even have to repeat it to myself out loud. Instead, with the woman in the next car looking aghast that the man in the car next to her is having an unduly animated dialogue with no apparent passenger, I figure maybe I should put a lid on it again, no more talking to myself. I'm beyond the point anyway where, even to myself, I really have all that much to say. . . .

Over the two days I spent moving into my new suite, I panicked. Not about the extra rent but because, situated in this apartment, in the big wide open front room with all the windows, I might be generally expected by others to become more productive, even inspired. I have no intention of becoming either inspired or productive; to the contrary I intend to sit in the dark at night in my big black leather chair staring out at the Hollywood Hills like a man gazing on an approaching tsunami. *Here comes the present.* On my monitor I run the same movies over and over with the sound off: *The Bad and the Beautiful, Out of the Past, Pandora's Box, I Walked with a Zombie.* Studying the films on my shelf, Ventura remarks that I don't own any funny ones. "What the hell are you talking about?" I answer in outrage. "You don't think *Scarlet Empress* is a funny movie? You don't think *Detour* is a funny movie?" Last time I was up the hall in Ventura's apartment I took a look at *his* film shelf, and *there's* a guy who doesn't own a single funny movie—except Charlie Chaplin, and he and I both know he doesn't watch *City Lights* because he thinks it's funny, he watches it because he thinks it's *profound.* The truth is I don't own anything but funny movies. Every one of them is hysterical.

On the walls of his apartment Ventura tacks little sayings written on paper, maxims he's scribbled from his readings, words of wisdom. He even has up there one or two things I've said. Starting at one end of his apartment and reading to the other, one comes away with a sum total of the Twentieth Century that's rather different from what the century itself might have concluded. Ventura has been having a dispute with the Twentieth Century, and now that it's over he just goes on disputing it, first the century and then the whole millennium. Ventura's whole life is a dispute with the Twentieth Century and I'm the moderator, the referee. I watch for the low blows, the groin kicks, the cheap shots, while trying not to get belted myself in the process. I'm neutral not only on the century and the millennium but on God himself; let's just say I'm reserving judgment.... Over the years Ventura and I each move from one apartment to the next in the Hamblin, trying to better situate ourselves, though for what I have no idea. He moves up the hall as I move down; he used to be in a larger apartment and moved to a smaller one, before I moved from my smaller apartment to the larger one. As he moves to smaller spaces he accumulates more and more pearls of wisdom on paper until there's no more room on any more walls, at which point he begins to layer over: he never throws anything out, God forbid. Just once I'd like to see him throw something out, one of these little pearls of wisdom scribbled on paper, just so I could see which one it was; I wouldn't even mind if it was mine. When the universe stops expanding and starts contracting, Ventura will start eliminating all these revelations until there's only one left— and *that's* the one I want to read. That's the one I want to take with me to my grave.

As for me, as I move to larger spaces I get rid of more things. I lose things as the universe expands; I'll start accumulating when the universe contracts. There you have it in a cosmic nutshell, the difference between me and Ventura. Soon he'll be living in a closet with more paper than the Library of Congress, and I'll be living on the roof naked in my black leather chair. This morning when I go up the hall to see him he's staring at his tarot, dealt out on the floor in the shape of a cross. He's contemplating the meaning of the Queen of Cups, at the nexus of the cross. On the broken-down table that stands in the middle of his ever-shrinking apartment is the usual volume of mail he receives for the column he writes for the newspaper. Ventura's sense of purpose is such that he will answer all these letters; he's been writing the column since the first issue of the newspaper almost fifteen years ago. But now, between his fan letters and his empty typewriter, sitting in his fedora and his cowboy boots and the same shirt that's always rolled up at the sleeves, he stares at the Queen of Cups. He almost always wears his fedora and cowboy boots, even in his own apartment; only very occasionally does he take off the hat, and every once in a while, if he's feeling really familiar, he may even be seen in his socks. Staring at the Queen of Cups, he's wondering who she is. He's wondering if she's his ex-wife or his current girlfriend or the woman who was his last girlfriend and may be his next. One of the most enduring and gratifying things about my friendship with Ventura is that when it comes to women, he's even more screwed up than I am, the best and most compelling evidence of which is that he actually thinks I'm more screwed up than he is. "I'm not going to ask," he says, "what it is they want. You haven't heard me ask that."

"No."

"I wouldn't dream of asking."

"Oh, go ahead," I say.

"No," he shakes his head, "I wouldn't think of it. It wouldn't even occur to me."

"Actually, it's easy."

"What?"

"It's easy. What they want. It's the easiest question in the world."

"It is?" For a moment he's alarmed. "All right, so . . . tell me."

"Everything."

"What?"

"They want *everything*."

An ashen look comes over his face. "Then we're fucked," he says hopelessly. Ventura is so confused about women that when I explain to him my Three Laws of Women, he actually writes them down. "One," I count off, "they're different."

"One, they're different," he repeats, jotting it down in his little notebook. He always carries a little notebook where he jots things down, so he can write about them in his column or tack them up on his wall.

"Two, they're crazy."

"Two, they're crazy." Scribble scribble.

"Three, they're funny."

"Three, they're funny." He reads it over. Ventura is convinced every woman is irresistibly attracted to him. "That woman's looking at me," he moans in a restaurant, "I wish she would stop. I have too many women in my life right now." Every woman in every restaurant, every woman on the street, every woman who exchanges two syllables or a burp with him, wants him. It's his burden in life to disappoint all of them. The ones he doesn't disappoint sooner, he'll have to disappoint later. Those are the ones he becomes involved with, the ones he casts in the movie he thinks he's living in; like him, they're larger than life. Each affair is a singular turbulent drama. "You two don't have a relationship," Viv said to Ventura one night at Musso and Frank's, about one girlfriend or another, "you have a weather report." Lately I've been noticing something. Every woman in Ventura's life gets larger and more mythic than the last, until the new one is the most remarkable of all, the smartest and most beautiful, the one who in another world was a movie star and is now reincarnated as a Sufi goddess—and then he breaks up with her, as always, for no reason I can fathom. He just broke up with one recently for the simple reason that there was *absolutely nothing wrong with her*; she was a woman with no vices whatsoever. "How was I supposed to be involved," he asks plaintively, "with a woman who has no vices?"

"You don't understand," I tell him. "*You* were her vice."

"That's it! That's it exactly! *I* was her vice. How was I supposed to be involved with a woman whose only vice was me?"

Weeks from now, of course, if not days, he'll regret it. "I was driving out of the desert," he'll explain, pacing his apartment in a frenzy, "when it hit me like a lightning bolt," and he'll hit the back of his head, nearly knocking off his hat, to show me what it was like to be struck by this epiphany: "I should have married the Sufi goddess."

"Do you know," I finally confess to him, "that in all the years I've known you, I've never understood a single thing about any of your relationships with any of your women? That in fact I understand your relationships with women even less than I understand mine? That's not the way it's supposed to work. Other people's fucked-up relationships are supposed to be easier to understand than your own. I'll bet," I pointed out, "that you think *my* relationships are easier to understand than yours."

"You're right. I do."

"You're supposed to. Except that, in this case, my relationships really *are* easier to understand than yours. Even *I* think my relationships are easier to understand than yours." I'm not a man of hidden meanings, he once said to me, there are no hidden meanings in my life. "It's interesting that the only time there are any hidden meanings in your life," I say, "is in your relationships with women." When we're this confused about women, we turn to the only option left us: we write. We write as though we understand everything and it's up to us to sort out the world. I only write about movies, but Ventura writes about Life. This morning, still contemplating the Queen of Cups, we head down to the newspaper. I drive because he doesn't want to take his car, an old sixty- or seventy-something Chevy that he also considers larger than life, even more larger than life than his women. All the way down to the paper he's in the next seat to me muttering it like a mantra: they're different, they're crazy, they're funny. And then: Shit! he exclaims, they want *everything?* "Well," I answer, "to be fair, we do too." I've worked at this newspaper about three years now, ever since things ended with Sally. It's published once a week out of the hollowed-out cavern of the old Egyptian Theater, not far from the mouth of the sunken L.A. subway. First few months I'd arrive to the theater every day to find that during the night someone had carted away another memento of the theater foyer—a pharaoh's chariot or a slab of fake hieroglyphics, or a mummy and its papier-mâché sarcophagus—until all that was left of the grand entrance was a dirt plot. Inside, amid the decor of tarnished gold that ascends in decay to the ceiling, the advertising department is located up on the stage where the screen used to be, and the editorial staff is strewn among the ripped-out seats of the audience section. The editor-in-chief's office is in the balcony and the receptionist works behind the snack bar. The publisher took the projectionist's room, small but offering an obvious vantage point.

My desk, happily, is near one of the old emergency exits. When I first arrived at the paper no one on the staff talked to me except some of the editors and the art director, a brilliant but tormented homosexual who was always raging at everyone. He admired a book of mine he read back in his more impressionable years and so we struck up a friendship of sorts, and I became the one others recruited to calm him down or negotiate various truces. I like the people at the paper but they tend to complain a lot about jobs I would have killed for when I was as young as they are. The level of envy is superseded only by the level of resentment. There's all the usual political infighting and turf warfare;

gossip pervades everything. At a party not long after I split with Sally, drunk and depressed and an all-around basket case, I wound up going home with one of the advertising reps, a cynical noirish blonde who chain-smoked and told me every last thing there was to know about everyone on the staff. Mid-seduction it occurred to me, in my drunken haze, that tomorrow everyone in turn would know everything there was to know about me, first and foremost that on this particular evening I was less than my most sexually formidable. Certainly enough, as Dr. Billy O'Forte put it to me later, "your wick wasn't wet twenty-four hours before phones all over L.A. were ringing." In the years since, every time I'm seen talking to this woman more than five minutes, the flames of rumor flare anew. People on the staff who have fucked everything that moves within the confines of the newspaper's walls sadly shake their heads and whisper to each other their "disappointment" in me.

What can I say? I'm a disappointing character. I only began to feel like I actually belonged at the newspaper when, having quickly mastered the art of disappointment, I went on to become completely practiced at the science of disillusionment. By now I've totally dismayed anyone still innocent enough to expect I'm capable of anything admirable, let alone heroic. When Ventura and I arrive this morning we immediately run into Freud N. Johnson, the paper's publisher. Johnson is a five-foot-five failed movie producer who publicly and bitterly mourns the world's lack of respect for him and deep down inside suspects he's a homosexual. He often ends arguments by whimpering, "I know you're right and I'm wrong. But you *always* get to be right." He's been trying to figure out how to fire the editor ever since I first came to this job, though what he'll actually do once he succeeds is an open question, since he doesn't appear to know the first thing about putting out a newspaper and all the best writers have said they would quit, something that in one of his stupider miscalculations he may not believe. I've made it clear to anyone who cares, for instance, that I would go, if only because the editor in question hired me against what would have been any more reasonable person's better judgment. In the meantime Freud N. Johnson constantly prowls the bowels of the Egyptian Theater, his entire being broadcasting a variety of messages in the neon of the psyche. "I'm not a homosexual!" howls one. "I'm tall!" squeaks another. "You're taller than I am and I hate you!" blurts a recurring favorite.

Freud N. Johnson regularly confides in Ventura, perhaps because Ventura has been around longer than anyone else. Johnson may think that when he fires the editor he can recruit Ventura into taking the job and pulling the paper together; and Ventura allows Johnson to take him into his confidence, he explains to me, so he can find out what's really going on. It's a strategy that seems to me obviously perilous, bolstering Johnson's nerve and implicitly encouraging him to believe he can do something rash and get away with it. Today, however, all that's neither here nor there as far as I'm concerned. Clearing my desk and tossing all my phone messages in the trash, I'm just waiting for Ventura to finish his intrigues so we can go home, because I had this dream yesterday morning I've been waiting to tell him. Lately I've begun to dream again, which is to say I've been having astonishingly vivid dreams that I remember in detail, when usually they only linger in my mind like smoke in the nostrils from a fire that's gone out. This one happened yesterday morning around ten-thirty or so. I had awakened briefly to find Viv curled up on her side of the bed rather than between my legs; and I went back to sleep and had this terrible dream—

We were staying in a casino in Las Vegas and my mother was with us, though in the dream I don't remember actually seeing her. A strange young woman had lured me from our hotel room to the swimming pool outside, and I was about to take off my clothes and go into the pool with the strange woman when I saw Viv watching from the window. I rushed back to the room where I found her lying on the stairs, sobbing. With great indignation I accused her of being jealous for no reason, and stormed out of the suite and began walking all over subterranean Las Vegas, through tunnels that connected all the casinos, until finally I surfaced on the outskirts of town. It was dusk. The casino where I was staying was not far in the distance. A large sweating man with dark hair and a scraggly beard said, "There's a Big One coming," and at that moment dust rose on the faraway hills and birds scattered frantically across the sky. I held onto a stop sign in the middle of the desert while the earth shuddered beneath my feet, and watched the high rise of my casino, which now resembled the Hotel Hamblin, tremble slightly. Then, just as it appeared the tremor and the danger were past, the casino completely collapsed. I was stunned. I ran back to the site, and by the time I reached it the sky had become dark and there was nothing left of the casino at all, no sign anything had ever been there; but even in the dark the sand glowed a dim red and people stood around staring at it, stupefied, until someone said, "We should try and dig." For a while we dug, pulling up planks of wood from beneath the sand. But soon we stopped because it seemed useless, it was so obvious that everyone who had been in the casino was buried, unreachable, hundreds of feet below us.

I was devastated. I was thinking what to do. I was thinking I would have to call my mother's friends and Viv's family, and I would have to call Ventura to come get me because my car was buried too, along with everything in it, and there was nowhere for me to go. I was very aware in the dream of my entire past being gone, and in the midst of my devastation there was also a sickening opportunism, that everything was behind me now. Then, in a daze, I was in another casino, stumbling through the halls, when I realized that at the very least I had to call out, to Viv or my mother, on the off-chance they might still be alive and hear me. I opened my mouth and started to call—

And woke myself up.

I couldn't have been more surprised. It never occurred to me I was in a dream, and now it stayed with me with defiant clarity. Viv was still curled up next to me, her back to me. "Oh God," I sighed, reaching for her.

She turned. "What is it?" she said, immediately conscious.

"Oh God. I had a horrible dream."

"What was it?"

I shook my head. "No, I can't. . . ."

"Was I in it?"

"No." I didn't really think it was specifically about her anyway, or even us. But what I woke to, what remained with me, was not how my dream had wiped my life of its past, but how I had spared myself in the dream by feigning indignation at Viv's jealousy and heartbreak, and bursting out of the room and the casino. In other words it was not my dishonesty that had doomed Viv and my mother, it was more complicated than that: honesty would not have saved them, it would only have destroyed me, leaving me entombed with them. Now in bed I took Viv, clutched her by her hair and lowered her to me. I slipped between her lips into that territory where my conscience can't reach me. I was convinced that if she had been there this morning when I woke, between my legs, her mouth wrapped around me, I never would have had this dream; she would have sucked the bad faith right out of me, it would have rushed out of me with everything else. Now she had to suck all the harder, stroking me as though to set me on fire, and I could still feel the small drop of conscience left inside me afterward, like the errant cell of a cancer left behind after surgery.

"But you aren't responsible," Ventura says this evening when I tell him the dream, "for what you *might* have done."

"I wanted to go swimming with the strange woman," I argue. "I wanted to take off my clothes and go into the pool with her."

"You aren't responsible for what you *wanted*. You're responsible for what you *do*." We're driving down Fountain Avenue through the blue corridor of cypresses that sag with clumps of wet ash, the turrets and towers north of us unlit in the night. The air is filled with this odd smell the city has taken on recently, not the common smell of sandalwood and hashish but a different smell I can't place, and as we sometimes tend to do we point things out to each other—the sites of famous suicides and old Hollywood love affairs—as though we're tourists, which, like everyone in L.A., we are. Sometimes we even make things up, though for all we know we're not making it up; in L.A. you think you're making something up, but it's making you up. After a while, looking at the dark towers and thinking about dreams and earthquakes, Ventura adds, "It's going to be very weird, when we're all driving around with a dead city in our psyches."

"But we're already driving around with a dead city in our

psyches," I answer. Those of us who are still in Los Angeles know the rest of you out there are laughing at us. Those of us who are still here—a million, half a million, a hundred thousand, no one really knows anymore—are already driving around with dead streets and dead alleys inside us, dead buildings and dead windows and dead gutters, dead intersections and dead shops, not the urban corpse of the present but the dead city of the future. We've already seen the end of Los Angeles the way the people of Pompeii watched their end rise in the smoke of Mount Vesuvius years before it actually blew. And walking around with a dead city in you either makes you just as dead or it thrills you, it makes you the most alive you've ever been, surrounded as you are by a landscape that's just choking for the breath of someone or something alive. . . .

The days right after the Quake. . . . Wandering from one dead apartment building to another, slipping past the red X's that marked the doors of buildings that had been condemned. Down at the beach an old huge aquablue building called the Seacastle greeted the brown waves that rumbled in, the basement long since flooded, the rooms now empty except for the other squatters that strayed from room to room until they found one to claim. From the street below, I could make out through the windows the apartments as they were abandoned: prim apartments, disheveled ones, some trashed when the earth lurched awake from its bad dream, and some unscathed except for the fact that the entire structure could teeter and crash at any moment. I headed for the top floor. People think that's the place you don't want to be in a quake but the odds can go either way, really, you can either be buried under the building or ride it on down. Deserted lives as I wandered from one apartment to the next, photos and letters, knickknacks and leftovers in the icebox, the disarray of the sheets that reminded me of Sally, whatever their pattern. From the top of the Seacastle I had quite a view, especially in the apartment that didn't have a wall, the ramshackle dead pier just a few hundred yards off to the south beyond the dangling dead cables of the now-exposed elevator shaft. Out of the shaft echoed the squawking of gulls.

I stayed at the Seacastle for a while, partly for the view and partly for the song of a parakeet still in its cage, until the feed ran out and I let him go. He flew directly into the shaft and never came out. But mostly I stayed for the disarray of the sheets, drawn not to the large king-size beds but the singles, where there was little chance that two people had ever slept together or had ever been there longer than the expanse of their ecstasy. . . .

The third night I woke with a start. At first I thought it was a tremor, or that an unusually large wave had rolled in; one of the reasons I liked the Seacastle was you couldn't tell the difference. In the western sky a huge moon hung level with my bed. I turned to the doorway and saw her form, glowing in the moon small and feral, nothing like Sally at all who the darkness always hid— and then the next minute she was gone. In that moment's recognition I realized I'd been seeing her ever since I got here, just out of the corner of my eye. I got up and searched the top floor of the Seacastle in the dark until I nearly tumbled over the edge of a jagged gash that ran down one of the hallways. When I went back to bed I lay there disgruntled, the moon way too big and the sea way too loud.

The next day I left the Seacastle for the afternoon. I stood in line over at Main and Ocean Park Boulevard where they were handing out sandwiches and fruit juice and vitamin packets.

When I got back to the Seacastle I found the pattern of my bed sheets disrupted. That night the same thing happened as before: I woke and there she was lingering in the doorway. Come here, I said, before she disappeared.

After that I saw her in the afternoon, in another room on the other side of the building. When she caught me looking at her, she didn't disappear or look away. Then I tried to ignore her awhile; a night or two passed and a day or two when I didn't see her; and I thought she was gone, thought she had moved on to another empty hotel up the coast, when I woke one night and found her kneeling next to my bed, her face inches from mine. "Jesus!" I cried, because she scared the hell out of me. She smiled at this, before she got up and walked out. Even in the dark it was obvious her eyes were green.

"Come here," I said, when I saw her again the next day. The sun was falling in the evening fog, a wet red blotch; she was in the room diagonally across from mine, facing the city rather than the sea. I moved toward her and she casually drifted into the next room. We kept moving in circles around each other. For a few minutes I couldn't find her, and then there she was on the north-west balcony, looking out away from the pier: she was leaning against the balcony watching the waves. I thought, You lean too hard it will break; but I didn't say anything. Let it break. Let her tumble into the water. I came up behind her and she turned her head slightly to register my approach, but didn't say anything, showed nothing on her face in exactly that way I would come to love. I hadn't been planning anything at all. Until I took off my clothes I really had no idea in my head what I was going to do. I reached around the front of her and unsnapped her jeans and she said, "What if I said no."

"I would anyway."

"No." I opened her up, standing there on the balcony, and she continued purring various refusals, No you can't, no I don't want you to, uh uh, mmmmm mmmmm, and the startled sound of her gasp when I came into her became the sound I always listened for whenever I fucked her, that little surprise I never understood that she expressed so inarticulately. So I never had an answer for her, from that first time until I could finally say, a year later, that I loved her, having decided love could be as different from what it had been before as Viv was different from Sally. Standing there on the balcony, naked from the waist down and staring at the charred cliffs of Malibu with me inside her, she seemed to drift out to sea on her little black Nos, dissolving into a stream of dreamy demurs. From the highest floor of the Seacastle, in the light of the sun setting into the ocean, with Viv in my arms, I could see the dead city to the east before it lapsed into the final darkness of night. But it's at night, on the other hand, that *my* Los Angeles, the dead city inside me, is especially beautiful in the light of the moon.

∞

She was gone the next morning, and when she didn't reappear over the next few days I left the Seacastle, not wanting to live any-more amid its memories. It was one thing when all the memories belonged to others, another now that I had one of my own. For a few nights I slept with hundreds of others in the circus tent that had been pitched on the beach for all the Quake nomads. I kept my eyes peeled for Viv. Then for a week or so I stayed with

Veroneek, who had a pet wolf named Joe and looked like a beautiful wolf herself, with short black hair and deep-set eyes that fixed on you without inhibition, and a low, resonant voice that so impressed the emergency officials they recruited her to read over the microphone. Inside the tent she sat behind a table calling the names of people who had frantic messages from friends and family out of town trying to find out who was alive.

Everything was haywire. A man who had been in jail on a rape charge was recaptured when he rescued an old woman from a collapsed building. A woman who had worked tirelessly on the relief lines threw her bound two-year-old daughter into the sea from the rubble of the pier; by the time the mother was apprehended, the little girl had washed away. It was not as if time had never before been populated with good people doing evil things or evil people doing good things, but that in the weird silver light expelled by the earth when it ripped open, the switch of the soul was flipped, autistic teenagers suddenly taking cool command of crises as corporation presidents and retired Marine colonels went completely mute with paralysis. I went mute myself, though by choice. I had lost my stutter, and had nothing to say until I found it again. I was a looter, not of stores or businesses but my memory: I rushed into its shadows and stripped it bare, leaving nothing but vandalism and random destruction behind me, until I was finished and light-headed. But now the words trickled out in an ooze I didn't trust, the fluid speech of someone just a single step in the past or a single step in the future, skipping or pausing to catch up with the staccato of the present.

Veroneek lived in an old wooden red house in Ocean Park. It survived the Quake while all the newer buildings around it crumbled. I slept in the basement, to the wolf's irritation, although eventually we had a meeting of the minds. Veroneek had a deep dark secret about a terminally ill friend who died under mysterious circumstances, and when she told me about it she looked right at Joe as though her late friend was riding inside the wolf; every once in a while she would pry open his jaws with her bare hands and bellow into his mouth, "Joe, are you in there?" When we slept together I was the first man she had been with in a long time, after affairs with women. When I kissed her between her legs it was the first man's mouth that had ever been there; it may be I was nearly as good for her as a woman was. Veroneek was trying to start a broadcasting station in L.A. and saw the Quake not as a setback but a golden opportunity, as though it had brought the airwaves crashing to earth along with everything else and now she could gather them up and launch them back into the sky on her own terms. She stared mesmerized at my laundered white shirt as it hung from a ceiling lamp in the front room of her house, turning in the breeze and glittering in the sun. Finally one afternoon she asked me whose message I was waiting for her to call in the tent down on the beach, and I told her about Sally; I just sort of assumed that, though we weren't together anymore, Sally would try and get in touch. Though it had been some time, I assumed she would just want to know I was all right, or would want me to know that she wanted to know. But as the days had passed and neither my name nor Sally's flickered across the monitor in the tent, my mild surprise had slowly transformed to relief: "So I guess," I told Veroneek, "it really is over then. So I guess I'm not really waiting to hear from her after all."

"Ah," Veroneek smiled, with that intense stare, "but now there's another."

And that was when I skipped into the present. I don't think it even occurred to me she might mean herself; I just assumed she meant Viv, and for all I know, she did. I went on waiting in the tent, watching the ocean waves through the flap and listening for my name over the speakers, and when it wasn't called I stood for hours before the monitors looking for my name anyway. Others waited too, with no reason to stare up at the monitor but to try and will into being a communication from beyond the wreckage. Finally, to no one in particular, I said, "I'm l-l-leaving," and was on my way out the tent heading down toward the waves when I heard Veroneek's voice over the speakers. The message wasn't for me specifically but rather any party that answered to the name Seacastle, signed by an anonymous party that answered to the name Bunker. Wh-Wh-Where is the Bunker, I asked everyone I met, and it was nearly midnight when I tracked it down, a huge white concrete conglomeration of artists' spaces on the edge of Baghdadville. I took the freight elevator up from the loading docks to the first level and walked down each hall in the dark, try-ing each door. None opened, nor any on the second level, and it wasn't until I reached the fourth door on the third level that one gave way. I had decided I would take whoever was behind any door that wasn't locked to me.

The loft inside was dark. Through a window on the other side I could see the glow of the distant bonfires on the freeway. Grop-ing around in the dark I found a circular staircase and made my way up to a smaller loft that overhung the larger one. She said nothing from the bed and I said nothing back. She didn't stir at all. It was only later, twenty minutes, maybe thirty, looking up from her thighs, that I was sure I identified the gold of her hair in the bonfire light from the window behind me. Up inside her, my tongue touched the tip of the long thin web of her climax. I saw her orgasm in the distance, somewhere beyond her shoulders; I inhaled it. She groaned and lurched. Her vulva burst with the last No left from the Seacastle, and I swallowed it. I still carry it inside me, like the note in a bottle.

⚮

For a long time we didn't say a word. That No from her vulva was the last sound between us except our moans. We rode in taxis down Crescent Heights, the sound of shakuhachi flutes drifting in through the open window. Headlights severed the trunks of the arching white trees and siamese-twin lizards joined at the head slithered up into the street from the sunken subways. Over the black shores of Wilshire Boulevard the caged nudes of the La Brea Tar Pits dangled in the wind; they watched from behind their wooden bars as we watched back. Viv and I had a silent agreement each of us would take of the other whatever we wanted whenever we wanted it. . . .

We've been together over two years now. Every once in a while this astonishes one or both of us, since not long after we met Viv made it clear she didn't need a mute for a lover, and I wasn't sure I could say anything at all, let alone whatever it was she wanted to hear. I was just being stubborn, is the way she looks at it now. Our last and most hostile separation was over a year ago, when I woke in the middle of the night to find her walking around the loft naked, searching for that last No she had given up so easily. Late one night four months later she showed up at my door a little drunk in her white lace top and little white boots; I think she just wanted to catch me at my most unsuspecting, see for herself if I had any women stashed away in the closet or under the bed. We went up on the hotel roof. Watching the fires in the distance we drank tequila and she told me about all the men she had known that summer or almost knew; she held the night close to her like armor. After an hour we went back downstairs and sat in her truck and talked a little longer, and I tried to explain how I had come to realize, over those four months, that I loved her, though I still couldn't explain to either her or myself exactly what that meant or, for the moment, make any great claims for it. For a while she didn't say a thing and then finally answered, angrily, "I didn't know you felt that way about me."

"I didn't know either," I said.

"Well, it just seems like you should have known." When we wouldn't or couldn't say anything more, when I figured I was just wasting my time, when I didn't have a clue what had brought her to me that night besides too much wine, I got out of the truck and was about to disappear into the hotel when she rolled down the window and called my name. We went back up to my apartment. It's still not exactly clear whether we had sex that night; I'm positive we did and she insists we didn't. Men and women apparently have entirely different ideas about what actually constitutes sex, but we won't go into that now. It doesn't really matter anyway, not as much as the fact that Viv was still there the next morning, or that we were together again the next night and we've been together since. Viv is quite sure all of this turmoil was my fault, and since she's more right than wrong, the details aren't worth quibbling about. I'm as disinclined to make excuses here as anywhere else. I accept that it's Viv's version of events we've decided to live by, and if you pin her down, Viv will allow that her version may not always be *completely* reliable. I remember one night in a gallery out in the Glow Loft District a conversation she had with the curator and how later, as we drove home, from the back seat she recounted the conversation line by line and, very calmly, not wanting to alarm her, I pulled the car over to the side of the road and explained with as little panic in my voice as possible that I had been standing right there when she had this conversation and that in fact it was *nothing* like she described now. He had not said any such thing to her and she had not said any such thing back; rather Viv's version was the subtitled version, the version between the lines as she read it. Of course, while Viv's version of reality may not always be entirely accurate, that doesn't mean it's *wrong*. It has just become Vivified or, if you will, Vivid.

Now our relationship feels oddly durable, as though having for the time being set aside the past and the future, we could just go on forever in the present. Every once in a while she likes to look at me and say, "Well, I guess you're not such a bad guy after all." I hope this is meant as a joke. I hope it's not meant to be reassuring. The defining moment of Viv's life may have come when she was five years old and, on a field trip to a farm with her kindergarten glass, was advised by the teacher that under no circumstances should she or anyone else touch the electric barbed wire fence, to which Viv of course responded by marching right up and grabbing a good hold of it. About half an hour later they finally revived her, and she's been pretty much electrified ever since. Years afterward, when too many people told her that under no circumstances should she abandon her unhappy marriage to one of the richest men in Los Angeles, she walked out on the marriage and the money to go climb Mount Kilimanjaro; and she's still the kind of woman who, feeling slightly neglected, can wake up one morning and announce she's leaving that afternoon for Tuva, when you don't even know where the hell Tuva is, or catch the next train out of Union Station regardless of where it's heading, staying up all night through the Mojave drinking Jack Daniel's with the porter.

Viv explodes with ideas and visions, which she writes down on her hand or arm to remind herself of them later. Soon she's a mass of notes, a five-foot-two memo to herself, which turns the bubbles of her bubble-bath blue, from which she emerges a blue blur. Not long after climbing Mount Kilimanjaro she returned to the United States intent on becoming either a film director or a metal sculptor, only to become both. . . . On the walls of her loft in the Bunker are dead insects. Ocean-colored butterflies, golden-winged beetles, flaming orange ladybugs, all encased in . . . hell, I don't know what they're encased in, some polyethylene something-or-other; there's also a Chinese chest, a pile of old hat boxes from the 1930s, a bottle of melted Kilimanjaro snow and blue mercury orbs hanging from the ceiling, an ostrich egg perched precariously on a stand, mannequins with neither heads nor legs mounted on wire frames, and the train of a Ziegfeld Girl's wedding dress hanging behind a lovely antique bed that threatens to collapse with every turn of one's body, which makes for an interesting night's sleep. There are also Viv's metal sculptures, geometric monoliths in the shapes of pyramids and obelisks and coffins and fortresses and sanctuaries with little slits that peer into tufts of fur and nests of bird feathers, and tiny doors that open on pearls coiled seductively in barely ajar pods that look like vaginas. One of Viv's sculptures is a six-foot-high tower with a stained glass window that, on closer examination, turns out not to be glass at all but small bits and pieces of butterfly wings Viv meticulously rendered in a stained glass pattern; for weeks after chopping up the wings of dead butterflies, Viv had nightmares of thousands of butterflies outside her windows flapping their wings maniacally at the glass. The stainless steel for these sculptures is fabricated by the same factory that makes the time capsules for Black Clock Park, and in the ocean sunlight Viv's monoliths gleam blindingly, and after nightfall their forms stand in the dark with the headless and legless mannequins like the street signs of a demonic topography. Viv isn't always entirely practical: there's no kitchen, for instance. When she found the loft and decided to take it, she said, Oh I like the space, oh I like the view of the ocean, oh look there's room for all my metal pieces; and then about the third or fourth week after moving in, she started looking for the kitchen and noticed there wasn't one.

After that first year and all the pain I caused her, I think I remain a somewhat dubious person in the eyes of Viv's family and friends. It's a wide circle, as opposed to my own family that now just includes my mother, and my friends that, with the exception of Viv and my pal Carl in New York and a few others, are limited to the Cabal. The Cabal is the subject of the newspaper's most prevalent and ludicrous gossip. The Cabal Theory, as articulated by the paper's resentful proles, is that the paper is run by four people, of whom I am supposedly one. The others are Shale Marquette, Dr. Billy O'Forte, and Ventura. The Cabal Theory has it that the four of us get together in the dead of night and hatch out various schemes and notions. None of us can remember when more than two were last in a room together, but this hasn't shaken the Cabal Theory by a single bitter whisper. As it happens Shale is the editor-in-chief, so one might expect he'd have some ideas from time to time about what the newspaper is going to publish. He came to L.A. from Boston by way of New York, or maybe it was New York by way of Boston, instantly sizing up the city and immersing himself in its history. I'm not entirely sure at what point he had been here long enough to finally understand that if there was ever a city where history counts for nothing it's Los Angeles, that in Los Angeles history is one of those things that will obscure your vision more than illuminate it. But at any rate he got to be a fucking expert about Los Angeles in short fucking order and sometimes it gets on everyone's nerves.

Of the Cabal, Shale is in fact the youngest. But he has that grown-up authority natural leaders have; when I'm talking to him I always feel I'm confiding in an older brother. He has a dark beard flecked with white, and a smile that affectionately tolerates your nonsense without being totally patronizing—though later you think maybe it *should* have been patronizing. Once Shale asked me what my great dream in life was, back when I still had one that was recognizable; when I asked him his, he answered, "To run a newspaper." Thus by the insistent light of his dreams he is incapable of running this newspaper with anything but complete dedication. Of course within twenty hours of his arrival the staff started griping about Shale: he was too familiar, he was too remote. He was too democratic, he was too autocratic. He was too attentive, he wasn't attentive enough. Those on the paper who had been around awhile quickly forgot that the editor before Shale was a certifiable psychotic who made even Freud N. Johnson look stable, while the adolescents who came after Shale's arrival never had a boss before and apparently think some of the things he does are de rigueur for a boss. If, for instance, someone is having a mental breakdown, Shale is the kind of boss who will give him or her time off with pay and have the newspaper pick up the psychiatric tab. Shale is the kind of boss who will refuse the publisher's order to lay off the pregnant fashion writer—even though he knows she's not really pulling her weight and that if he doesn't cut costs sooner or later, *he's* the one who will be laid off—because the father of the child just walked out on her and she has no other prospects for work. Shale is the kind of boss who routinely throws his body before the bullets from the higher-ups, protecting those below him and putting his own job on the line, just because he believes that's what a boss is supposed to do. The children not only seem to believe all bosses do this but, by the time it gets around to the cynical noir blonde in the advertising department I slept with, rumor has it that Shale is actually trying to get the pregnant fashion writer fired.

There's no Cabal because none of us who are supposedly part of this Cabal—except Shale—gives enough of a fuck to even deny there's a Cabal, let alone be in one. Dr. Billy O'Forte is the most popular guy on the staff, maybe the only person on the staff everyone likes. One night when he was drunk and just sober enough to hope I was too drunk myself to remember it the next day, he confessed to actually having a Ph.D., if you can imagine such a disgrace; he was even more chagrined to report he had written his doctorate on something called "Modern Thought in American Literature." He swore me to secrecy and I assured him that of course I would tell no one. I didn't, however, promise not to openly call him doctor, so now everyone calls him doctor. Besides working for the newspaper Dr. Billy is also trying to get financing for a film documentary he is making about sex addicts in Guatemala; this project follows his last, a documentary about sex addicts in Copenhagen, which followed his magnum opus, a documentary about sex addicts in Bombay. At one point a few years back he was awarded a grant by a mysterious millionaire in San Francisco, the terms of which were that he would tour the world for a year with his wife Jane and make a documentary about international sex addicts. Soon after the money came in, the millionaire died and Dr. Billy sort of forgot about making the documentary and just took the world tour. Rio de Janeiro was nice I hear. The newspaper seized on this freakish development to name Dr. Billy its "international" correspondent until, weary of all those tedious stops on the itinerary like Bangkok and Barcelona, he returned to America in a fit of ennui, whereupon the paper instantly named him its national correspondent. Now he drops into the office every once in a while to groan about the onerous task of traveling the world on a dead millionaire's money. Dr. Billy is about five-and-a-half feet tall, which is only worth noting because everyone who reads his work thinks he's six-and-a-half feet tall. His favorite scam is to always tell everyone what a bad writer he is and what a duff story he's just written, and every single time I'm sucked in by this routine—there is, after all, no happier occasion for a writer than another writer writing something bad—until I read it and then I want to jam his fingers in a pencil sharpener. For someone who's supposedly such a terrible writer he seems to be the guy all the paper's other writers routinely steal their wittiest one-liners and most insightful observations from, as I've done myself many times.

Then there's Ventura. Ventura started the newspaper when he first came to Los Angeles from Texas fifteen years ago. He's written a column for it every week since day one and became one of the most famous writers in L.A. doing so; over the years he's refused at least three serious offers to become the paper's editor. In his spare time he's written four or five books and three or four movies and tosses in a volume or two of poetry when he feels like he's been under-productive. He is entirely self-educated and his working knowledge of everything from geology to the Chinese economy to the novels of Willa Cather and D. H. Lawrence is too intimidating to be around very long; I've long since given up on any possibility I will ever know or have read as much. He's a seer and crank, the star of his own movie, writing all the dialogue and giving himself the best lines. He drives a puke-green Chevy he thinks is beautiful, with half a million miles on it, which he keeps rebuilding and restoring; his symbiosis with this piece of junk was born about the time he crossed the L.A. border, and has been getting more twisted ever since. He thinks his movie is a Western and this car is the horse. "The voices are telling me not to park in the garage tonight," he intones after an earth tremor that shakes the Hamblin right down to the beams of the underground garage. He's not worrying about the building falling on him, he's worrying about it falling on the car. The "voices" are always talking to Ventura, telling him what's transpiring in far reaches of the universe. "The voices," I say, "are telling you that you worry too much about your car."

"That's not what they're telling me."

"That's what they're telling me."

"*My* voices are talking to you about *my* car?"

"Yes."

"No they aren't."

"Yes. They've told me to tell you that they're tired of hearing about your fucking car."

"They're not saying that. Maybe they're talking about *your* car."

"My voices don't talk to me about my car. My voices have more important things to talk to me about than my car."

"Your voices don't talk to you at all," Ventura retorts. "You haven't been on speaking terms with your voices since you were toilet-trained." The voices are a big thing with Ventura. When he founded the newspaper he found himself in the inky placenta of its birth, as both a man and writer; the two have become intertwined ever since. He likes to think of himself as some kind of living local legend, which is total megalomania of course—except maybe not total because, on some level, though I'd never tell him this and would probably have to kill anyone who did, he *is* a bit of a legend. He's one of the few people about whom you could coin the word *Venturaesque*—though I always thought *Venturian* had a nicer ring to it—and make it sound ... well, I was going to say legendary, but that would be positively Venturaesque. "See this?" he says, pointing at something on the refrigerator.

It's a clipping of an article he saw on page twenty-six in this morning's paper, a couple of hundred words about some volcano that went off in Bora Bora and displaced the shoreline three thirty-seconds of a millimeter, according to some scientific study. But what those scientists aren't telling us, Ventura explains, his mouth just beginning to turn up in its familiar crazed grin, is that a three-thirty-second millimeter rise in the ocean tides off Bora Bora throws the entire seismic gyrations of the Pacific Rim completely out of whack, and ... and by the time Ventura's done he's got the earth splitting open and everyone tumbling into fiery crevices and swallowed up in craters the size of Long Beach— people, animals, buildings, bad movie producers who cheated him out of twenty-five hundred dollars years ago, everything except his damn car which is a totem of the cosmos and our only chance at salvation. What is Venturaesque about this planetary exegesis is not the inevitable apocalypse of Ventura's speculations but the absolute *glee* with which he recounts it; in his heart Ventura believes the human race is too arrogant and fucked up to go on surviving with impunity. He can't wait for all of us to be put in our place, wherever that happens to be.

In the end, however, no matter how many years go by or where they take us, my friendship with Ventura remains in *its* place, where we were at the beginning. When I was a nobody in this town, a writer barely on anyone's consciousness, Ventura, the most famous critic in the city, reviewed my first book. It was not only one of the smartest reviews I ever got, which anyone would have expected, it was also the most generous, at a time when he hadn't a thing in the world to gain by building up a potential rival. His intellectual integrity simply demanded that he do it. He has renewed the generosity over and over, time and again, and I don't know anyone—once you get past all the mystic tough-guy posturing—better-hearted, or anyone—once he's cornered with no escape—who will laugh harder at the puncturing of his own pretensions. As a crank and seer, two out of every three things he writes may be ridiculous, but one of them is likely to be something no one else has thought of before or said in just that way. In other words, a completely original thought. Who else these days has one completely original thought out of three? Who else has one out of *twenty*-three? The same passion that mesmerizes those who love Ventura also drives other people fucking bananas, because if there's one thing that sends people right over the edge, especially among the current zeitgeist's self-anointed watchmen, it's a passion that never surrenders, and accepts none from anyone else. Ventura's passion draws a line in the sands of our time. People get on one side or the other, but no one can straddle it.

Last time I caught a glimpse of my career as a novelist, before it disappeared altogether in the dark, was in New York City. I had been cordially invited by a local arts group to give a reading in Central Park with another author, all expenses paid including my hotel tab and the train fare east. For the first leg of the trip, from Los Angeles through Arizona and New Mexico, up into Colorado all the way to St. Louis, I had my own compartment, quite a spiffy little compartment too, where my meals were brought to me and my bed was turned down for me at night. "Why, I'm a big shot author!" I thought to myself in amazement, ordering vodkas and waving grandly from my window to startled passersby like I was the president. Circumstances deteriorated, however, as we advanced east. Somewhere beyond St. Louis I was transferred to another train, and as we slipped out of Chicago across Illinois my accommodations got rather less impressive, until I woke one morning in Pennsylvania to find myself sharing a cabin with several mops and a fire extinguisher. No one brought my meals and no one turned down my bed. "What do I look like," the porter growled at me when I ordered my vodka, "the fucking porter?"

Just arriving in New York, just breathing its air, seemed to confirm that my trajectory had taken a decided dip. As with Los Angeles, if you're not actually from New York it becomes, every time you go there, a greater and greater monument to what you've achieved or, more to the point, failed to achieve—the urbanology of your own particular success or failure. On the way to the reading in Central Park I wound up snatching a taxi from a woman who had been waiting for one some time; and as I was sitting in the back seat feeling bad about this, the taxi just narrowly avoided a head-on collision with another. Contemplating flaming, metal-crunching death I thought not about how I should have let the woman have the cab but how she would never know that if some asshole hadn't stolen her cab, she would be dead. I couldn't stop thinking about this all the way to Central Park, wondering if I should die in an accident in this taxi cab how I would let the woman know what a reprieve fate had narrowly granted her; I imagined clutching the paramedic's arm and croaking out a description of the woman and making him swear to track her down and explain it all to her. And then I got to thinking about all the fatal accidents I didn't know about that I must have missed in *my* life, and how the present is just a culmination of all the unknown near-misses that are part of an unknown past, and . . .

In other words, I had worked myself into quite a state by the time I reached the park. The other writer the arts group had paired me up with was a science-fiction novelist of phenomenal renown. He had virtually invented a whole school of science-fiction single-handedly and was always being quoted in important magazines. A very nice guy, actually; from time to time, in one place or another, he had said some kind things about my own work. We had met before in Los Angeles and hung out at the Cathode Flower admiring a beautiful Eurasian stripper named Kiyo while trying to have one of those simpatico literary tête-à-têtes that aspiring big-shot authors always imagine having with other authors, I envying his phenomenal reputation and staggering success and religiously devout world-wide readership and him envying . . . well, I don't know what he was envying of mine, but I think he was feeling frustrated at having become hopelessly mired in the science-fiction genre, and if there was one thing I could take solace in, it was that I wasn't hopelessly mired in the science-fiction genre. Anyway I fully expected he would be the event's main focus of interest, which he was, though I suppose I didn't need to have it so emphatically reinforced by the write-up in the local paper where, after several hundred words about him, my own presence was acknowledged in as cursory a fashion as possible. I also assumed that, as the bottom of the bill, I would read first. But backstage the publicist for the science-fiction author argued with the program director that his guy should go on first "because everyone wants to leave early." Since I was only two feet away when he said this, it seemed obvious he just didn't realize who I was, so I thought I should try and make my presence known, clearing my throat, shuffling my feet, yawning lustily, humming obnoxiously, moving furniture, rattling dishes, blowing my nose and waving my book in the air, all to no avail.

When all was said and done, however, I wound up going on first. I had given readings before but never like this: outdoors, in the dark, on a high stage with lights shining in my eyes so that I was reading to blackness, without a clue whether two people were in front of me or two hundred or two thousand. Every once in a while from out of the black, but as though from far, far away, would come a response of some kind, a titter of laughter for instance at a line which I may or may not have intended to be funny. But otherwise there was only the stillness of what I liked to believe was rapt attention, though it might as easily have been the stillness of empty seats. Then, at a crucial moment in the narrative, exactly half way through, all the lights suddenly went out.

I stood in the dark, waiting for them to come back on. The minutes ticked by, everyone silently sitting in the darkness, waiting. Finally, all I could say was, "I'd go on, but I can't see."

Well, I suppose it served me right for ever having thought that writing novels was a "career" in the first place. Reviewing movies, on the other hand, now *there's* a career, and when I started at the newspaper I suppose I was almost passionate about it. For whatever reason, I made it my particular specialty to defend those movies about which the critical establishment had already put out the dreary word, movies where some poor deluded filmmaker tried to reach for something the cultural mavens could have told him was far beyond his grasp. In fact, I quickly came to have little use for any movie that didn't completely embarrass itself. For a while I got something out of this, extravagantly championing displays of incompetent audacity; but enough time has gone by now for the culture to bleach out any embarrassments of real consequence, which is to say the sort that actually disturb anyone, and Shale has recently hinted that I've gone off-track. Lately it's all I can do to write anything at all. I've taken to just staring out my apartment window at night watching the helicopters drift in and out of the plumes of smoke, listening to *Now, Voyager* and Marrakesh drums on Station 3 and wondering what failed third career awaits the failure of my second. . . .

At first it was simple. There was only one rule you had to know about being a critic, which was that everything that isn't underrated is overrated. You can plug into this equation any movie or director or actor and stake out a position accordingly, taking into account of course that something is underrated right up to the moment it becomes overrated, which it remains until the inevitable backlash and it becomes underrated again. The point where the culture's adoration or contempt is finely balanced, suspended in a place of perfect proportion, does not exist; some years back I myself was both underrated and overrated at the same time. Beyond this simple algebra I admit there was a brief period when, secretly, naively, I held out hope for something more. I hoped that in the city of no politics, no identity, no moment and no rationale, a new cinema would present itself, which I called the Cinema of Hysteria. I was convinced that throughout the Twentieth Century this clandestine cinema was already forming though no one noticed, since by its very nature it was scattered and entropic and found only in outposts represented by such movies as *In a Lonely Place*, *The Shanghai Gesture*, *Bride of Frankenstein*, *A Place in the Sun*, *Gilda*, *Gun Crazy*, *Vertigo*, *One-Eyed Jacks*, *Splendor in the Grass*, *The Fountainhead*, *The Manchurian Candidate* and *Pinocchio*. These are movies that make no sense at all—and we understand them completely. These are the movies that would be left when the bottom fell out of America altogether, the cinema that would rip itself loose of its moorings and stutter across an American screen that remembers nothing. In an age riddled with uncertainty by technological acceleration, financial upheaval and the plague of exchanged bodily fluids, when we're panicked enough to root ourselves in anything we can still pretend to recognize—a job, a girlfriend, a heavily annotated calendar or Rolodex updated with correct area codes—the undercurrent of the age pulls us to an irrational truth, for which only an irrational cinema is sufficient. In the end this cinema resides at either the bottom of the psyche or the very top, the final shrill expression of a truth beyond words and thought, addressing the concerns of obsession and redemption that are beyond the rational calculations of technology or the rational price of finance or even the rational ravishment of plague.

It was only later that I realized there would be no such cinema for the very reason that made me a movie critic in the first place.

As time and passion dwindle to a pinpoint, the audience has come to understand that it no longer need subject itself to the actual experience of art but can subsume and synthesize faster and more efficiently art that is already processed by critical inter-pretation. Even better and more efficient when, as the second critic responds to the first, the art is twice removed; even better, as the third critic responds to the second, three times removed. When it became clear to me that reviewers, commentators and professional observers of all stripe were the true wise men of the new epoch, I could also see that with each new exponential twist of the ongoing cultural logarithm, the artist was approaching that ideal utopian moment when he or she would vanish altogether. Well I'm no dummy. As a novelist I felt myself getting less corpo-real with every passing moment. Except that ... except that after a while the tedium of reviewing movies that could neither be over-rated nor underrated, that were not worth rating at all, started driving me crazy. So I couldn't get it out of my head, my Cinema of Hysteria, when I sat down last week to review the revival and restoration of the long lost hysterical silent masterpiece *The Death of Marat*, by the legendary director Adolphe Sarre, who made the picture when he was twenty-five years old and never made another film. It was one of my best pieces. In fact, it may have been the best review I've ever written. Brilliantly analyzing the construction and montage, eloquently conveying the power of the lead actress's performance, I surmised in breathtaking terms how the entire his-tory of film might have been affected if *The Death of Marat* had gotten its due when it was first released; I even quoted an inter-view with D. W. Griffith in which he acknowledged the impact of *The Death of Marat* on his own work. All in all, watching this pic-ture was one of the highlights of my career as a critic, I assured the readers—"an unforgettable movie experience"—and at the end of the piece I posed the haunting question as to what had become of Sarre, who must now surely be dead. I could only hope, I concluded, that he lived long enough to see his vision vindicated. Reading over this final coda practically brought tears to my own eyes.

My only real concern about the review was that there is no such movie as *The Death of Marat* and there is no such director as Adolphe Sarre. I made them up. Borrowing here and there from the French Revolution, I made up the movie's plot, though only in bits and pieces, of course, since the critic never wants to give too much away; I made up the actors, I made up the sets, I made up camera angles. I made up cinemascope. The one thing in my review that was real was that there was indeed a filmmaker named D. W. Griffith, though the interview referred to I made up as well. By the time I got home from the newspaper after turning the piece in, I was already beginning to wonder what I was going to say when I was confronted with the fraud, as I would be in short order, if not momentarily. My best hope was that Dr. Billy O'Forte was the assigned editor on the piece; he would get the joke right away and maybe a good laugh out of it too, and then the two of us would have time to figure out what to do about my jape. We could just tell Shale I'd reviewed something else and gotten hopelessly bollixed on the job, and dump it altogether. Shale wouldn't be happy about it but, all in all, not reviewing any movie was probably preferable to reviewing one that didn't exist. A quick call to Dr. Billy, however, determined that he was not the editor on the piece, but that in fact Shale himself was editing. Shale wasn't so likely to laugh about it. It would be like the time I wrote about that strip joint as the spiritual center of L.A. and had it thrown back in my face, with the difference being that there actually was a strip joint.

Any minute now Shale was going to call. I kept turning the telephone off and back on, figuring I might as well get it over with. This is the last straw, he would say, except—being Shale—he wouldn't say it like that; he'd be tactful about it, sensitive to the deeper personal despair that had led me to this moment, his heart heavy with journalistic responsibility. Finally the phone rang. It was an odd conversation. He talked about trimming the second paragraph and rewriting the first sentence of the third; he argued that the middle section of the last graph was unnecessary. "Good piece," he concluded.

"Uhm. . . ."

"Coming into the office tomorrow?"

"No, I. . . . Shale?"

What? he said; and Nothing, I said; and we hung up. For a while I sat there trying to figure out what was going on, and then it hit me: of course he was going to shame me into confessing. He was going to see how far I would let things go before I stopped them myself. Or. . . . Or it was a joke, I thought. He was turning the whole thing back on me, and there was no way it would get that far anyway, once it went to copy editors and fact-checkers and the art department. Was there a chance in hell that one of those anal-retentive twenty-year-olds in fact-checking would let this get by? So for the next forty-eight hours I jumped at the phone every time someone called, half mortified and half relieved I'd been discovered. When I didn't hear from the copy editors at all, I actually relaxed, because that *had* to mean Shale killed the piece; the copy editors always had some complaint. But then one of the fact-checkers phoned, a particularly constipated kid who was constantly trying to argue with me over things he knew nothing about: "I want to ask you about your film review," he mumbled, timorously since I've always made it a rule to take an especially nasty tone with fact-checkers. "Our reference book says he was twenty-four."

"Who?"

"Adolphe Sarre."

"Reference book. . . ."

"He was twenty-four when he made *The Death of Marat.*"

At first I went blank. Then suddenly I understood: "Sure," I answered, laughing, "twenty-four, huh? I don't know how I missed that one. Anything else?"

"Uh, no, everything else checks out. . . ."

"Oh good. That's fine. I like it when everything checks out," I went on, congratulating the hell out of him.

"OK," he hung up, baffled. For half an hour I laughed about it, and then an hour later the art department called to ask if I had a still shot from the film they could run with the piece, and now I *knew* it was a joke; Shale even had the fact-checker and art director in on it. "Twenty-four in the reference book"—very funny. "A still shot to run with the piece"—hilarious. But after I was through laughing I started steeling myself again for the inevitable; sooner or later, once I had my fun and he had his fun, Shale would insist on a serious life-questioning discussion about whatever corroding inner rot was driving me to write about spiritual strip joints and non-existent movies. It wasn't that he'd fire me, of course; like I've said before, Shale's the kind of boss who gives you every chance before it comes to that. And in a way that made me feel all the more sheepish, because I'd taken advantage of his reasonableness, the way I always thought other people took advantage of it. I had indulged my boredom at his expense and the newspaper's, and felt infantile about it; and over the next few days I kept meaning to telephone him and beg forgiveness, like a school kid whose teacher is waiting for him to own up to his transgression. For a week I dialed his number and hung up before he answered, increasingly tortured right up to the morning I picked up the new issue of the paper on the street and there it was on page thirteen, no photo but otherwise big as life: ADOLPHE SARRE'S HEROIC RESURRECTION was the headline.

I just stood there on the sidewalk staring at it in horror and disbelief. Shale would never have taken it this far; his editorial integrity was such that he might make a joke out of me or himself, but not the newspaper. That stupid "fact-checker" obviously looked up the wrong entry. He got my made-up movie completely mixed up with some other movie, and now the thing was in black-and-white in a hundred thousand newspapers. Before the day was out studios and theaters would be screaming, maybe threatening lawsuits; now it was entirely possible I *could* lose my job or, worse, Freud N. Johnson would demand it and Shale would once again throw his body in front of me like he's done for half the other people at the newspaper, knowing it could lose him *his* job. I had precipitated a spectacularly foolish crisis, and I rushed back to the Hamblin and down the hall to Ventura's apartment where I rapped desperately on the door. But he wasn't there, so I went back to my suite and called Dr. Billy, but he didn't answer either.

The hours passed. The phone didn't ring, Dr. Billy didn't answer, Ventura wasn't home. Evening came, darkness fell, and still nothing happened; and then the night passed and the dawn came and the day passed again, and still nothing. And then the weekend passed and the beginning of the new week arrived and there was still only silence, except that at one point I could hear Ventura back in his apartment playing bebop on his stereo. But now I didn't know what to say to him, since four days had passed without a word from anyone; I felt too stupid about the whole thing to even tell Viv. So I said nothing. . . .

But that first night after the *Marat* review hit the streets, as I was still waiting for the angry telephone to ring and my fraud to catch up with me, I had a thought I hadn't had in years. For some reason or another, perhaps for no more reason than the fact that if I lost my job I wouldn't have anything better to do, I began to think about actually writing another book, one last book I had reconciled myself long ago to never writing. Up out of the sea of my psyche ripped the glacier of my conscience, beneath the sky of memory; and in my mind I began to record the story of that traveler who is always trying to get across that glacier, scale its walls one more time as I had tried to do so many times before, before the exhaustion of passion, faith, energy and courage led me to give up. Lying on my bed in the dark I followed the traveler's journey in my mind's eye until he was out of sight. I followed him into my sleep, to the horizon where the white of the ice becomes the white of the sky and he disappears from view: "He disappears from view," I think I muttered to myself before drifting off. But that doesn't mean, a dream answered, he isn't still there.

ೢᢞᢊ

Woke up a few days ago with one of my headaches, the first I've had in a long time. At first it isn't so bad but then it comes over my brain like a swarm, for two days, then three, then a week. . . . I went to see my acupuncturist in Little Tokyo; in a tiny dark room with the shades pulled I lie on a table and she sticks me with pins from the top of my skull to the toes on my feet. Since I always keep my eyes closed I can't be sure what it is she uses to tap the needles in, but tap them she does, in my legs and my arms, in my shoulders and my face. I picture her with a tiny little hammer pounding the needle into my forehead: tap tap tap. Then she sets all the needles on fire. I hear her lighting them and I feel the heat. She leaves the room and I lie anxiously awaiting her return, my eyes closed tightly, twenty little torches blazing from my body, like an albino porcupine on fire.

As I anticipated, Abdul has been sacked. Rather, the jihad for whom Abdul works, the other Palestinian terrorists, have been sacked, by whatever bank or lending institution holds the mortgage on the building. Everything is thrown into chaos, which alarms the other tenants. I just go on like a man blithely walking through a battle, bodies and bullets flying all around him. My guess is that financially Abdul ran the Hamblin into the ground with his grand designs. He had big plans for redecorating the hotel entry-way, putting hardwood floors in all the apartments, garbage disposals in all the kitchen sinks. Given enough time he would have installed a swimming pool on the roof, with a tennis court. Of course it also took him six months to get the elevator and the plumbing fixed—but Abdul isn't the kind of man to waste time on plumbing. What's plumbing next to hardwood floors? Abdul is a landlord of vision, he can't be bothered with mere *repairs*. He actually did lay a new hardwood floor in my old single apartment I just moved out of, which he then rented to a pretty girl from Indiana. Or, more likely, he laid the floor *after* he rented it to her, just so she wouldn't have any doubts as to what a smooth character he is. Now Abdul is out as manager, figuratively if not literally out of his palatial apartment where he schemes his inevitable comeback, waiting for the financial and legal problems to be resolved and control of the building once again to be within his grasp. "It's all bullshit," he says with a sniff, contemptuously waving away the recent events. "*Tactics.*"

⌒⌖⌒

In the months after I left Sally and returned to Los Angeles, I had many unusual dreams. I wrote some of them down. In one I had the distinct and certain sense that the only option left to me in my life was suicide. This sounds more melodramatic than it felt. In my dream I wasn't conscious of any unbearable pain, just that my identity was irrevocably dead, that my life was over even as my body went on living, out of sync with the reality of my life. Killing myself was the only way to get myself in sync. It wasn't an emotional decision but a practical one. I remember saying to myself, I wish this were a dream; but I knew it wasn't. It was like the dream I had about my father after he died, in which we met and, knowing he was dead, I argued with him over whether it was a dream, and he kept telling me it wasn't. Now, in this dream, I was looking through a window on a large yard, trying to read a notebook with words written close together in blue ink; a fleeting memory says Sally was in one of the rooms of the house....

A murdered woman, lying in the corner of my apartment, who I had the vague sense of having known.... There was an instant, however, when she seemed to turn her head; and when I looked again she was gone, and in her place on my apartment floor was my desk lamp, lying on its side, the tall metal one that Viv says looks like the kind used in gynecological examinations. For a moment I was elated by the possibility that this murder hadn't happened after all, but part of me wouldn't accept this; and in the months after Sally, I constantly had dreams like this, that questioned themselves and their own dream-nature, dreams built on memories rather than visions—not a vision of a woman being murdered but the memory of it. Memories, in other words, of things that not only never actually happened but that I had never even dreamed before; and yet in these dreams the memories were already there, delivered from some place that was neither consciousness nor unconsciousness.

In a little gallery in Baghdadville not so long ago, I found these silver balls. About four inches in diameter, and breathtaking in their uselessness. You can't look inside them to see colors, like in a kaleidoscope; you can't put them to your ear and hear the sound of the sky, like shells on the beach that hold the sound of the ocean. As artifacts they're distinctly uninteresting except for how uninteresting they are: round in shape, and nothing *but* round; silver in color, and nothing *but* silver. They don't stay in one place but roll maddeningly back and forth from one end of my shelves to the other. I bought half a dozen. It was only later that Viv read to me an ancient Chinese legend from the Tsui Dynasty, about winged dragons that flew over China snatching white mares up into the sky and mounting them. Drops of the dragons' semen spilled to earth, freezing into silver balls that littered the hillsides. Now, after hearing this story, when I put the silver balls to my ear, I hear the sky after all. Now when I gaze into their reflection, I see the embryos of little dragons swirling in a sea of sulfur. At night, when I'm in bed between Viv's legs, they drop from the shelves to the floor and roll into the moonlight, waiting for its cold gleam to evaporate them homeward. . . .

Sally is married. I found out a couple of nights ago in a bar from someone who, like everyone else, had been waiting for someone else to break the news to me, and assumed that by now someone had; thus, given the half-life of a rumor between the time it is rumor and the time it is truth, one can calculate it must have happened a while ago, perhaps as far as last spring. I gather that Los Angeles is full of people who have known about Sally's marriage for some time, and wondered how long it would be before I found out. She called a couple of months back, right after bumping into Ventura on one of his trips to Austin. When he got back to L.A. he told me he'd seen her, but not much else; maybe he knew and maybe he didn't. She left a couple of messages and I called back and left a message with whoever it was that answered the telephone; then I didn't hear from her again. Then I ran into this woman in a bar, a good friend of ours when Sally and I were together, and we were talking and she let slip about having been Sally's bridesmaid. "Bridesmaid?" I said, not sure I heard right over the clatter; but even in the dark I could see her face go from one shade of white to one of red and back again.

I'm not really so angry that no one told me sooner. I'm the world's biggest coward myself in such situations, and figure it isn't my responsibility to bring the news that someone else should have brought, just because I happened to have had the bad luck of being in the time and place to have heard it. I'm not even so angry that Sally didn't tell me. The truth is that, even though Sally should have been the one to tell me, I wouldn't have wanted to hear it from her. I would have felt the need, for either her sake or mine, to find an eloquent or graceful way of expressing my feelings, when I wouldn't have felt particularly eloquent or gracious. My rage about the whole thing—and it *is* a rage, no one should have any doubt about that—my rage about it isn't that I've been waiting for Sally to come back to me, because I haven't, or waiting to go back to her, because I wouldn't, but that this marriage is a lie; and while in a world of liars I'm a liar too, this lie is too profound for even me. I last saw her a year ago. She was in town and came by to leave off some things that were mine that she had never gotten around to returning, or that I had never gotten around to wanting back; when I answered the door her face was still that mix of anger and guilt and sadness it had been since I left—or was she the one who left? Down at the corner café, as the flames of the third ring began rising over the hill, she asked, "But why is it I mess everything up? And how is it that I messed *us* up?" and when she said it, it was with the same deathly sadness that was on her face almost five years before, when we were at the beginning rather than the end, sitting in a little bar on La Cienega and staring out the window. "Another man," she said quietly then, meaning me, naturally, "that I'm going to make miserable." I laughed it off, not having a better response. I didn't have a response this time either. The part of me that could never be unkind to her wanted to give her an answer: "Well, you did the best you could"—that sort of thing. Take her off the hook. But I don't take anyone off the hook anymore. So I had no answer for Sally. Guess the silence must have been devastating. Maybe it was in that silent moment that Sally's marriage became inevitable. We finished the coffee and left, before the heat of the backfires in the distance became too unbearable.

I once loved a woman named Lauren. Now in retrospect there

seems a very clear connection between Lauren and Sally, though they could not have been more different, and though there were ten years between my knowing them. Sally dark, Lauren light, one a singer and the other a child therapist, holding in common only their confusion. When Lauren finally went back to her husband, many things about me weren't the same after that, and some things were dead a long time. For a long time after Lauren there was no believing in love, not the love that makes you a force of nature; for years after she went back to Jason, every now and then she would call to say hello, and I couldn't hear her voice without turning inside out. I never blamed her. "Well, you did the best you could." I knew, and still know, that nothing she did was out of malice, but rather turmoil: which of us always knows our heart so well, or follows it so bravely? And then, a full decade later, just after I had left my own wife and fallen in love with Sally, the phone rang one night and it was Lauren. I don't think her husband had been out the door—or her life—all of five minutes before she called me. And I couldn't see her then, not with my own marriage in shambles and a new love affair I hadn't even begun to decode yet. So over the next two years we talked, and finally I went to see her after things fell apart with Sally; she was living near the beach, and at the first sight of her in the doorway I knew someone can turn your world upside down and then enough time can pass that she can't turn it right side up again. We had dinner. We didn't make love. I held her and she slept in my arms. "I'm not expecting anything," she lied when I left.

That night after I got home I had one dream after another, each connecting into a long tunnel at the end of which I could see the past. It was an insane night, everything in turmoil, the turmoil of Lauren revisited in the midst of the turmoil of Sally. In the weeks that followed she left a number of messages, which I answered only after deliberate and growing delays. Leaving the country on a long-planned vacation, she phoned within hours of returning; it was a week before I called back, gracing her phone machine with an excuse so feeble it infuriated even me. Her reaction, on my machine the next day, was as startling as it was brief: "I've been thinking," she said carefully, "we've had a long history together. A very long history." And then she paused. "I don't want you to ever call me again." And then she hung up.

I told you, I don't let anyone off the hook anymore. The woman took eleven years to decide she wanted me back. I took a week to return her phone call—and she never wanted to hear from me again. So I didn't call, as she had said not to, though I suspected she didn't really mean it; and six months later I received yet another message on my machine, one she was obviously reading from something she had written out, an extraordinarily bitter piece about what a liar I was. And the love of years before, when I loved her more than I had ever loved anyone, when she changed forever how I loved people, exploded, its shrapnel still hurtling down the years of my life. I knew she was terrified now, alone and alienated from a past that was embodied by a husband to whom she had sacrificed everything. Now she was living with the horror of having made the wrong choice; when I couldn't unmake it for her, she hated me. "It's been a year since you asked me never to call you again" I finally wrote her. "I've often thought it was a mistake that I didn't anyway. I'm not writing now to get in the last word on anything; if you really believe my love was a lie, I don't think there's much I could say that would change your mind. But after a year it's become too much for me to live with and not answer it: though for the time being it may have become necessary for you to believe differently, I had to write and tell you that if there are ways in which time has changed or misled either of us, or if we both wound up letting each other's love down, my love was real, and I always knew yours was as well, and I think deep down you know it too."

Well, perhaps. I don't know what's real about love anymore, except that the last thing I want is to sound cynical about it. Perhaps you have to get to the end of your life to know what's real about it or maybe, as my mother did with my father, you have to spend a life with one person to know how real is the turmoil of love as opposed to how glib is the turmoil of romance. I sent Lauren the letter and a week later it came back, unopened; I still have it, sealed in the envelope with the postmark, as though sometime I expect to have to produce it for a judge or jury, to prove that it really exists, and that I really made the effort of writing it. Lauren called yet again, months later, getting in one last cut: "I guess," she said, "I stayed with Jason because at least he was honest." And maybe you really believe that, Lauren. Maybe for the moment you've convinced yourself that's true, so I won't try and convince you otherwise, except to say you're going to have to spend a lifetime convincing yourself of that one, because you couldn't convince anyone else for two seconds. He abused you, he cheated on you, he lied to you on a daily basis, and you still stayed with him, *and it isn't my fault*. It breaks my heart, and I'm as sorry as I can be, truly sorry, not the sorry of contempt or even pity but the sorry of empathy with another human soul who can botch up her life as efficiently as the rest of us. But it isn't my fault, and I'm done apologizing to people for their bad choices. I've never expected anyone to apologize for mine.

Trained by a world of men who stop caring about them once

their youth and beauty run out, the women who have been double-crossed by time look around, all of their possibilities suddenly vanished, barely retaining what a vicious world trained them to consider their assets, and then they savagely reassess their situations. Thinking back, squinting hard at a memory, they reconstruct in their minds a hazy image. Then they say to themselves, Well, actually, he wasn't so bad. He never hit me. He was faithful, far as I knew. He didn't take my money. He listened to me as though I was more intelligent than an ashtray. In bed he could make me come, or at least tried to, and when I cried he took me in his arms and, not often, but every once in a while, even cried with me. He wasn't, in other words, absolutely the most selfish, loutish individual I've ever known. There were even a few of my friends who thought I was a fool to let him go. No, now that I think about it, he wasn't so bad at all; in fact, now that I think about it, I wonder if I still have his phone number, from all those years ago. . . . And so they call. Desperation on their lips and in their throats; and it just makes me feel lousy. I'm appalled by their terror, and the part of me that's still left from before, back around the time I got married, from my idealistic days which even my best friends cannot bring themselves to believe I've so brutally discarded, that part of me wants to take the terror out of these women and cast it aside for them. I swear. I want to assure them their lives aren't over, that they won't be alone all the time, which is the thing that scares them shitless—and that if they *are* alone, it won't be so bad. But I'm in that minority of people who believes it's better to be alone than with someone you despise, unless, of course, the someone you despise happens to be yourself.

Not long after Lauren went back to her husband, I moved into a little upstairs-downstairs studio in a cul-de-sac near MacArthur

Park. On this street lived the last of L.A.'s elite, professors from the nearby art school and the inheritors of Old Money who had been there fifty years, since a time when this was one of the city's most exclusive neighborhoods. Now of course the neighborhood was overrun by the hordes: punks and students and aspiring artists, of whom I was one. Next door lived a young couple, a day laborer named Roy who had been laid off about a year before and sat around all afternoon listening to the radio and doing drugs until his wife got home from work, when they would head off for the clubs in Chinatown. I fell in with them, I don't even remember exactly how. He complained one night about how loud my music was through the walls, but appreciated my taste and decided I should come along on their nightly rounds; or maybe it was her idea all along. Her name was Madeline. She worked for a secretarial temp agency that sent her out to one law office after another, where eventually the moment arrived when the head partner propositioned her and she had to move on.

It never took long. That she ever rejected such overtures at all—and I don't know for certain she always did—may be a little surprising, given not just the generous financial benefits that were usually implied but her chameleon sexuality, as depraved one moment as it was demure the next. She had overripe red lips and wide brown eyes, under a storm of auburn hair. Those nights in Chinatown when the clubs' crowds were dense and everyone was packed together and, from the shoulders down, everyone's hands and fingers lived a secret life, she danced with me way too irresistibly, and reached over and unbuckled me and took me in her hand even while Roy stood there right next to us, since no one could see anything anyone was doing. Obviously I should have extricated myself from the situation. But I made the mistake of looking too long into her amazing face, which rendered anything her hands did or didn't do irrelevant; and pretty soon the morning arrived when he was passed out from the night's drugs and Madeline was on my doorstep. I promise I resisted her at first. But soon there was no resisting her. She offered herself again and again, provoking and taunting and humiliating me all at once; only looking back do I realize with surprise what she really wanted. She wanted me to hit her. She wanted me to hit her the way Roy had hit her, and perhaps the man before him and the man before him. Looking back it's as clear as water that's what she wanted, all the infuriating things she said to make me desire and hate her, all the infuriating things she said to make the two inseparable. But since I've never hit a woman the idea was incomprehensible, and instead our fucking got more crazed, as he listened through the wall next door; it tore at the last shreds of whatever I had left from Lauren, whatever I could still bring myself to remember, until one night in the dark when I slid myself into her, she glared back at me over her naked shoulder and hissed, "You're *such* a beast," and it exhilarated me. At that moment the rest of my life tore itself loose from everything that had come before, and I was free of what I had been, of my innocence and pain, everything awash in pitch-black but for the translucent squiggle of my semen.

A few years back, right after the Quake but before things really began with Viv, I was in a bookshop vying with a woman for the most advantageous position among the shelves from which absolutely, positively, without any doubt whatsoever, it could be determined that the store didn't carry any of my books, when I looked over at the woman and said, "Sam?" Sam was a strawberry blonde I knew back just before Lauren. It had been nearly fifteen years since I'd seen her, and her cruel waif's beauty had grown tired around the edges while remaining, after all those years, as remarkably uncomplicated by self-consciousness as it ever was; there wasn't an idea in her head someone else hadn't put there. Even her "wit" had a hand-me-down quality: "Just a sharp intake of air," she would say when she yawned, that sort of thing. Now all these years later in the bookstore her eyes still tended to dart around her like they had always done, but a little more frantically, as though in fifteen years she'd learned how little her beauty counted, how the watching universe was less impressed with every passing moment. She stood in the aisle of the bookstore holding the last copy of my last book in front of her as though it were a shield, and I guess we exchanged a phone number or two, because she called me not long afterward, and for a while I tried to dodge my own impulses, which is easier to do in the daylight than the dark. Finally one night I decided to drive down the coast to see her.

She lived in a trailer park. She was rather mysterious about what had happened to her in the last fifteen years, but lying around the trailer were the distinct remains of a marriage gone bad. Pages in fashion magazines of photos of beautiful young girls who might bear resemblance to a younger Sam were dog-eared a little too ferociously. Hanging around the trailer and then going out to get a bite to eat quickly reminded me that we never really had a thing in the world to talk about, that our best moments were the silly ones; and as plainly as I honestly could, as delicately as whatever feeble code of honor I still have allowed me to, I tried to explain what I was *not* there for. And in that familiar tarantella of feminine ambivalence Sam decided to let me go home with barely a kiss, and in my rearview mirror I watched her watching me leave from behind the trailer's front screen door.

Before I met the highway, however, I turned back. The night was just too dark—that darkness where memory becomes the only thing you see before you. The window and doorway of Sam's trailer had gone black by the time I returned, twenty minutes after I left; I didn't knock, I didn't call out. I made my way through the darkened trailer back to the bed still thinking about how she looked and felt all those years before, the arch of her back, the wideness of her hips, that silky undeveloped feeling of her labia that still suggested forbidden adolescence; and now I couldn't quite tell if she was awake or the sound I heard in the darkened trailer was the rustling of her sleep. If she had said no or begged me to stop I swear I would have; I'm almost sure of it. But when I saw flash across the white of her back the sputtering glow of the broken streetlamp outside her window, and as the sound of the screen door I had neglected to latch behind me blew open and shut in the wind and mixed with the little half-asleep sounds she made as I fucked her, there was that same old feeling in me of memory going up in smoke, of the future going up in smoke, of nothing to be remembered that had come before or would come yet, that feeling of being lost to myself and the past and the future, that delirious amnesia which, because Sam was practically a perfect stranger to me again, was all the purer, as though she was the purest drug on the street now racing through my veins. I don't confuse it with love. But I don't deny either that it might be a kind of love. It's the last truly anarchic act left to us by the millennium, the last opportunity to seize love back from the sexual ideologues whose only real love is power anyway: and who knows what was filling Sam's head at this moment, all the memories that flushed and deserted her? Who knows if her eyes were filled with the faces of young girls from fashion magazines and whether she was thinking in this moment of obliteration that she was not just one of those girls but all of them, rows and rows of young girls on rows and rows of beds? Maybe her head was filled with majestic insights I could never imagine, maybe she was solving one riddle of the damned cosmos after another and I was nothing but the generator of all her revelations. I didn't finish with her but left still hard, planting a kiss in the small of her back.

On the highway in the middle of the night, I pulled over to the first pay phone I could find. I phoned Morgan, who I hadn't seen in a couple of years, and who didn't answer; then I called Dory, who lives on the floor below mine in the Hamblin, and whose husband works at night for the phone company. She didn't answer either. Then I called Ylana with our signal—one ring and then hang up, and then call back. I never quite understood what the point of this signal was or who was being deceived, but I used it anyway as she had always asked me to. I had met Ylana in a bookstore too, like Sam; she had just been caught trying to shoplift a book. Mortified, she was insisting to the store manager that she had simply put the book in her bag without thinking, when I piped up in the middle of the confrontation, "I'm sure she didn't mean to steal it." We were all standing in the doorway where she had nearly made her getaway, Ylana and I and the grim store manager and the weasely little clerk who caught her.

"Do you know this woman?" the manager asked me.

"No."

"Then we'll handle this," he snapped.

"But, you see ... I wrote this book." And I had. It was one of the earlier books that could still be found in paperback before going out of print. I had never seen anyone buy a book of mine, let alone steal one. "This is me," I went on, pointing at my name on the cover.

Of course, no one had any idea whether it was really me; that was the first thing. The second thing was, What difference did it make to the situation at hand? And yet the startled manager sputtered, "Oh, well. . . . Yes, then, I guess. . . ." Ylana quickly paid for the book and I hustled her out of the store. As with the store manager, it never occurred to her I might not really be the author of the book; she instinctively knew it was so, and when we got to the car she turned triumphantly with her witchy mouth in a half smile and half pout, and touched my face. In that moment I knew she would give me anything I asked for that didn't involve more than two or three hours, and that moreover she expected nothing in return. So now, calling her from the phone booth on the highway in the middle of the night, she answered, having gotten the signal; and without my saying a word she breathed into the receiver, "The beach," and hung up. Before I got back in the car I called my own number to pick up any messages off my machine, and there was one from Dory. "I know it was you who just called," she said, "I'll be waiting. The door will be unlocked. He won't be back till morning. . . ."

Halfway up Pacific Coast Highway, heading for my rendezvous with Ylana at our special beach, I could smell the ash of Los Angeles through my window, I could see the red midnight sky in the distance, and I thought about these women who gave themselves to the sensual moment that lived inside them, to the hunger that resided where their legs met and whatever hands rapturously gripped them by their hips. It would be an insult to simply compliment them for the courage of their carnal convictions; that courage came to them so naturally as to not even involve the calculation of petty courage. Rather it was the unthinking, unconscious surrender that inspired me; for its one brief moment I was almost good enough to be inside them. Driving up the coast highway in the night I might have been completely overcome by gratitude if I'd had the time, it might have driven me right off the highway, but I was still hard from Sam and I had to get to Ylana and our special empty beach, and an hour later I pulled up and parked the car and stumbled down the hillside in the dark, wandering along with the ocean in my ears not able to see anything, groping like a blind man—when a hand reached up out of the dark and took mine. She pulled me down on the sand. She was completely naked. She unbuckled my pants and slipped her mouth onto me and I heard her giggle because she could smell Sam on me, and there was no way she was going to let me get away with *that*. She pulled me into her before she was completely wet and scissored her long legs across my back, and of course now I had a predicament, which was that Dory had left a message on my machine that she was waiting, and so, as with Sam, I was committed not to finish with Ylana; I held back as much as I could. But then a cloud moved and the moon was exposed and flooded the beach with light and in the wind off the ocean was the smell of blood and body oil, and on top of me she swayed against the pandemonium of the stars behind her. And when she brought her long hair up to completely cover her face and said, "Would you like me like this, to be nothing but a body for you?" I could barely make out in the moonlight the wild little smile that was on her lips, but I knew my scheme about holding out for Dory was at great risk, and as I tried to maintain control of the situation the wench gave the slyest little wiggle of her hips; and it was all over. *And she laughed.*

So now twenty minutes later I was back in the car speeding through the Palisades down Sunset Boulevard. I was exhausted, depleted, not an impulse of desire lurking anywhere from my brain to my heart. I wanted to go home and go to bed but of course I couldn't do that, because Dory was waiting and while I could pretend I hadn't gotten her message until it was too late, and while she might not be in any position to complain about it, given the husband who worked for the phone company, I might be able to deceive her but I couldn't deceive myself or the obligation I had to her. It didn't matter that my desire was gone or that it would have been easy to ignore hers, it didn't even matter that we were barely acquaintances, crossing paths at the mailboxes one afternoon when she was mad at her husband and grumbling at her mail and we started talking and wound up going up to her place for a glass of wine. . . . What mattered was that I had telephoned her tonight because I wanted her and she had answered, and now I couldn't just forget her because I had been satisfied by someone else. I was obligated by my desire for her of earlier that evening and though the desire had passed, the obligation had not, because I was obligated by desire's memory; she had offered herself to that desire and for her it wasn't just a memory, it lived and breathed in the moment, it was still a part of her present even as it had already spurted into my past: even desire has its laws. So you can see how when I reached the hotel and pulled the car into the garage I had no choice but to head up to her apartment; the door was unlocked. I had no choice but to make my way into her bedroom and turn the top sheet back and run my fingertips down her belly; she shuddered. I pulled her to the edge of the bed where I knelt so I could separate her thighs and open her with my fingers and press my mouth against her; even in my exhaustion I couldn't help loving the moan that answered. Half asleep I slipped my tongue inside her. I don't know how long it took, maybe it was minutes or maybe it was hours, I just remember kissing her when she came and her purr of response before she fell asleep. . . .

Tonight, before I fall to sleep, looking at the city's scattered lights and gapes of blackness outside my window, thoughts of Sally return. And I know, in my exhaustion and fulfillment, that it wasn't all Sally's fault. With the strange, hallucinatory clarity of fatigue, I suddenly understand how the burden of my romantic expectations was unendurable to anyone but me; there isn't a woman on earth who wouldn't have felt buried alive under them. We both knew she wasn't capable of reciprocating in full. When the receiver can barely return what has been given, then the giving is not really about giving but power. In both our minds Sally could only repay my "gift" with her very life, since her love couldn't possibly be big enough; it was too much for her to live up to, and part of me knew that and demanded it anyway. Now I find myself saying to her, "Your love was a lie," as Lauren said it to me, and maybe this is where love's journey always ends, in the land of liars. Maybe now she writes me a letter, as I wrote to Lauren, to say: I'm sorry, but they were your expectations, not mine, *and it isn't my fault.* And she's right, it wasn't her fault, not all of it anyway; maybe it wasn't even mostly her fault. I don't know anymore. Now the most profound regret I have is that Polly, Sally's little girl, who I raised during those years with Sally as surely as did her mother, must have forgotten me. Little Polly is seven now, her little life doubled since I last saw her; if I was to see her on the street I might not even know her, except for the way she must look more and more like Sally. If I talked to her on the phone, hers would be a voice I've never heard, communicating things she could never conceive only a few years ago. When I think of how I've surely slipped altogether from her memory— "Who is that strange man? I think perhaps I knew him once"—I can barely stand it, and it was my own doing, of course. . . .

What the hell. At least I got one good laugh out of the whole thing. Drifting off to sleep I have to laugh that the city out there beyond my window is eaten up by the "secret" of Sally's wedding. People wondering and worrying when I'm going to find out, staying clear of my intersections with my secrets and waiting for my collision with the biggest secret of all. I see them scurry from shadow to shadow, avoiding any conversation in which the Big News could manifest itself at any moment. Suddenly, in retrospect, a thousand unfinished sentences make sense, a thousand abrupt questions that I have been asked—"Uh, heard from Sally lately?"—suddenly have a reason for having been asked. Revealed in a new light are a thousand awkward pirouettes and nimble dodges that struck me at the time as a little odd. The sap in me, of course, wants to take them off the hook as usual, wants to relieve them of their anxiety, call them all up and assure them: It's OK, I know now. You can come out of hiding. But I'm going to resist that impulse for a while. I'm going to let them stew awhile, the longer the better. The fact that it's *not* a secret anymore is now *my* secret. I'm not so angry they didn't tell me, but it does seem they ought to pay a price for it. If it were me, I would expect to pay such a price.

I wonder whether Viv knows, and if not, whether I should tell her. For such a long time she has felt herself in the shadow not so much of Sally but my love for Sally, the two of which become more distinctly different as time passes. Maybe she's thinking, How will he feel when he finds out? How do I tell him without sounding gleeful . . . ? Or, if she doesn't know and I tell her, will she then wonder what it *means*, imagining meanings that don't even exist? To tell Viv interjects Sally into our lives in a way that does us no good—or ejects Sally from our lives in a way that frees us forever . . . but right now I don't know which. So for a while I will leave Sally in the soundless shadows, and spare Viv the one last entrance Sally must make before she makes one last exit.

Goodbye. It's one thing to have gotten over you. It's another thing to get over having loved you. Now I say goodbye to our past that I could never quite say goodbye to before, and to whatever dubious future might have once been attached to it. I put it with all my other dubious futures; I have a vast collection of them, lined up on my shelves in empty silver balls. I pick them up, shake them and they don't make a sound, and that makes me smile. Every once in a while someone tries to slip one in that rattles with a false promise, like a petrified dead bug trapped inside; and I just open the window and heave it to the Hollywood Hills, where by now there must be a junkyard of such futures that rattle with one false promise after another. I'm back to the present, the one true living moment in a continuum of death—dead pasts, dead futures, dead memories, dead expectations. In an ironic world, you will think I'm being ironic when I say it's good to be alive. But there's nothing ironic about it. I would like to think I haven't become so bankrupt as to replace a dead innocence with a dead irony, the first of which distinguishes children, but the second of which distinguishes monsters.

It was in Berlin when I first came across the American Tarot. The cards were tacked up on the wall of a German punk's flat. A year or so ago, driving home one afternoon from my acupuncture session in Little Tokyo, my body buzzing with the bedlam of toxins pricked loose by all the little pins I'd had stuck in me, I stopped in Hollywood and stumbled into a tattoo joint on Ivar. I wandered from one wall to the next staring at the hallucinatory designs. The young woman who ran the tattoo shop had jet black hair and eyes that lit up like the sun through the dirtiest pane of a stained glass window; in the fashion of the neighborhood all her teeth had been filed to points. Talking with her about the designs on the walls, I asked her about the American Tarot. She had never heard of it. There and then I made it up for her, the major arcana and the suites, the Snakecharmer and the Boatman and the Moll and the Slave, the Witch and the Bounty Hunter and the Black Lieutenant and the Salem Mistress, the King of Stars and the Knight of Bridges and the Queen of Rifles and the Princess of Coins. The tattoo artist started drawing them as fast as I could come up with them, until the counter was papered with them; and we hatched our plot then, that she would tattoo the whole tarot on the women of Los Angeles, until the entire deck was dealt and wandering the city. Every once in a while I drop by the shop on Ivar to see how it's going. And when I'm driving the streets and I see the young hookers and runaways and waifs who are all fleeing their names, I name them: I imagine that this one is the Blind Hitchhiker and that one the Ripped-Dress Debutante, their secret personae etched on them in secret places. The last time I went by the tattoo joint I had a revelation. It was filled with that peculiar odor I had been smelling in the streets of Los Angeles for some time, without being able to identify it; and I realized it was the smell of color soldered to flesh. . . .

America recedes into the past. History recedes into the future. From my rooftop at dusk in ravaged L.A. I see America and history in the distance, a horizon of dust pulling farther away. On the monitor every once in a while I pick up a broadcast from back east where, among the rest of the nation's populace, L.A. has become just a dim recollection. Out blips the image of some politician, making the usual stern proclamations the dead make to the living.

They kept telling you it was a war for the soul of America, but you didn't believe them. They kept saying you were the Enemy, but you wouldn't accept that, because you just didn't feel like an enemy. Now you know they meant every word, and more. Now, as the Twentieth Century slips America's hold on it, you have become the Enemy they always said you were; and in the receding history that you see from your rooftop, you can't help being impressed. No one with a highly developed sense of his own hypocrisy can help being impressed how the amoral have become the New Moralists, how the spiritually malevolent have become the New Righteous. You can't help being impressed how the New Patriots have consolidated their power and profit in the name of an idea someone had for a country a couple of hundred years ago, or the name of a cracked visionary who died for love a couple of thousand years ago. Of course it might prove embarrassing if he were to actually return as they claim to believe he will, living among the very trash these paragons hate and despise: the hookers and junkies and abandoned teenage mothers and muttering crazies who have nowhere to live but the street, the once-beautiful young men emaciated by plague, the suffering and forsaken souls he would cradle and comfort as they die the agonizing deaths in which the "moral" and the "righteous" and the "patriotic" revel. But the New Paragons have probably concluded that there really isn't all that much danger of him showing up any time soon; and so every one of them can come beaming in on the airwaves these days with a little more confidence, sounding a little tougher and sitting a little more ram-rod straight, like he has a ruler up his ass to measure to the last millimeter not only the distance from his rectum to his heart but which of the two is smaller and tighter and more constricted. And then after a while you have to admit maybe you're not so impressed by them anymore. After a while you have to admit maybe you're beginning to get your fill of these gibbering corpses, and you just wish there was another thousand miles of Mojave between them and you. You have to admit you would just as soon set the desert on fire and rip up all the highways leading into town and lay a black smoke screen across the eastern sky, so there was no possibility whatsoever any of them could ever get in.

In other words, I couldn't help saying yes when Viv asked me to write her movie. I couldn't help but like the idea of such a movie flickering in and out of monitors all over America. Network Vs. signed her to make a short fifteen-minute pornographic film about a woman artist who paints portraits of nude female models while they tell her their fantasies; then at the end of the film when we finally see the artist's paintings they aren't portraits at all but scenes of fire—sparks, blazes, infernos, tendrils of flame rising skyward. . . . It was all Viv's idea. I take no blame nor credit for it. "That sounds great," I said when she explained it; I could see the whole thing in my mind.

"You really think so?" said Viv.

"I can see the whole thing in my mind."

"You can?"

"Absolutely."

"In your mind? The whole thing?"

"Absolutely."

"Good," she said, "you're going to write it for me." Sneaky little vixen. Now I was stuck. It had been years since I'd written anything but movie reviews, unless you count that *Death of Marat* business, and at first I tried to hem and haw my way out of it. Later, after I actually started writing, my doubts only grew. Over the days and weeks I turned out many pages of splendid camera shots, amazing dissolves, spectacular fades: desolate lunar plains turning into bare thighs, spheres over sand dunes turning into breasts over bed sheets, a background rumble of ominous machinery revealing itself as the murmur of voices, all interspersed with images of paints being mixed and brushes splattering furiously upon white canvases. In my last scene the repressed artist finally attacks the painting with her hands, her fingers running through the fiery reds—which Viv later pointed out a real painter would only do at the risk of toxic poisoning. After three weeks I had written two minutes worth of the damnedest cinematography you've ever seen, leaving thirteen minutes in which I realized, to my great resentment, I was expected to supply characters who actually said things to each other and activity that bore some vague resemblance to a narrative.

By the time I knew I'd gotten in too deep, it was too late. The station fronted Viv some money and drew up a production schedule, which meant I had to finish a script by the end of the month. In search of an inspiration I started crossing back and forth from one time zone of the city to the next, prowling the clubs and coffee houses and topless joints that spring up overnight in the ashes of the Black Passages; I don't know if I really expected to be inspired or just hoped that by a stroke of good fortune someone would mug me and bash in my brains and put me out of my misery. I didn't get *that* lucky; but almost. I was at the Feverish one night, down at the corner of Fountain and Formosa, when Jasper walked in. Now populated with punks and musicians and after-hours strippers, the Feverish was a Chinese opium den back in the 1910s that became a Hollywood bar in the 1930s; yellowing autographed photos of expired B-movie stars line the booths, and a pool table sits in back next to a platform where every once in a while someone gets up and recites the worst fucking poetry you've ever heard. On this night I was there, in came this big disheveled rag doll of a girl. Tall and defiantly round, with blonde hair and torn stockings, she wore around her neck a necklace that didn't match her earrings that didn't match each other, none of which matched the three or four rings on her fingers.

She strolled over to the table next to me and sat down, ordered a glass of wine and smoked a cigarette awhile. I just scribbled nothing at all in my note pad in order to appear busy, until she looked over and said, What are you writing? at which point I told her a little of the story about the artist and her models, and waited for her to ask a couple of questions. It was all I could do not to leap across the table, grab her by her enormous breasts, rip her open and reach inside and pull out an inspiration, because the moment I saw her I knew she had one; I was desperate, and just barely canny enough to know this wasn't a woman who appreciated anybody else's desperation but her own. We talked awhile and I ordered us another couple glasses of wine and nearly sprayed mine across the table when she said, "You must know a lot about women to write a story like that."

I looked to see if she was joking. "Well," I pulled myself together, "let's say I know just enough to know I'd have to be an idiot to say I know very much about women."

It only got worse when she said, "I mean, comparing women to men, for instance." She had this way of slipping in and out of a sly look, the same way she slipped in and out of a slight accent, which sounded German; the look she did with her eyes, narrowing them and then growing wide with them again before she smiled, "Leaving aside the obvious."

"Well ..." I started, and couldn't think of anything that wouldn't say a lot less about women than it did about me. I went for an easy one first. "Women are braver than men," I finally suggested.

"Everyone knows *that*," she answered.

"They have more imagination."

"Really?"

"I don't mean they're more creative. I don't know whether they're any more or less creative. I mean that, more than a man, a woman can reimagine herself."

"Women are always changing," she nodded. "And after a while men don't change at all."

"No," I had to agree, "for most men the train pretty much pulls into the station about the time they're twenty-five. Whereas for women it continues on down the track for the rest of their lives."

"Yes."

"They're stronger and more resilient," I offered, another easy one.

She sipped her wine and waited. "Those are the good things."

"Yes."

"You didn't suppose," she smiled, "you could fool me by just mentioning the good things, did you?"

"Well . . ." I fumbled. "Women are less forgiving."

"Yes."

"They're less willing to take responsibility for their contradictions."

She didn't say anything to that.

"They're less romantic."

"They're less romantic?"

"Of course that isn't necessarily a good thing or a bad thing."

"Women are less romantic than men?"

"Yes."

"I don't *think* so."

"Actually, it's the only thing I'm reasonably certain of."

"I don't know any woman who would agree with that."

"That's because for a woman, romanticism is a pattern of behavior, or maybe even ritual, whereas for a man it's a matter of life and death. Assuming he's the sort of man who was ever willing to die for anything in the first place."

"Yes, well," she answered witheringly, lighting another cigarette, "maybe women haven't always had the luxury of dying for romance."

"Well, there you go."

"Anyway, you're generalizing."

"That's what you asked me to do, remember? Your contradiction, your responsibility."

She widened her eyes ferociously. She asked my name and I told her, and she said maybe she had heard of me; I told her I doubted it, and she asked if I wrote some books once, and I admitted I had. "I read a review of one, maybe," she said. "The last one."

"That was a while ago."

"The pretentious one."

"All my books are pretentious," I assured her. "The last one was just especially pretentious."

"My name's Jasper."

"Interesting name."

She was bored with how interesting her name was. "It's a name without a reason," she explained. "No, my parents didn't think I was going to be a boy. No, they didn't conceive me in a town called Jasper. No, they didn't name me after Jasper Johns or an Uncle Jasper who left them a million dollars...." On her finger was a ring in the shape of a cat, curled around a red stone. She held her hand up and even let me take her fingers in my own so I could examine it. She looked at me like she saw right through me. "It matches the one in my labia."

"Pardon me?"

"It matches the ring in my labia."

"I don't believe you."

But of course I did. I believed it completely. She appeared genuinely unconcerned with whether I believed her. "Well, I'm not going to prove it to you," she said.

Inspiration was at hand. Not because I was in control of anything but because her control was so complete she found giving something to me easy, a gesture of sexuelle oblige in lieu of the evidence that there was a cat ring in her labia, which was the only thing that matched anything else she wore, namely the ring on her finger. "In my story," I said to her as calmly as I could, "the artist poses a question to each model, who is a stranger to her."

"Yes?"

"Where does he touch you?"

She nodded.

"There's no preface to the question, and the 'he' referred to is irrelevant. Sometimes the model is surprised by the question, sometimes she's amused or threatened. In each case the artist assumes she's taken control of the situation by catching the other woman off-guard, until one night she meets a model who answers as though she's been expecting the question all along."

Thinking only a moment Jasper said, "Under my breast. Below my nipple."

"Which one?"

"The left." She said, casually, "When his hands are raised to my breast, you know . . . he's exposed to me. Disarmed."

"Disarmed?"

"Like in the gangster movies. When the bad guy puts his hands in the air."

"Or the good guy sometimes."

"Or the good guy."

"Is he the good guy or the bad guy?"

"He's the good guy," she answered, "when I'm the bad guy." She leaned back where she sat and looked me in the eye. "Last night I went to this opening, a little gallery downtown out near the third ring. I thought I might see myself there. I mean, in a painting."

"You mean you actually *are* a model?"

"—but I was walking through the exhibit and by the time I was halfway, I'd had a little wine, and was feeling a little. . . ." She smiled and widened her eyes again that way she had; in moments she suggested complete dementia, in others almost unearthly composure. "So maybe I was there after all, and I just didn't recognize myself."

"What does it mean when you see a painting of yourself and you don't recognize it?"

"It means the artist ought to give up painting, as far as I'm concerned. Did you think it meant something else? You didn't think it meant something deep and psychological, did you? I don't think too much about the meaning of things. Halfway through the exhibit I bumped into him or he bumped into me, I don't remember.... He acted like he knew me, but as far as I know we've never met. It didn't matter. We went back to his place. I went into the bathroom and took off my clothes. When I came back he was passed out on the bed, so I undressed him and blind-folded him, and tied his wrists to the bedposts with my stockings. I found his keys and turned off the lights and went to this little bar I like, down by the beach. There's a good jukebox there. I was drinking and started talking to this woman, I don't remember her name—she was quiet, like someone who was dying to be wild but just didn't know how, and we had another drink and I said, Let's go see this guy I know. So we went back to the apartment. He was still tied to the bed. We did what we wanted. Sometimes we kissed each other, sometimes we touched him. Sometimes we just left him there and didn't pay attention to him at all. We'd wander around his apartment and look at his things and drink his liquor and stand naked on his balcony, looking out at the ocean, listening to him thrashing on the bed inside trying to get free. The more desperately he thrashed, the more we liked it. I could tell she was holding back, waiting for me to let her know that whatever we were going to do was all right, and finally we went back to bed and I got on top of him and then she did, and then we both did at the same time. I know what you're thinking. You're thinking it's every man's fantasy. Every man thinks it's his fantasy. But when I held his face between my thighs and put myself in his mouth to make myself come, I could tell he realized it wasn't his fantasy, it was *my* fantasy. Afterward the other girl got on top of him and it was taking her longer, so I started whispering in her ear, telling her I was a man and how I was going to fuck her from behind. That made her come. We finished and put on our clothes and went back to the beach bar where we had another drink. We were still laughing about it. He's probably still there, tied to the bed."

I believed all of it, the way I believed the bit about the labia ring. But while I had been given everything I could hope for, somehow she was still in charge; sort of like she said, I thought it was my inspiration, but now I realized it was hers. She got up from the table and finished the last of her wine.

"Maybe you'll write another book someday," she said on her way out, "even more pretentious than the last." And then she disappeared through the door and I sat there staring at it for five minutes, just to be sure she wasn't coming back. Then I swallowed the last of my wine, gathered up my notes and rushed back to my apartment, where I bolted the door and turned out the lights and by the glow of the desk lamp wrote down every single word, every single thing about her I could remember, every single thing she said. . . .

❧

We call our movie *White Whisper* because it doesn't mean anything at all, at least as far as we can tell. "But just where," Viv asked one night, reading the finished script, "do you propose we find an actress with a cat ring in her labia?" Her eyes narrowed suspiciously. "Do you actually *know* a woman with a cat ring in her labia? Also," she added, flipping back several pages, "women are a lot more direct."

"What do you mean?"

"When they talk to each other. A woman doesn't say breasts, she says tits."

"Are you sure?"

"Of course I'm sure." I replayed in my mind my conversation with Jasper: did she say breasts or tits? So over the next several days I revised the script, making the second draft more explicit, to which Viv objected that now it was *too* explicit. "I mean, think about it. Would a woman say *that?*" So I revised the script again, taking things out, to which Viv complained it now needed something more, something else. To which I became irritated and suggested maybe Viv didn't really know what the script needed, to which Viv answered I didn't need to get so temperamental about it and anyway she was just trying to anticipate what the head of the network might say, to which I proposed maybe the head of the network ought to write the script and we'd see whether *he* thought women said breasts or tits assuming he thought women had anything to say at all, to which Viv pointed out that the head of the network wasn't a he but a *she*. To which a little bell ought to have gone off in my head right then. Sure enough, when we went down to the network to meet the head honcho, who should be sitting behind the desk but Veroneek; next to her, Joe the wolf began howling the second I walked in. Veroneek grabbed him by the jaws and hollered down his throat, "Keep it quiet in there, Joe!" Hello, she said, looking back up at me.

Hello, I answered, a little astonished.

Hmmm, Viv said, looking back and forth between us.

Veroneek had apparently succeeded in her campaign to seize the L.A. airwaves. Isolated in an abandoned lot on the edge of Beverly Hills, Network Vs. was a charred black satellite dish that fanned out over a single red elevator that led down to an underground broadcasting station that beamed sensual propaganda to America on a twenty-four-hour basis. Over several evenings Viv, Veroneek and I conducted auditions for *White Whisper* as the elevator unloaded one bevy of women after another into the dark network hallways lined with flickering monitors. The women had been assembled by a fat casting agent who unbuttoned his silk shirt low enough to reveal a prominent hickey on his chest, which over time metamorphosed from red to purple to black like the larva of an insect; he insisted on attending the casting session in order to take nude photos of the actresses—for "the files," he explained. There were shy girls from Maryland who turned off the light in their own bathrooms to undress, and seasoned professionals who were out of their clothes before they were inside the door, only to realize with shock that there was actually dialogue in this movie they were expected to read. There were women who would only take off their clothes for Viv and Veroneek, which meant I had to leave the premises, and women who would only take off their clothes for me, which meant Viv and Veroneek had to leave the premises. There were women with cropped hair and braces on their teeth who appeared to still be virgins at the age of thirty, and Chinese lesbians who traveled in pairs, one with the hard look of experience and the other an eighteen-year-old who had yet to shed her baby fat. This last cherub in particular excited me. She had about her that perfect blankness of youth that begs to be defaced. For the rest of the week I wracked my brains trying to figure out how to work Chinese lesbians into the movie.

Any sentimental notions I might have had, however, about surveying a parade of naked women quickly gave way to reality. The harsh light of the network's underground offices cast a dead pall over even the loveliest, let alone fortyish over-the-hill actresses apologizing for their various birthmarks, scars, piercings and the ravages of particularly brutal C-sections. The spectacle was dismaying not simply because all the plastic in their faces and limbs and breasts had hardened to the point of petrifaction, but because their bodies wore their panic like their eyes; all Viv and I could do was cringe. No, really, we pleaded with them, you look beautiful. We wanted to take them all to dinner and buy them drinks and convince them they were still ravishing, with long careers and many acting opportunities ahead; our movie just wouldn't be one of them. Within forty-eight hours the message was out in the world of erotica: we were the *sensitive* pornographers. Come audition for us and we would feel sorry for you.

We cast the two less significant models first. As one actress after another failed to make the cut, a character we originally imagined as latin became black and finally a redhead. For the role of the "shy" model we chose a tall doe-eyed brunette who mumbled inaudibly and held her arms close to her; this introvert, we later learned, had a reputation for happily sucking any cock in Hollywood to get a part. The two lead roles eluded us. We offered the part of the painter to the virgin with the braces, who gave a very good reading even if she did insist we clear three or four city blocks before she allowed Viv, and Viv alone, to gaze upon the sacred splendor of her nakedness. That evening she went to her theater group where the other actresses, any of whom would have taken the part in two seconds if she had the chance, shrieked in disbelief that any self-respecting thespian could possibly think of performing in such a project; she hastily reconsidered and so informed us the next morning. Two days before the shoot was scheduled, I finally convinced Viv to cast a young woman named Amy Brown who had just rolled into L.A. from Tennessee a couple of years back, right before the Quake. Amy had curly black hair, a small mouth with slightly crooked teeth, and didn't at all fit the image Viv had of the character. But she was alert and intense, and I liked the way she kept leaning into the wall when reading her lines, like a girl trying to act tough but unconsciously trying to hide from everyone. I also liked the way she took off her clothes; she was determined about it without being altogether casual. Maybe the thing that most impressed me was that her name was Amy Brown as opposed to Diamond or Starlight or Snowflake or all the other names we'd heard in the past few days, and I figured any woman who had been in L.A. two whole years and still thought Amy Brown was a good enough name to make famous suggested a sense of her own identity that, along with a steeliness of purpose, we could use right now.

Then there was the character of the model that I had modeled after Jasper. Marshaling all my powers of invention, I had named this character Jasper. By pure default our best prospect was an actress Viv and I called Catwoman, who arrived at the session in a tight little black body suit. Her lips were inflated like they'd just been blown up with an air-hose at the gas station down the street, and her teased hair appeared to have been styled with a toilet plunger. As she read her lines she would slink along the wall and dig in her nails as though she was going to hump it. Faced with Catwoman's growing inevitability, Viv was beginning to cover her face with her hands and groan a lot, and we became so desperate to find a Jasper that even the screwiest ideas began to seem like a brainstorms. I thought, for instance, I had quite an inspiration when, driving home from Network Vs., there at the end of Melrose Avenue as I came around the curve off La Cienega, the Red Angel of Los Angeles rose like an answer: Justine as Jasper! Of course I wasn't entirely certain anymore that there even was a real Justine, though once twenty years ago I thought I saw her driving a red Corvette north on Rossmore where it turns into Vine. And if there *was* a real Justine, I thought now, was she as timeless as her billboard, or ancient, hiding her face in shadows and encasing her body in an aerodynamic cathedral of undergarments that attempted to launch her fantastic breasts into eternity? So when I got home and called her, still remembering the phone number on the billboard, I never figured on anyone actually answering. I figured I'd get a long ring into nothingness, or a recording telling me the number wasn't in service, or maybe a machine that simply exclaimed, in the manner of her billboards, "Justine!" Instead I was stunned when a woman's voice answered "Hello," and I didn't doubt for two seconds it was the Angel herself, and I was so startled I hung up immediately. . . .

By the fourth day of the auditions I realized I had to try and find the real Jasper. I didn't have the courage to tell Viv there *was* a real Jasper, because she would want to know how I could have let her slip away in the first place and also about the labia ring business, which didn't sound like the kind of thing someone just confesses in a bar. For several nights at the Feverish I waited for her to show up. I asked various people if they had seen her, and wasn't entirely surprised that no one had the slightest idea who I was talking about. The waitress who had served us our wine that night didn't remember, no matter how much I harassed her, nor did the bartender, no matter how much I badgered him, as though she was my hallucination, as much an illusion as Justine— the ragged doll muse who enticed me into her room high at the top of the tower of inspiration and then slammed the door, took the key, and folded the stairs up in a suitcase when she reached the bottom.

The final night before the shoot, as I was about to give up on Jasper and leave, I was distracted by a conversation behind me. People at nearby booths were talking about this and that, and there was nothing about this one conversation in particular, about the talkers or the tone or volume of their conversation, to necessarily draw my attention ... but when my ears caught a familiar reference I couldn't place at first, I had to listen several minutes before I realized the movie they were talking about was *The Death of Marat*. I turned to peer over my shoulder, thinking maybe it was someone from the newspaper. But it was a man and woman I had never seen before, and they looked back at me as if to say, What's *your* problem? The more they talked and the more I listened, the more it sounded— Well, the more it sounded like they weren't talking about the review I had written, but a real movie. The more I listened, the more it sounded as if ... well, they were talking about the movie as if they had seen it. They were talking about scenes I never mentioned in the review— scenes, in other words, that never existed in my imagination, let alone on a screen. "The use of lighting in the monastery sequence was extraordinary," the guy said. Monastery sequence? I thought to myself, truly alarmed, until finally I lurched to my feet from the table, almost tipping it over; people at other tables looked up. "I guess the whole damned city's in on the joke!" was all I could sputter at them. "Jerk," I heard the waitress behind me murmur as I left. "Asshole," confirmed the bartender.

∽⤫∾

I'm not exactly sure how, since I tried to be circumspect about it, but soon it seemed the whole newspaper had heard about my new vocation as a writer of pornographic movies. The Cabal in particular was fascinated. Ventura read my tarot and drew huge life lessons from the event. Struggling to remain non-judgmental, he never directly addressed the question of whether it represented a major turning point, or just my final fall from whatever state of grace one could consider my life to have occupied. . . .

There wasn't going to be anything glamorous about the filming of *White Whisper*. Given its length and a budget that was almost visible to the naked eye, it would have to be shot in one night, with every scene afforded no more than one or two takes, maybe three if we thought we could push it. The actresses had only a few hours of rehearsal in Viv's loft, with me reading Jasper's lines, since it wasn't until the last possible minute that we finally reconciled ourselves to casting Catwoman, who had the personality of a cat if not the labia ring. The day before the shoot, Viv, Veroneek and I frantically scoured the city scouting locations in abandoned factories and dingy alleys, casing rundown rooms that were distinguished mostly by the tell-tale signs, on rumpled beds and stained floors, of other productions that clearly had been even less elegant than ours. I admit that as each place smelled worse than the other of piss and semen, it gave me some pause about the whole project. I admit that for a moment or two I felt downright disreputable, just the way the New Paragons would have wanted me to. We finally decided to go with one of the Glow Lofts that appear after sundown in the industrial district east of Downtown, a white windowless cavern like the inside of a huge egg, with curved corners and cubbyholes lining the perimeter that could instantly be converted into dressing rooms, rehearsal spaces, an office and kitchen. Its preeminent virtue, however, was that it didn't smell.

On the big night, the minute the sun fell and the loft came into view, Viv's crew backed the vans up to the loading dock and moved in. Within the hour the dolly tracks were laid and the cameras and lights and booms were up as well as the set—a makeshift artist's studio with easels and a paint table and a platform where the models posed. The crew was Viv's usual circle of bohemians and drug addicts. The cameraman was a big burly Texan named Harris and the makeup woman a former "cosmetics technician" from a local fashion magazine; the paintings were supplied by one of Viv's ex-boyfriends. The producers were Lydia and Niles, a wife–husband team from New York who used to be in the theater. Lydia was intelligent, dedicated and pleasant, and Niles was a putz of the first order. Viv, Veroneek and I were all saddened to learn Lydia had lovingly tattooed Niles' name on what presumably had been an otherwise perfectly acceptable bottom. Niles expounded on his vast knowledge of everything from art direction to makeup to sound editing, walking around the set in a stupid baseball cap barking meaningless orders into his walkie-talkie and quickly managing to insult Viv's ex— who only did the paintings in the first place as a favor to Viv— and grope all the women on the set he didn't happen to be married to, the most prominent of whom was our star. Waiting for our other actresses to show up, Viv decided to shoot the film's last scene first in which Amy Brown, as the repressed painter who comes to exchange roles with her model, stands naked on the model's platform; as everyone prepared the shot, a simple zoom-in on Amy glowing in the lights like a trailer-trash Modigliani, Niles was determined to give her his personal supervision. In and out of the scene he darted between takes to "fix" Amy's hair, constantly brushing a curl from her brow as Lydia grew more and more visibly enraged, Niles' name blazing away on her ass.

Probably the only reason it didn't escalate into an out-and-out marital crisis was that Lydia and Viv were currently preoccupied with a bigger problem. Catwoman hadn't shown up. After several hours trying to track her down Viv finally placed a frantic phone call to the casting agent with the gangrenous hickey on his chest who, just before midnight, lined up another actress. Thirty minutes later Viv came over to say later the new actress had arrived and was looking over the script: "We have a new Jasper," she announced, an odd look on her face.

"You have an odd look on your face," I said.

"Well, it's funny."

"What's funny?"

"She really *is* Jasper."

"What do you mean she really is Jasper?"

"I mean, her name is Jasper." And sure enough, sitting in a chair in the shadows as though she appeared out of nowhere, the way she appeared out of nowhere the night I met her, was Jasper. She wore a different dress, simpler and looser—an altogether less imposing incarnation, but as cool and slightly ethereal as she was at the Feverish, my script in her hand rather than a glass of wine.

Viv introduced us, and Jasper just looked up from the script and said, I like the part about the labia ring.

You don't happen to have one, do you? Viv laughed.

I'll surprise you, Jasper laughed. Viv laughed some more. They both laughed together and then, looking at the expression on my face, laughed some more. In no time at all they seemed to be getting along famously, and then Viv returned to the set and I sat with Jasper trying to explain the script. I was explaining the character to her, which is to say the character I stole from her in the first place; I was explaining the things the character said— which is to say the things she originally said. She gave absolutely no indication of realizing any of this. She gave no indication of ever having met me at all. She read the lines like they were completely new to her, like she had never heard them before; she even analyzed and interpreted them as she went along, trying out different inflections. "I don't like tits," she said, "I'd rather say breasts." Given the circumstances, I told her she could say just about whatever she wanted as long as it followed the general drift, and that we were going to have cue cards and someone to prompt her, so there was nothing to worry about. Oh no, she insisted, I'll learn the lines, I'm a very quick study. Finally I left her alone to go over the script by herself. I was happy to leave her to it. There was something about her now that unnerved me, as though the night I met her she had stepped out of my id but tonight she stepped out of someone else's. A few minutes later she was in makeup, still poring over her lines, and soon we were ready for her. The minutes passed as everyone waited; in the meantime we were shooting everything else that could be shot—scenes with the other actresses, close-ups of paint brushes, close-ups of canvases with Amy and canvases without Amy, close-ups of thighs that looked like lunar plains and breasts that looked like spheres over deserts. Viv kept going back to the makeup room to check in on Jasper and kept coming back without her. The crew grew mutinous.

Jasper finally appeared. She glided onto the set like she did into the Feverish. She moved as though not walking through the real world but through the corridors of her imagination, where she might pick up one of its artifacts, casually admire it and then, bored, toss it over her shoulder. She didn't so much drop her robe as let it slide off her, ascending naked to the model's platform; she took off everything but the cat ring on her finger. The crew, men and women alike, were stunned by the sight of her. She was impossibly lush; you could practically hear last night's semen still sloshing around in her. I had two reactions to her. The first was that I wanted to fuck her, because not to fuck her would be to insult God and slander the divine order of things, and the second was I wanted to get the fuck *away* from her, because it was about to become clear, as I suspected from the first, that she was absolutely crazy, the Abyss Walking like a Woman, madness so generic it practically had a bar code on it.

We had written all of her lines on cue cards, and script assistants were at the ready to prompt her. We began filming. She got through the first line of her monologue—the one I had transcribed practically word for word from that night at the Feverish, about picking up the guy at the art gallery and tying him to his bed—and then forgot the second line. The script assistant prompted her but she refused to take the cue, asking instead that we begin again. Viv called cut, we took a break. After a couple of minutes Viv called action again and we started from the top; Jasper once again got through the first line and once again forgot the second, and once again refused to take the cue. Once again Viv called cut. When Viv again called action, Jasper now forgot her first line; the cue card was waving in front of her face but she refused to read it; Viv called cut, we took a break, Viv called action, Jasper began: "I was at a gallery the other night, thinking I might. . . ." She shook her head. Now Viv told Harris the cameraman to just keep rolling. Jasper started again. "The other night, at this gallery, I was there and—" Over and over she started and stopped, the camera constantly rolling: "At this gallery the other . . . at this. . . . I was at this gallery where I thought. . . . I—" Suddenly she dissolved into sobs. It's all right, it's all right, Viv assured her, and Jasper nodded Yes, yes, OK, and she took it from the top and actually got several lines into her speech before she lost the train of thought, at which point she collapsed naked on the platform like a woman having a fit, before suddenly leaping back to her feet: "OK, OK, OK! I'm all right, really, I can do it," and beginning again at the top, camera still rolling, she once more got several lines in before everything fell apart.

By now Harris the Texan and the rest of the crew just wanted to rip the film out of the camera, tie a noose and toss it over the highest rafter. Every breakdown pushed them closer to vigilante justice. Viv was cool beyond belief. People were screaming at her and she was making fifty decisions a minute while always keeping her eye on the big task at hand, with the calm authority of someone so comfortably in charge she never had to raise her voice or make a demonstration of her power. Now I heard her voice in my ear. It was a *soothing* voice; she was smiling a little too broadly, beaming a little too brightly. In the monitor behind her I could see Jasper pulling on her robe and lighting a cigarette. "What?" I said uneasily.

"Well. . . ." I didn't know why but I already had this feeling Viv was about to say something very peculiar. "I think we've gotten as much out of Jasper as we're going to get. We almost have enough to intercut with scenes of Amy. But we still don't have Amy's scenes with Jasper. . . ."

"Shoot Amy's scenes in close-up," I suggested helpfully. "Someone else can read Jasper's lines off camera."

"Exactly." Her calm was as terrifying as it was awe-inspiring.

Suddenly I saw the light. "Forget it."

"You haven't even heard what I'm going to say."

"Forget it."

"You haven't even—!" Furiously, she spun on her heels and began to stomp away.

"All right," I succumbed, "tell me. . . ."

"Never mind."

"Tell me." This was Viv's genius; I was now begging her to tell me this idea I knew I wasn't going to like.

"All you need to do is read with her," Viv said, fists on her hips.

"Why can't someone else?"

"Fine. We'll get someone else."

"You could do it."

"Fine. I'll do it. I don't have anything else to do right now, except direct a movie."

"Veroneek can do it."

"Fine, Veroneek can do it. I just thought maybe *you* would do it, that you would *want* to do it, because you wrote these lines and you understand them. I thought you would be able to see how much better it is for Amy to act with someone who knows how to read the lines and what they mean."

"But wouldn't it be better for a woman to read the lines?"

"Why would it better?" She threw up her hands. "No, *fine.* We'll find a woman to read the lines."

"All right, all right. I'll read it."

"I just thought it would be easier for Amy."

"I'll read the lines."

"I think you should take your clothes off."

"I'm sorry?"

"Amy is supposed to be a repressed painter, remember? You wrote it. Remember, she's exploring her own psychological nakedness, through the physical nakedness of the model she paints? She's *affronted* by that nakedness."

"It's a naked *woman* she's affronted by."

"I know it's not ideal. . . ." Viv agreed.

"It's not ideal?" I said. "Personally, I think it's distinctly less than ideal. That's just my own personal opinion, you understand. No, I would say we're in agreement on this, that a naked man playing the part of a naked woman is not ideal. And somehow—I'll grant you I'm biased on this—somehow the fact that *I'm* the naked man makes it *really* not ideal."

"Yes, well," Viv retorted, "I don't have the *luxury* of *ideal* right now. You know, it's not like you haven't read with Amy before—you did at the casting session, if you'll remember. She'll be comfortable with you."

"See, at the casting session? *I had my clothes on.* That was the big difference there. I'll bet Amy is a lot more comfortable with my clothes on than my clothes off. Ask her."

"Amy!" Seconds later Amy was at Viv's side. "He's going to read the lines with you so we can get your close-ups. Given that your character is supposed to be responding to a naked model when you hear these lines, doesn't it make perfect sense that he should take all his clothes off?"

"Absolutely," said Amy.

"I just thought," Viv turned back to me, "you wanted this movie to be good. I thought you cared as much about it as I did. Don't you think I'd be very happy right now to have an actress who could play Jasper without falling apart? Don't you think, at this point, I'd even be happy with Catwoman, for God's sake? But I don't have a Jasper or a Catwoman, what I have is you. I don't imagine Catwoman would hesitate two seconds to take her clothes off."

"I'm sure Catwoman wouldn't," I said bitterly. "If she had bothered to show up, I mean."

"I have no more time," Viv calmly answered, as though explaining the sunshine to a three-year-old. She spun on her heels again. "Think about it a minute and let me know what you decide, so I can tell everyone whether they should just go home and I can figure out how I'm going to give Veroneek back her money."

That was her crowning blow, because she knew that in the end I was incapable of letting her down. Christ, if the Cabal ever hears about this I'm cooked, was all I could think thirty minutes later on the model's platform. Around me was a great flurry of activity and preparation. The crew bustled with heavily suppressed hilarity; they couldn't wait for me to finish so they could all explode with laughter. Only Amy, focused as ever, never cracked a smile. In my mind I kept going back to the beginning, to the night Viv first proposed this project. I don't think it occurred to me then that I would wind up naked in this movie. In fact, I'm sure I had it in my head that it was *other* people who would wind up naked in this movie. Action! Viv barked behind the camera and, behind her canvas, Amy asked, "Where does he touch you?"

"Under my breast," I sighed, "below my nipple."

"Which one?" said Amy.

"The left." Out of the corner of my eye I was watching everyone around me. Everyone around me was looking not at me or Amy but the ground and their feet, trying to contain themselves; the only sound I heard was snickering, a solitary chortle from back in the shadows of the set. After a moment I realized it was Niles. It was Niles snickering and a certain peace came over me, because now I knew that in a few seconds I was going to kill him, just as I had been wanting to do, and it would make everything worth it. Thinking about it now I was glad I was naked, because it would just make Niles' demise all that much more humiliating, to be throttled in front of all these people by a naked man. "When his hands are raised to my breast," I went on, "you know . . . he's exposed to me. He's disarmed."

"Disarmed?"

"Like in the gangster movies, when the bad guy puts his hands in the air."

"Or the good guy sometimes."

"Or the good guy."

"Is he the good guy or the bad guy?"

"He's the good guy when I'm the bad guy." Later it would occur to me that this was one of those common primal dreams, to be the only one naked in a room full of people. I don't remember what it's supposed to mean, beyond the obvious sense of exposure and vulnerability; and I certainly don't know what it meant that in this dream I was not only naked but in the role of a naked woman, talking to another woman about which breast I preferred having touched. Interestingly, as we did take after take, moving on from one section of dialogue to the next, everyone else on the set fell away from my consciousness and I became lost in what Amy was saying and what I was saying, until I had almost forgotten that my voice would not be on the film at all, that nothing of me would be on the film, that I would have been only the ghost who revealed himself, herself, whatever my self was at this moment, for the sake of the look on the face of that person who witnessed my revelation. At this moment, everything and everyone else was exposed to me. I was free of the threat or possibility of any further exposure, as naked on the outside as I was inside, and everyone cowered before me, prisoners of their pride and secrets.

❧

But later, going over the footage and looking at Jasper's scenes on the monitor, Viv and I both noticed something right off. Mid-air, between her nervous breakdown on the set and the image caught by the camera lens, Jasper transformed into the woman I met at the Feverish—the spellbinding eyes, the vague German accent and strange stillborn smile. . . . The effect was electrifying. "Jeez," Viv shook her head, unabashedly infatuated, "she *makes* the movie." She called Jasper into the network a few days later to overdub some lines, and for the next week Jasper was all Viv could talk about.

I think it was mostly Viv's obsession with Jasper that gave us the idea for the party. In order to coax Jasper into her lair, Viv decided to have a Nude Artists Ball on Halloween at the Bunker. We would invite all of Viv's friends, painters and sculptors and photographers and curators, plus some of my pals and their various women and wives, plus Veroneek and Joe and the crew who worked on *White Whisper*, and the other actresses and maybe even a select few of the auditioners, the Chinese lesbians perhaps, and perhaps Sahara and some of the girls from the Cathode Flower. Hell, we might even invite Catwoman and then tie her to the floor and stand around spilling wine and tequila on her and eating hors d'oeuvres off her body. Viv created invitations out of parchment and feathers and foil, drawing an elaborate image of a genie emerging from a pod with stupendous, dripping breasts like Jasper's, and a penis I had the funny feeling I'd seen somewhere before, ejaculating a blue pool that bled around the card's edges. It was left to me to write the announcement. But going over it in my mind it occurred to me I wasn't sure how many of these particular people I really wanted to see nude, even at a Nude Artists Ball; the Cabal, for instance, I felt reasonably certain I didn't want to see any of *them* nude, whereas I kind of liked the idea of Niles— invited in the first place only out of deference to Lydia, whose bottom was tattooed with his name after all—turning out to be the *only* person at the ball who was nude. So I made some adjustments in the invitations, customizing them, so to speak.

The closer the party got, the more elaborate it became. Viv's loft didn't need a lot of extra ambiance, given the metal coffins and pyramids and mannequins and dead bugs on the walls, but she unpacked an exotic array of artifacts anyway from her various travels: masks and dolls and strange figurines from Africa and South America and the Middle East. Overcoming her dread of even imaginary spiders, she draped makeshift webs from one corner of the ceiling to the next. On the monitor intercut with Network Vs. broadcasts was an ongoing montage of *Metropolis* and *Vampyr* and *Kiss Me Deadly*, Louise Brooks and Val Lewton movies, outtakes from *White Whisper* and selected blasts from the Cinema of Hysteria; and in the center of the room, on a low glass table, burned a huge candle, which was actually the once-melted, twisted mutation of many candles. By Halloween night we had turned the whole Bunker into a maze, confiscating the bulbs from the light fixtures and throwing the corridors into blackness, extending the winding passages into the loft so that if people took one turn they wound up on the main level and if they took another they wound up on the upper platform looking down. Not intelligent enough to become truly confused, the first person actually to make it all the way through to the end of the maze was the dim little eighteen-year-old half of the Chinese lesbian couple. Three minutes of social intercourse confirmed she had the vocabulary of a parrot and enough brains to fill a shot glass. The other lesbian was lost somewhere on the Bunker's second floor; all night we heard her distant screams. "You're getting closer!" someone would shout into the passage every now and then, just for the sheer hell of it.

People arrived in baffled, agitated bursts, spewed from the Bunker's concrete aqueducts in general states of dishevelment. It was hugely entertaining to watch them tumble in on top of each other, snapping and snarling like trapped dogs. The women were in varying degrees of nakedness, costumed as leopards or birds or in nothing more than a striking shade of blue or white champagne and glitter. Some of the more brazen men wore only cod pieces while a few were in evening attire, escorting nymphs on their arms. Viv was resplendent in nothing but white stockings and white shoes; I wore my black boxer shorts with the dancing orange skulls and a green D'Artagnan hat with a purple feather. In his hat and boots the only thing different about Ventura's usual appearance was the look on his face that said, Now will somebody please explain to me what the fuck I'm doing here? Per my plan, the only completely naked man was Niles, arriving as bare as the day he was born. Dangling obliviously, and eagerly scanning the room for Amy Brown, he didn't have the sense to be mortified; rather he had about him the air of someone who couldn't believe the dumb luck of all these women that there should be one singularly naked man for them and it was him.

One of Jasper's thighs was blurting across the monitor when she arrived in person. Taking her cue from Viv's drawing on the invitation, and perhaps recognizing the inspiration of her own breasts, she came as the genie herself, completely bare in a deep bronze tint with a huge phallus strapped to her that waved wildly from her pubic hair, which was dyed white like the hair on her head. Her eyes were made up to accentuate their light, and her lips were a metallic blue. Behind her was a guy in a loincloth and turban whose ankles were bound by chains and who lugged behind him, on another chain, a huge papier-mâché lamp from which a genie presumably could emerge. I have no idea how they got the lamp up through the Bunker corridors. I couldn't help wondering if this was the guy who wound up bound to his bed the night Jasper went barhopping, assuming Jasper's story at the Feverish was true or that she had ever really been there at all; he had on his face the look of a man who has been down at the bottom of a deep amniotic shaft so long and is so dazed and dithering from the experience that the only thing he can imagine anymore is returning there. At any rate, the entrance made a big impression. Where Jasper stopped in the middle of the room the temperature rocketed twenty degrees, and everyone stared, not knowing whether to swarm over her like Bolivian jungle ants or back away cowering from her as some kind of unholy vision of sex. Instead they rushed to the refrigerator and gulped down the pitchers of tequila I had laced with cognac.

After this the only two things that could happen to the ball was that everyone would clear out altogether or explode in a drunken frenzy, and since people were too transfixed by Jasper to navigate their way back down through the Bunker, and we could *still* hear the cries and thuds of the other Chinese lesbian trying to grope her way toward us, a drunken frenzy it was. The party became a night-long din of breaking glass and shattering lights and ripping fabric and bodies hurtling from the overhanging loft. Several times in all the blind inebriated confusion I considered weaving my way over to Niles and giving him a good kick in the nuts. At one point someone got the idea of hauling the huge centerpiece candle up to the rooftop and casting it to the street below, and so the whole party became a caravan staggering its way up through the Bunker's pitch-black arteries to the overhanging night, from where we could see in the distance the freeway bonfires and dark Magritte ocean slowly rolling in toward the city. Off the side of the building went the candle in a streak of fire, its flame flickering valiantly all the way to the bottom, where it smashed and erupted in a white rain of wax.

I turned from the rooftop's edge to look right into Jasper's eyes as she stood behind me. In the moonlight her hair and lips and eyes and phallus glimmered, and she took my hand to lead me with the others back down through the Bunker to Viv's loft. When she pulled me past Viv's doorway, deeper into the black halls toward the bottom of the building, I tried to pull back: "Wait," I said, because I didn't want to go without Viv, especially with Jasper. But she fastened her grip on me. I couldn't see her or anyone or anything else before or behind me. At the bottom of the building the door opened and we emerged onto the street where I found, to my mystification, that it was not Jasper attached to my hand but Viv— "What . . . ?" was all I could start to say; I looked over my shoulder to see that Jasper had somehow wound up behind me. Her slave was nowhere in sight, having tangled his chains on a drainpipe up on the roof. Let's go to my place, Jasper suggested. Let's go, Viv agreed. We could still hear from the third floor of the Bunker the noise of the party along with the stray cries of the lost Chinese lesbian who, on our way up and down, must have passed through us like a ghost.

We got in my car. Viv and Jasper sat in back. North of Baghdadville the second ring was burning so I headed out Pico Boulevard and then cut up to Sixth Street, driving east on Sixth through the dark knolls of Hancock Park and slipping through a Black Passage just beyond MacArthur Park. On into Downtown we continued past the Glow Lofts to the industrial veldt of the switching yard that lay before the old gothic stone bridges of East Los Angeles. The smell of the ocean fell behind us, the smell of backfires wafted through the window. . . . Half a mile from Jasper's house we could see it, growing alone out of the wasteland of the railroad tracks next to a junkyard of twisted metal, disposed concrete beams and the abandoned hulls of tanker trucks, in the middle of a circle of low but constant fire. The fire never rose more than a couple of feet, and never went out. I could feel the heat a couple of hundred yards away and it was blasting in through the body of the car when we pulled to a stop. Jasper got out to voice-activate the huge iron door that let us into a concrete tunnel, which led the remaining fifty feet to the house itself. "We keep the fire burning," she muttered from the back seat of the car, when she got back in, "to discourage the vandals and gangs. . . ."

"We?" I said.

At the entryway of the house a small parking foyer opened up. An antique car shone in waiting. "Let's drink something!" Viv chirped, launching herself from the car before it came to a complete stop. Jasper had become much quieter since the house came into view. We followed her in; the front door was small and unassuming, like a service entrance. Immediately beyond it rose a concrete stairway to the second level, where the whole house opened up into a skyward-spiraling mass of turrets and gussets and beams shooting off in diagonals and parabolas, so that you were inside when you thought you were outside and outside when you thought you were inside, except for when you were both at the same time. This level forked off into several other directions, including a kitchen, another set of stairs and an elevated outdoor patio; disappearing another direction out into the open air, from where we could feel the heat of the fire moat, a metal catwalk curled around the outer circumference of the house. The stairs led up to a study from where came a light, and then the bedroom, and from there another series of stairs again led out into the night and up the side of the house's tower to the top. By my count there were about four levels to the house in all, except for all the half-levels in between, the top two overlooking a huge circular living space on the second level that was lined by glass from one end to the next. The glass alternated between window and mirrors that ran from the ceiling to the floor, each window confronted on the opposite side of the room by a mirror so you could look out on the city and see your own face floating above it. In the middle of the room, where the floor was slightly sunken, a low black sofa and two matching black chairs surrounded a low black table, and the whole room was filled by an icy blue light like the color of Jasper's lip gloss. Shooting up the middle of the house like a metal spine was the disembodied hull of a tanker truck, an open chute that exposed the night far above us.

The house must have been eighty feet high. From the windows of the living room was a panorama of the scrapyards, the surrounding hills, the ravine cut through by the black Los Angeles River, the old baseball stadium that had been taken over by coyotes and homeless people and fourth-generation descendants of the blacks and latinos who had been displaced by the stadium in the first place, and just beyond the flames of the house's moat the trains that slithered through the switching yard in the dark, one coiling silently by just at the edge of the fire. We stood over a pool that invaded the living room from the elevated patio outside. This too was made from the tank of a fuel truck, a narrow oblong canal of water leading out to a much larger pool. The pool lights were on and the water was red with the light of the fires; the reflection of the distant city skyline floated on the surface. Hovering just beneath the skyline and the surface of the water, in the middle of the larger pool, was a large module, with aortas and ventricles like a huge mechanical heart, roomy enough from all appearances to hold a couple of people. There appeared to be portholes on all sides. Through the water I could see on top of the module a glass hatch. "What is that?" I said.

"It's a bathysphere," Jasper answered. She was now distinctly sullen, and made her way straight to the table in the center of the room that held glasses, several crystal liquor bottles, and an ice bucket full of melted ice. She kept looking over her shoulder at the pool and then up at the stairs toward the study where the light was coming from the doorway. Viv was humming and dancing from window to mirror while Jasper poured her a drink; she handed the drink to Viv and asked if I wanted anything, and I said no. "Where did you find this house?" asked Viv.

After what seemed a long moment Jasper said, "It's my stepfather's. He built it. He's an architect." She added, rather caustically, "His bathysphere, too."

"You mean he built the bathysphere?" I asked. Almost in response a flurry of bubbles exploded on the surface of the pool. The three of us watched from the dark of the house as the bathysphere surfaced in the bubbles' wake, where a motor kicked on and navigated the craft to the side of the pool. The motor shut off and after a minute the glass door on the top of the bathysphere opened and a distinguished looking man in his early fifties got out, fully dressed. Even in the light of the pool his tawny resemblance to Jasper was unmistakable. Stepfather? I was thinking, watching the two of them, when he looked over to the living room from beyond the glass and now seemed to notice there was someone in the house. "Jasper," he said, not like a question or even a greeting but a perfunctory accusation, with a demeanor that rendered everything an accusation. He circled the pool, ascended the outer steps and entered the house on the next level up, looking down at us. There was no rail; I had already noticed that none of the landings or stairs had rails, as though rails had been deliberately omitted from the design so no one could ever get completely comfortable or secure. In front of the light from the study, the man's frame was silhouetted. Viv staggered a little but not particularly engaged by the moment; both she and Jasper had been naked enough of the evening to have seemingly forgotten about it. The man on the balcony also appeared not to notice that standing in his living room was a blonde in nothing but slightly askew stockings, wobbling on a pair of high heels, and another blonde, his stepdaughter, saluting him with a plastic penis, the only thing about the evening that hadn't begun to wilt.

He looked from me to Viv back to me with clear disdain, and then back to Jasper, who returned his look and then turned her back on him, walking around the end of the black sofa and plopping herself down, staring out into the night at the ring of flames in the distance and drinking her drink. From the top of the stairs the man looked at me again, and then vanished back into the study.

"What's happening," Viv slurred vaguely. She was a little pickled.

"Nothing," Jasper answered, and then, after a minute, suddenly brightened, in one of her now familiar psychotic shifts. She leapt up from the sofa so fast her dildo nearly knocked over a bottle of scotch, and grabbing Viv she pulled her giggling toward another room beneath the stairs. For the next half hour I could overhear Jasper showing Viv her life. She was hauling out yearbooks and poetry journals and glossy magazine photo layouts from younger days, and newspaper stories of beauty competitions where triumph was only a smile away, though it sounded like it usually wound up being some other girl's smile. The recounting had about it the desperate wistfulness of a valediction to a life that was already over. At one point, very clearly and soberly, Viv said, "Jasper, don't do this," and then after a few minutes they returned. I was sitting in one of the chairs and Viv and Jasper were slouching on the sofa.

For a few minutes we were quiet in the dark. Viv sipped another drink and Jasper absently flicked her phallus with her thumb, lost in thought. "My father is not a good person," she finally felt compelled to explain, breaking the silence. "That's why I was rude. I didn't know he would be here tonight, I thought he was out of town."

Neither Viv nor I was sure what to say. "Your stepfather," I finally clarified.

"What?" said Jasper.

"Your stepfather, you mean."

"That's what I said."

Viv turned to me. "That's what she said."

I didn't argue with them. I waited for Jasper to go on but instead, after several more minutes, she started to talk about when she had lived in Berlin with a man named Rudi, during the time when all the animals from the Berlin Zoo were running wild in the streets. One night, when Rudi was out, she had picked up the phone and started dialing numbers at random. She kept dialing until she reached someone who didn't hang up on her; they had sex on the phone and a couple of nights later she called another number and did it again, and went on doing this for weeks until finally she got an American who lived in a nearby hotel. As with all the other numbers, she had just pulled this one out of the air, and then pulled out of the air a room number when the concierge answered. The American was shy, not at all sure what to say when she told him she wanted to take him in her mouth. He asked if she would wait while he closed the window shutters. On the phone his orgasm was frightening and, for the sound of that frightening orgasm, she called him back, always around the same time of the evening until, finally, he insisted he would no longer do it on the telephone. There and then, by sheer impulse, she agreed to meet him in the most anonymous of circumstances: she would go to a hotel the next night and take a room, and call him from the room with the name of the hotel and the room number, and leave the door unlocked for him, with all the lights off. They would say nothing to each other. He would fuck her and then they would leave, first one, then the other. And that, Jasper said, is exactly what happened. When she called him the next night, from a hotel not far from his, he answered the phone without saying a word; a little less than an hour later, waiting for him in the dark naked on the hotel bed, she heard the door open and shut, followed by his approach. Never saying a word, nothing but a dark form, he waited by the side of the bed as she unbuckled his pants and slipped him into her mouth, and just when she could feel he was about to come, she turned on her hands and knees and knelt before him, and reached behind her and put him inside her. As he was fucking her, she realized she was going to leave Rudi. "There was no doubt in my mind," Jasper said, "that I would rather feel the hands and cock of a complete stranger than Rudi's dead heart for another single minute. When I cried out I could feel his excitement. He was a beast, of course—I could have told that from the wound in his voice on the phone. But you know, when the heart is broken and the dream is gone, annihilation is delicious. All I really wanted was to feel whether his orgasm was as frightening as it sounded on the telephone."

"Was it?" Viv said.

"No."

"How do you know," I said, swallowing hard, "that it was the same man?"

For the first time since I had known her, Jasper seemed profoundly bewildered. "What?"

"The same man as the one you talked to on the phone."

"What do you mean?" she said. Viv looked confused too.

"How do you know the man in the room was the same as the man on the phone—?"

"How do I know it was the same man?" The question almost incensed her.

"Forget it."

"It's a very strange question," she said, upset.

"Yes," Viv said, looking at me, "it is a very strange question."

"Why wouldn't it have been the same man?" Jasper asked. Both she and Viv were looking at me, waiting for an answer that made sense.

"Well . . . it was dark," was the best I could offer.

Viv said to Jasper, "But he must have said something. Afterward."

"He never said anything," Jasper answered, disoriented. "He finished and I got up and dressed in the dark, and left him there."

"So you never saw him at all," Viv said.

"No. I tried to call the next night, and . . . no one answered. And then I called the night after that, and the night after that. And I never talked to him again."

After that, none of us said anything. We all sat in the dark staring out the windows where the flames in the distance had begun to smear in the dark fog that blows in from the sea every night and turns the sky red. The blue light of the room and the pool outside where the abandoned bathysphere now bobbed mixed with the red to turn the night to wine; from the house, sitting in this low chair in the middle of the sunken floor, there was no sense, gazing at the windows and mirrors, of any city out there whatsoever. Closing my eyes I thought of Berlin. I hadn't thought about Berlin for a long time, and now I was trying to remember exactly how long it had been since I was there: was it right before my father died, or right after my marriage? Was it right after the end with Sally, or right before I went to work for the newspaper? I had lived in a little hotel in Savignyplatz where every night I waited in my room for the ring of the telephone, which had so shocked me the first time, since I didn't know anyone in the city and no one in the city knew me. Lying on the couch in Jasper's house now, I was trying to remember why I had gone to Berlin in the first place, and all I could think of was that I had gone for the very thing that happened there, so that the part of me I couldn't live with anymore could die there, without witnesses. I had gone to Berlin because it was as far east of L.A. as I could get before the millennium came roaring down the autobahn. . . .

Next thing I realized I had drifted off awhile. Maybe it was minutes and maybe it was an hour; but the light in the door at the top of the stairs had gone off, and someone had turned off the light of the pool, where the bathysphere floated like a dark tumor. Looking around I was a little surprised to find myself alone in the living room, and I got up and started wandering around, peering into the unlit room where Jasper had shown off to Viv her mementos of the past. I made my way up the stairs. I passed the dark study where Jasper's father or stepfather or whoever he was had disappeared, and kept moving up the stairs toward the bedroom at the top, just barely conscious that there was no rail to catch me if I misstepped and tumbled down some random shaft that would deposit me God knows where, in a field of flames or off the side of a cliff or somewhere north of San Luis Obispo.

The bedroom was dark as well. Even at the top of the house, sixty feet above the ground, I could feel the heat of the surrounding moat. Before the windows and the vista of the faraway hills that embraced the city like the ridge of a volcano's crater, something was happening on the bed. Jasper was lying on her back, no longer wearing the phallus that now lay beside her face; her profile shone in the blue light. Her eyes were open but she was so still and unblinking I thought she could almost be dead except for the sound coming from her, a gorgeous low rattle that was not from her lips but all of her. In the blue light of the room I could see her whole wet body shudder as though she was going to crumble into pieces any minute like a fractured statue. The sight of her brought roaring up from the middle of me this dark scavenger appetite ready to swoop down on the rubble of her; in her hands she clutched something between her legs like a nest, and I half expected a bird to fly out of her. Then I saw it was Viv's hair in her hands and Viv was drinking her. Her eyes were closed. Jasper tried to pull her up inside her. She began to thrash to the rattle coming out of her, and Viv was holding her down to the bed by her wrists when the rattle burst and I could hear everything inside Jasper wash out in a tide. "My God, stop," Jasper groaned as Viv continued. Finally Viv stopped. Still nestled in Jasper's thighs she opened her eyes, staring straight at me. When she pulled back from Jasper I could see, just beyond Jasper's pubic hair, the swollen glint—from an unaccountable light much brighter than any inside this room or out beyond the windows—of a ring, in the shape of a cat.

On the way home, the first pink shred of sunrise peering over the canyon, Viv, who was sitting in the front seat for a change, suddenly began to sob. What is it? I said. Suddenly she was crying violently and all I could do was pull the car over to the side of the road. What is it, what is it? I kept saying, trying to clutch her to me as she leaned into the car door. I might have expected her to answer anything else but what she did. "No one will ever love her!" she cried. "The only people she'll ever know will be the ones who don't really care about her at all. She'll just wind up all by herself, all alone." Come on Viv, I muttered, trying to pry her loose from the door, and she hadn't been in my arms five seconds before the crying stopped and she was fast asleep.

∽✦∼

It was a few days after Viv's party, and the night at Jasper's house, that I saw the Red Angel of Los Angeles in her little red Corvette. It was only for a moment, and she was pulling out of an alley right at the end of Jacob Hamblin Road, which couldn't have been more incongruous. I was in my own car and for a while I tried to follow her, swerving in and out of traffic to keep up as she headed east toward Hollywood, until she suddenly seemed to disappear into the red air of the backfires....

After that, Justine became my quest. I think I knew, somewhere inside me, that it was really a search for something else, though I didn't know what; for so long I had barely been aware that there was anything I wanted to search for. But lately I had felt the chasm between me and memory closing when it seemed it should have been growing wider, and I figured if anyone had transcended memory it was Justine, who for twenty years had fixed herself to the L.A. moment. I called back the phone number I had called before, when she had actually answered with the most unexpected Hello I ever heard; this time she didn't answer, this time there was the machine I thought I would get the first time, banally identifying itself as the number for the International Justine Fan Club and inviting me to leave my name, number and purpose for calling. I told the machine I was a newspaper writer looking for an interview, though I could just imagine what Shale would think of *that*, on the heels of rejected pieces about spiritual strip joints and reviews of movies that didn't exist. For several nights I went to one club after another on the chance I'd spot her making the scene. But that really didn't make any sense: Justine didn't make the scene, she *was* the scene, and the best that could be hoped for was that she would happen to cruise by in her red Corvette just long enough for those coming out of the clubs to say they had witnessed her, like one witnesses the Miracle of Fatima or the streak across the sky of a UFO.

Then I returned home one night and there, on my machine, was her voice. She sounded just like she should have, like the very image of herself that was on the billboard. She left an address she said was "in the Hollywood Hills," but no date or time; as someone with a memory for dates and times, I'm sure of that. I had never heard of this address, so I pulled out a map and started looking. It was nowhere to be found. In the hills I conducted personal reconnaissance missions, driving around figuring I'd stumble on the street sooner or later, but I never did, at least not until the one night several weeks afterward when I was returning from visiting my mother in the Valley and was forced by a backfire to take a detour; and there it was. It was just off Ventura Boulevard, hardly on the glamorous side of the Hollywood Hills, or what anyone really thinks of as the Hollywood Hills.

I don't want to get your hopes up, so I guess I better mention right now that I never did see Justine. I know you're anticipating a big rendezvous, but you might as well forget it. Instead something else happened, not as interesting as Justine, I grant you, but.... I found the address, an old white Spanish style house; one look at it and it was obvious no one had lived there for years, certainly not for as long as Justine had been popping up on billboards all over L.A. Nonetheless I got out and walked around in the dark peering through broken windows and over the fence that ran alongside the house, when it finally came to me. It came not in a flash or a sudden rush but rather in bits and pieces that gradually arranged themselves in my head—at which point the chasm between me and memory vanished altogether; and I couldn't have been more shocked.

It was the Stutter School, or what I used to call the Stutter School when I came twice a week at the age of nine, once in the morning when it was just myself and a counselor, and then once in the evening with the other kids. I had forgotten it completely and now, pulling myself over the fence and wandering around the backyard in the dark, under the overhanging tree where once had been a swing and around the abandoned jungle gyms that now seemed tiny replicas of what I had once climbed on, I wanted to forget it again. Not because it was so bad; actually it wasn't bad at all. The people who ran the school treated me well and I remember getting along all right with the other kids too, though I never understood why any of them were there, since none of them stuttered as far as I could tell at the time. As far as I could tell at the time they might have all been rounded up just to keep me company. ("He's coming today! Round up those little kids!") In the morning sessions with the counselor I don't remember any serious, wrenching, painful discussions of childhood traumas or torments, I just remember playing in the house or out in the yard, whatever I wanted to do; the only requirement was that I had to talk, about anything, the counselor interjecting himself just enough to keep the monologue going. Soon it was like talking to myself. I don't remember the subject of stuttering ever coming up, though even then I understood that was why I was there. And it's because that was why I was there that I allowed it some time ago to recede into the red air of memory as quickly as it wanted to; and now here was the Stutter School at, of all places, the address Justine had given me. I had been searching for the moment to which Justine fixed herself in defiance of memory, in the same way L.A. itself defies memory, and instead I was confronted by a memory I had long forgotten, and it seemed like quite a trick, like people chattering about a movie they know perfectly well doesn't exist.

I didn't hang around very long. I certainly wasn't going to get nostalgic about it. I left after awhile, and I didn't look for Justine anymore.

❧

I'm sitting in the dark drinking tequila, listening to a Mongolian soprano on Station 3 and what sounds like a dance orchestra from Venus. I am concentrating on the sound of my breath, because when my head is in the future and my body is in the past, my breath is the one thing I know is in the present. My apartment does not exist in the dark; when I turn on the lights the walls appear—the shelves, the furniture, the panes of the window, the metal beams that bolt the walls to the floor so that, when the earth shakes, the two do not become separated—but when the lights are off, the suite takes on its true nature, which is as a chamber of night, the lights and hills of the city rushing in through the windows and the walls blown away by a howling sky no metal beams can stop. . . .

Under a moon the color of flesh, that shines behind the smoke and a cloud that appears about to explode, L.A. surrounds me in amnesiascope. It stretches from the quays of the L.A. River to the holographic pissoirs of Burton Way, from the eucalyptuses of Jacob Hamblin Road etched so sharp before the streetlamps they look like smashed glass to the domed mosques of Baghdadville, shimmering in the light of the stars. Gazing due west from my apartment window, about halfway between me and the sea, I can actually see the spires of Black Clock Park, the time capsule cemetery that lies just beyond the rafters of the old freeway. There aren't many visitors to the park anymore. I don't even remember the last time I was there. People used to wander the knolls from one stainless steel tombstone to the next reading the dates when each cylinder had been buried and was scheduled to be unearthed, in fifty or a hundred years or, among the more optimistic, a thousand. But now only the fallen white leaves of the barren white trees blow along the rows of the graves, and birds peck at the earth in pursuit of a mystery memento within: an interred photo or scrapbook, a diary or confession, a newspaper clipping or the ring of a broken engagement or the tape of a favorite song played on a night of sex.

I live in the Border Time Zone of Los Angeles, which is more commonly called Zed Time, because on a map the zone is shaped somewhat like a Z. It runs in a long strip along the southern edge of Sunset Boulevard from Bel Air out to Crescent Heights, where it slashes down all the way to Venice Boulevard and then cuts east again to Downtown. At one point or another it borders Mulholland Time in the Hollywood Hills, Hollywood Time in the east, and Ocean Time in the west and Compton Time in the south. Out beyond the Glow Lofts and the Los Angeles River and the Downtown Time Zone is Daybreak Time, and out beyond the Ocean Time Zone, running up from Baghdadville to Zuma, is Oblivion Time. After you've lived in L.A. long enough you learn to work the zones so as to keep yourself in net plus time; if you hit all the green lights driving out on San Vicente Boulevard, for instance, you can arrive where you're going twenty-three minutes before you left. In our early days Viv and I always arranged our various rendezvous and assignations in whatever zone would get us a few extra minutes together, and up on Sunset near the corner of Jacob Hamblin Road, in front of the Chateau Marmont where the hookers flag down traffic, a girl can walk across the street to Mulholland Time if she wants to move the night along a little faster, or cross back to Zed Time if she wants eke out a few extra minutes for a few extra dollars....

Tonight Carl calls from New York. Lately he's been calling every week or so. Carl is some kind of computer traffic guru in Manhattan, mandating and eliminating roads and bridges with the snap of his fingers. I imagine him in a huge war room of sorts, surrounded by four towering wall-size flashing grids of streets and bus routes and subway tracks. Carl is the brother I never had, which somehow makes it appropriate that he is so far away and that the distance matters so little; for twenty years the life of our brotherhood has been formed of conversations every two or three weeks or months, two or three letters a year, visits every year or two when we simply pick up wherever we last left off. We met in Europe where I was always bumping into him on trains—trains to Toulouse, trains to Venice and Vienna and Brussels—and we wandered the streets of Paris ridiculously fashioning ourselves as romantic figures, unwrapping sugar cubes in cafés and wishing they were women. We are the opposite poles of our dialectic brotherhood, East Coast-worldly-bon-vivant-doubting-Jew and West Coast-antisocial-misfit-deist-by-default, and since we met he's been waiting for me to write a novel about a subject truly worthy of my time and energy; giving it a great deal of thought he's even come up with a title: *Carl's Story*. These days Carl calls with news of Los Angeles. It's the nature of L.A. that the local news is broadcast to observers three thousand miles away who then report it back to us. It was Carl who informed me when the city was under martial law, which accounted for all those tanks and Jeeps I saw on the streets the night I was late for Dr. Billy O'Forte's wedding. Thus only those outside of Los Angeles know what's *going on* here, while only those inside know what's really *happening*. Carl beseeches me to get the hell out. "Are you still there?" he says frantically, each time I answer the phone.

L.A. is all that's left of America the Delirious. Long ago, in the movie theaters of the land, L.A. collectivized the American dark; it cleaned up the depraved whispers and messier impulses of America's deeper recesses and reduced them to archetypes or, even better, commodities. L.A. insisted that the subconscious didn't own us but we owned it; a more American aspiration is hard to imagine. Now east of L.A. rolls America the Mean. The thin membrane between the delirious and the mean, between L.A. and the rest of the country, is an America of the mind that will explode any moment, if it has any life left in it at all, or will expire with a hush, if we should be so lucky. Beyond L.A. is the new America that got sick of being America, and of its own sentimental promise; for years you could feel every passion slipping away except rage, you could hear every conversation about the meaning of America framed by the decadent on the one hand and the repressed on the other who shared the same common belief that sensuality was meaningless beyond mere sensation or sheer procreation. This was the new America that came to feel more beset by freedom than invigorated by it, that was ready to hand everything over to anyone who would just fucking *take charge*. Now in L.A., street by street, block by block, step by step, door by door, all that's left of the old America is under siege. I catch sight of it from time to time: a fleeting glimpse at the top of the stairs, or outside rustling in the bushes. This is the old America of legend and distant memory, that invested no faith in the wisdom of history and no hope in the sham of the future, the old America that invented itself all over from the ground up every single day. It is the brazen America, the reckless one, the one with the lit fuse, the America that ejaculates not by habit but for the intoxicating pleasure of it, the America where no precaution is sufficient and nothing will protect you, no passport or traveling papers, no opportune crucifix or gas soaked torch, no sunglasses or decoder box or cyanide capsule, no ejector seat or live wire or secret identity or reconstructed tissues or unmarked grave or faked death. It's the America that was originally made for those who believed in nothing else, not because they believed there *was* nothing else but because for them, without America, nothing else was worth believing.

I've tried to leave L.A. before. Tried in Paris, tried in Amsterdam and Berlin; even lived in New York years ago for about six months, until I woke one morning to the sound of a strange hiss in my head and realized it was my imagination turning to dry ice. But L.A. has always pulled me back, and it wasn't until I saw it dying, wasn't until I saw it in its last throes and its last exhilarating thrash for life, wasn't until my eyes were flush with the glow of its overripeness and my lungs were filled with the perfume of its rot, that I loved it. Now when I leave L.A., it's only for the sensation of returning. Now I've become a very bad traveler, nervous on the road and out of sorts with myself, when I'm gone from L.A. too long. Now when I return, as soon as I cross the city line, I know I'm back in L.A. because I recognize it by its women; they're not like the women of anywhere else, they rampage in a way that's endemic to Los Angeles, wild like the animals that flee a fire in the hills. They emerge from out of the city's cinder heaps glistening with menstrual smoke, and recently Viv and I have noticed that every single one of them looks familiar. We've racked our brains trying to place them, before realizing they all auditioned for us: the hostess in the restaurant is the one who just arrived from Maryland, the woman at the next table is the one who wouldn't take off her clothes. And the one laughing at the bar, wasn't she the one who . . . ? That they're all beautiful, these women, means nothing. They're *auditioning*, that's what makes them Los Angeles women, and they're auditioning for more than a movie, for more than fame or success. In L.A. famous people are a dime a dozen and beautiful people a nickel a dozen, which makes people famous for being beautiful barely worth a red cent; in L.A. both the awe of and contempt for beauty have been raised to an art form. The contempt is for a gift that time and experience detract from rather than enhance, a gift that reaches its zenith in a single dazzling moment, a day or an hour or a minute when a woman blossoms to her most impossibly beautiful, whereupon the autumn of age begins, instantly and indiscernibly, to weather the petals. The awe is far more complicated. Of course it goes without saying that this awe has a distinctly male gasp to it. It goes without saying that it's men who get particularly silly about beauty—to which I offer this familiar, pathetic male whine: we can't help it. As Ventura puts it, a beautiful woman is the face of our dreams. Those dreams may span the psychic spectrum from primal to infantile to transcendent but they're our dreams nonetheless, and down in the ego-muck of the barbaric male that dream is likelier to be embodied by a beautiful face than any other vision. And as Viv puts it, Los Angeles is the Ellis Island of beauty, not just because beauty crosses its borders on a regular basis but because, like those who once came to Ellis Island not just for a new home but to be part of the American dream, beauty immigrates to Los Angeles not just to trade on its surface allure but to become the face of people's dreams. Manhattan and Paris and Milan may teem with beautiful women who are also in the business of beauty, but in Los Angeles that business is more than selling merchandise. L.A. is where the objectification of beauty is tethered directly to the subconscious.

There are so many beautiful people in L.A. that no one becomes famous *just* for being beautiful. L.A. is the city where, if it's to mean anything, mere beauty must transcend itself. Ten years ago I met a photographer who told me a startling story. It was about a young woman he knew who had just arrived in Los Angeles from South America; not long after, he began taking pictures of her, which he distributed to various agencies and magazines. Because the young woman was very beautiful, the pictures were well received. But the woman began to come unraveled by the sight of her own face, first in the photos, then in the mirror; she wound up institutionalized in a mental hospital near Ojai, where the photographer was still visiting her weekly. She had literally been driven crazy by her beauty, which had so little resonance in her South American village, and so much in Los Angeles. The streets of L.A. abound with women and men who are *clearly* mad from their beauty. They're clearly mad from the burden of becoming the face of our dreams, and from their compulsion to carry this burden. They invest everything in this mission that money can buy and technology can achieve, until they're plastic from top to bottom, bone and cartilage and fat carved away to make way for more plastic—until there isn't any more plastic left. When the plastic is gone, the doctors fill them up with whatever's handy. Open up any one of these beautiful people that you see on the street, any one of these people whose life is an audition, and inside you'll find anything you could want or need for modern existence: lighter fluid, dish soap, cognac snifters, bookends, collapsible umbrellas, matching monogrammed bath towels, dog biscuits, remote control, margarita mix, the Sunday comics, the collected recordings of Bessie Smith. Almost everyone in L.A. positively glows with the bric-a-brac and spare parts of the millennium. In the city where there is no time, the most transient of gifts— beauty—strives to be endless, added to or subtracted from not by time but at will. One invents one's beauty as one invents one's name or destiny or dream; and a thousand exchanges transpire between the dreamers: I will be the face of your dream, if you will be the dream to which I can give a face.

Beauty no longer drives the stake through my heart it did

once. I've become inoculated to beauty; I got a good dose of it, and came out of the fever still alive. The Hotel Hamblin that has Jean Harlow's name scrawled in the sidewalk in front teems with beauties. They lurk in the hallway shadows hunting for a dream to which they can attach themselves: some are sweet and some are neurotic, some are nervous and some are melancholy; some are frivolous, most seem intelligent, a few may even be deep. They eye me warily at certain times, hopefully at others, perhaps because I'm one of the few men in the hotel who doesn't appear to be a homosexual, and perhaps because they sense the inoculation and recoil from it. I don't know whether to feel badly for these dream-forsaken women or terrified of them, afraid that if I so much as meet their ravenous gaze, I'll find them in the morning sleeping at the foot of my door, their nails wedged into the wood.

At any rate I don't really think the women in the Hamblin are much interested in me. What they're interested in, from what I can tell, is their pound of flesh, and that flesh, I'm happy to say, is not mine. Unhappily for him, it's Abdul's. Since he lost his job as the manager of the building, there's nothing to protect him from the wrath of women who got sick of him showing up in their apartments in the middle of the night in his smoking jacket with a cigarette in one hand and a glass of champagne in the other. Now they want him out of the hotel altogether, and maybe in jail at that, for breaking into their apartments and going through their underwear when they weren't there, or greeting them in the shower when they were. Abdul denies all of it. One day he pulls me aside in the hall and asks if we can talk; in a shaken voice, with a face full of hurt, he recounts the rumors about him. "Can you believe this terrible shit?" he says, outraged. In the meantime he's moved out of the palatial penthouse on the first floor and in with the girl from Indiana—the one whose apartment he graced with a new hardwood floor. Following a minimum of dallying and a maximum of dalliance, she is now pregnant. "You see," he smirks when confiding the news, "even the sour fruit has a sweet bite," or some fucking idiotic Arab proverb, meaning I suppose that the sour fruit is the situation with the Hamblin in general and the sweet bite is the one he gets on what are now his very own hardwood floors. The mother-to-be is inscrutable; it's hard to know what she thinks of all this, maybe because she doesn't know herself. But as all the drama swirls around, her eyes take on the strange haunted look of a woman for whom everything depends on believing the best, even as thirty women are circulating a petition that charges the worst. Soon enough the petition comes my way. "No," I tell Dory, who presents it for my signature.

"Why?"

"Because he's not the manager anymore, and kicking him out of the building is just vindictive."

"The man has been harassing every woman here for the last two years," Dory answers angrily. "There are women who felt compelled to move out of the hotel because of him—because in a sense he drove *them* out."

"That may be," I answer. "It's also true they had other reasons for moving. I know, because I talked to some of them. They didn't like the rent or they didn't like the problems with the plumbing or the elevator or they were leaving L.A. like everyone else. So maybe he drove them out and maybe he didn't."

"It doesn't bother you that he was breaking into women's apartments?"

"It bothers me if it's true. But I don't know for myself that it is true. I never heard it firsthand from anyone who knew for a fact that he had been in her apartment, other than a feeling she had about it. I also don't know that it's *not* true. To be honest, it wouldn't surprise me if it were."

"So what are you saying?"

"Has he ever come into your apartment?"

"No."

"So."

"So what are you saying? Because he didn't come into my apartment and accost me when I was coming out of the shower, I shouldn't do anything?"

"Yes, that's what I'm saying. Let the women he did it to make the accusation. Let them get him thrown out of the hotel or worse. Until then he's just another tenant living with his pregnant girlfriend on his hardwood floors."

"You men all stick together," Dory viciously concludes.

"Someday someone will say something unpleasant about you. If it's a rumor, I'll be on your side. If it's a fact, you'll be on your own."

"Oh thank you Abraham Fucking Lincoln," she sneers, stomping off. "What a bunch of sanctimonious crap," Viv agrees with Dory, expressing that dead-on sureness of hers I can only envy: "He's guilty and you know it." Soon I have the same problem from the other side; Abdul comes around wondering if there's any time we can "get together and talk." I hedge and dodge; I can hear *this* conversation coming a mile away. He'll want me as some kind of character witness for him, in whatever forum this is going to be thrashed out: "Abdul, the smooth Palestinian, breaking into women's apartments?" with the proper tone of astonishment and indignation. So now I keep my eyes constantly peeled—for the women, for Abdul. Soon I'm hiding out from everyone, the women and Abdul and the fact-checkers at the newspaper who would confront my fraudulent movie reviews, the zombie America that stalks my streets. Only in the windows of my suite thirty feet up do I put myself on complete display to the world; and Carl still phones with bulletins, and warnings: "For God's sake, *get out of there.*"

∞

My Cinema of Hysteria grows. I've cleared my shelves of everything else, with the sweep of my arm. All the "masterpieces," all the "landmarks," all the films good for one's edification, tossed them out and replaced them with nothing but my deeply hysterical movies. *The Big Combo, Phantom Lady, Humoresque, Leave Her to Heaven, Autumn Leaves, Duel in the Sun, The Curse of the Cat People, Land of the Pharaohs, Some Came Running, Written on the Wind, Kitten With a Whip, When Worlds Collide.* I run them on the monitor all the time twenty-four hours a day, with the sound off, even when I'm not here.

For a while, amid Carl's warnings and the pleas of auditioners, I heard other voices. I heard them everywhere, in bars and cafés and theaters, in the aisles of bookshops and the checkout lines of grocery stores and up and down the street, people talking about my movie, and I don't mean the one I made with Viv. Everywhere I went I heard it until I thought I was going to go nuts, endless discussions of spectacular tracking shots and the revolutionary triptych effects and the exciting montage and what a wonderful performance Adolphe Sarre had gotten from the lead actress, the "fabulous" lighting and the "authentic" costumes and the "stun-

134

ning" set design, blah blah blah. It was bad enough everyone was a film critic now; worse that they were critiquing a film entirely written, directed, acted, photographed and produced in my head.

I'm sure everyone thought it was pretty damned funny. I'm sure it was all quite amusing to everyone. Every once in a while, sitting in a theater listening to a conversation about *The Death of Marat* in the row behind me, I was tempted to turn in my seat and confront the matter head-on. I was tempted to say, to whomever was prattling on about it at the moment, "You really thought the costumes were that good? The editing's a little slack in the middle, wouldn't you say?" And if they tried to argue with me I would yell back, "Yeah, well, I'm the guy who made up the movie in the first place! So don't give me a lot of crap about costumes!" One night I was about to do just that when the woman who was discussing the film with her boyfriend or husband or whoever said, "Did you read that piece about it in the newspaper? I thought the reviewer really missed the point." I was so dumbfounded all I could do was sink into my seat: I had missed the point of a movie I invented. After that the voices just got louder; I woke to them in the morning as though they were in the next room, having a party. . . .

Tonight Network Vs. is showing *White Whisper*. As it happens Viv is on the set of another shoot, and I choose not to watch the movie without her. I go to sleep with the movie on the airwaves, floating above me in the skies of Los Angeles. It snags on my dream and catches in a dream-loop, playing over and over just beyond my windows, where I sit hovering in the sky naked on a model's platform as Amy paints away and asks if I'm the good guy or if I'm the bad guy. Just as I'm about to answer, and before I know for sure what my answer is, the dream begins all over again.

Lately I've been getting letters from a woman in Virginia who I'll call K. Actually it is one letter, written on the backs of postcards, all of them numbered and sent one by one though, given the vagaries of the postal system in L.A. or what's left of it, I receive the cards in random order. Number five arrives before number three, followed by thirteen, nine, seven, twenty-one. For some reason there are no even-numbered cards, just odd ones. As K writes these cards each breaks off mid-sentence, which is completed on the next card that begins mid-sentence. She's writing because she's read a couple of my books, one several times, each time from the point of view, she explains, of a friend or acquaintance to whom she recommended the book but who didn't have the time or inclination to take her recommendation. When I first began receiving these cards I answered with my usual perfunctory response, thanking her for her comments; but then I became almost inexplicably intrigued by her questions, about art, life, love, sex, what food I like to eat, what movies I like to watch, my favorite color.

Now I try to answer more regularly, though there's no way to keep up with the stream of cards that keep coming. I got forty last month; in the last twenty-four hours I've received nineteen. She's literally writing them faster than I can read them, and I'm running out of space to put them. The drawers of my desk are crammed, the closet is full, I'm boxing them up and renting storage bins. I'm shipping them off to far lands because L.A. can't hold all of them. On the front of the cards are pictures of cats, elephants, trains, boats built in the shape of guitars, punk riots in London, a river that cuts through a valley like sulfur, a woman in a black dress clutching her child watching a ship on the ocean in the distance, a man on fire plummeting to earth, two apparently naked bodies folded into each other beneath a bed sheet, and a gallery of familiar icons, Billie Holiday, Tom Mix, Marcel Duchamp, Miles Davis, Cab Calloway, Greta Garbo, Albert Einstein, Bob Marley. "How do you define culture?" she asked early on. "Appealing to the intellect is always a selective process, isn't it?" Lately, however, the tone has changed. "I'm twenty-five, long-legged, large-breasted, golden-haired, green-eyed," she taunts. "I've got a Ph.D. in American literature, I act and model part-time. I'm a photographer and filmmaker and I've got my pilot's license and fly cross-country solo. I've never been married, hence never divorced, never had either a child or an abortion, never been engaged. I've never made love. I'm a virgin two times."

I've gotten the order of K's cards hopelessly mixed up. I warned K that our correspondence is bound to be one-sided; nonetheless she has seduced me somehow, even as the continually arriving cards raise certain questions in my mind. Is she obsessed? Is she insane? Is she homicidal? Will she appear any moment at my door? Nonetheless from the distance of Virginia she has found the secret passage into the secret room of my life. My life's secret room has been empty for some time, like my life's literary room. From time to time I pass through the public room, but over the last several years, since the Quake and the backfires and meeting Viv, I've lived almost wholly in the private room, with communications issued from wherever it is I write the movie reviews. Since the secret room has been empty my life has been much calmer, but it's also true I've come to miss it; and I've come to realize that it's only when I'm either in the secret room, or when the secret room is completely empty not only of myself but guests, that I'm entirely in the present. Now I think that maybe I hear sounds coming from the secret room. I wonder if they're K's. I wonder if K has invaded the secret room and that unsettles me, not only because I have no idea what she's really like—I'm skeptical of the leggy, large-breasted, green-eyed description—but because I have no idea what password she used to get in, among all the words scribbled in tiny writing on the back of countless postcards. She's becoming a figment of my imagination, like *The Death of Marat*, and as a result of her invasion I've been thrown a step back into the future. Our correspondence, one-sided or not, has both the utter innocence and profound danger of secret life.

What I find both irresistible and frightening about my correspondence with K is that, inside my secret room, she is the secret, not me. Though I've come to feel I can trust her, I still can't be entirely certain in the dark what weapons she might hold or whether the glint in her eye is desire or murder. So I push her away with one hand and pull her to me with another, as I've done with so many women; in the secret room I want to have my way with K as she's tied and bound. I want to walk away from her after I'm finished until whenever I'm ready to come back, and not have to think about her in between, because if I did my conscience would be tormented, and long ago I became so tired of all the things and people, significant and trivial, that torment my conscience. I am aware, of course, that I created the secret room in the first place so I could pretend its forbidden activities happen not in the real world but rather a dream that has four walls. And I personally know of secrets, not mine but those held by others, that are beyond the pale even as fantasies, secrets that cannot be absolved no matter how large or small is the room of the psyche in which these fantasies find life, no matter how dark the room is or how light. Compared to such secrets my correspondence with K, who I have never met and am not likely to ever meet, is barely worth being a secret at all, for which I may or may not be held accountable any more than the world can hold me accountable for the desires of my dreams. Only moral totalitarianism refuses to make the distinction between a secret that announces the death of the soul—watching a snuff film, for instance, or the defilement of children—and the secret of a one-sided correspondence that does nothing more than suggest an illicit affair of the mind. Still, I'm stirred by my contemplation of just where moral rationalization ends and real damnation begins, I'm stirred by how even the imagination is not entirely guiltless. I'm stirred by consideration of just how many layers really lie between the blackest secret and the most harmless, and just how thin they are, and by the membrane between the impulse that only lurks and the impulse that is realized. I can only bring myself to ponder, without ever actually pursuing the answer, whether I would really pursue my darkest impulses if I was sure I could get away with it, or whether my conscience would still know itself, even if the defining lines of civilization were so scrambled as to allow the unallowable. . . .

There is a little blonde hooker I see now and then on Sunset Boulevard. She is always there at dusk in Zed Time, on the corner across from the Chateau Marmont: I call her the Princess of Coins, from the American Tarot. She glistens conspicuously. Get close enough to her and she's younger than you thought; the girls on this stretch of the Strip are always either younger or older than you thought, if you ever get that close. At any rate she's young enough to still be on the street, before the law of desire either places her in some guy's penthouse or renders her old, or kills her: she glistens too conspicuously to remain on the street for long. I look for her whenever I drive by this way. I have no serious thought of employing her, but since she's more appealing than most of the hookers I've seen, and since she stands not four blocks from where I live, I find myself wondering what it would be like to buy her and take her home. I can still remember years ago walking down a street in Amsterdam past all the women in the windows, one in particular sitting in her window in black hair and a soft white turtleneck sweater, smiling and saying nothing, knowing I wanted her but had neither the money nor the nerve, and knowing as well that years later I would vividly remember the missed opportunity. But the Princess of Coins, years later on Sunset Strip across from the Chateau Marmont in Zed Time, is too young and unwise to smile like that. Hers are the young smiles that vanish instantly in my rearview mirror when I pass her by. . . .

I was at Viv's one evening and had what I thought was a dream. The sun was going down and I was about to leave, because Viv was expecting some friends over in an hour or so for a Night of Women; but I went up to the overhanging platform and lay down on her bed, and I must have drifted off. I don't remember being so particularly tired. At some point I woke, or I dreamed that I woke, and the women had arrived and were down below the loft, talking; I wasn't conscious enough to make out what they were saying. I don't know if they were indifferent to my being up there or had just forgotten it. But slipping in and out of sleep, I woke again to the flickering of candlelight on the ceiling above me, and turning over I peered over the edge of the bed at all the women below me who, eight or ten of them, were naked. Some of them I recognized. I was pretty sure I saw Veroneek and Lydia and even Amy Brown, along with several of the artists who had been at the ball. They weren't saying much, just whispering among themselves while they shaved each other. Little bowls of soapy water sat between the legs of the four or five women being shaved by the other four or five who very intently dipped the tiny razors into the water and continued until the work was finished. There was nothing especially precious or ritualistic about it; rather the bare, glistening women seemed to be mapping, between the lines of a commonly held secret, their own country that was inviolate to any man, whether or not they knew or cared that he might be up in bed on the platform above them watching. I was lulled by the sight and silence of it; and I can't remember if I just turned away and closed my eyes or kept watching, but I could see emerge through the pubic hair as it was shaved away the tattoos that had been hidden underneath, the Nine of Bridges and the Ace of Rifles, the Six of Stars and the Five of Coins. In the juxtaposition of their bodies I read my fortune—a foggy destiny and newly revealed crossroads, where the name of the bridge before me was written on a sign in an amalgam, and right before waking I almost deciphered the letters long enough to make it out. Later when I woke the women were gone. I went downstairs in the dark and turned on the light, and there was no sign of razors or bowls of soapy water, but looking closely at the floor I ran my finger through the small silky hairs that had slipped by the women's effort to remove all traces of what they had done.

Not long after our night with Jasper, Viv showed me her plans for a new sculpture. She calls it the Memoryscope. It is to be twenty feet long, cylindrical like a telescope and made of steel, and will stand perched in the sky. Lining the inside along the bottom will be a mirrored strip that runs from one end to the other, so that when the sun rises to a certain point, the telescope will flash a blinding light. In this light, Viv explains, one will see the memory he or she has most forgotten. Once she has finished this telescope she'll determine the coordinates of its aim, wherever that might be—the Rockies, Chicago, Nova Scotia—and build there another telescope, aimed back at Los Angeles. Obviously it is an impressive, ambitious plan; Viv has spoken to Jasper about erecting it in the moat of fire that surrounds Jasper's house, or maybe the junkyard beyond, within view of one of the garrets. I sense this is Viv's gift to Jasper, to revive Jasper from what she perceives to be the deluded despair of her memories even as it would revive Viv herself from her own doldrums after the Artists Ball and the filming of *White Whisper*, not to mention a growing ambivalence about the direction of her life, the sense that something is slipping through the cracks. . . .

Last week I had dinner with Dr. Billy O'Forte, in a little steak joint near the old pier. "You know," he said of Viv, "she's better for you than anyone you've ever been with," and once I was too young and stupid for that to have meant anything. But then life passes by and, almost unnoticed to you, the curve in the hill that has always been upward suddenly turns downward, and what and who are good for you means something. Viv is my Queen of Stars. She's the face of a dream that waits for the flash of sunlight along a strip of mirrors before it explodes into recognition, which may be to say that Viv is not the face of my dream but that my dream is the face of Viv: at any rate she is the face of my reality, which has become a much better thing than my dreams. Part maternal caretaker and part eternal ten-year-old tomboy, part romantic commando and part sexual guerrilla, Viv careens between the extremes of scandal—it's all one can do to hold her back from jumping on the Cathode Flower stage and taking her clothes off with the strippers, and there was one month she seriously considered a job as a go-go dancer in Tokyo—and a kind of saintliness, giving a bum on the street her last twenty because she has nothing smaller. For the first year, we were together only because we couldn't stay apart, our bond made not out of dreams but our irresistible fucking; sex bound us when everything else, the past and future in particular, tried to break us down. And then not so long ago came the moment when both the past and the future rushed into the present and all the wounds I inflicted on us and all the promises that had been implied between us presented themselves to be answered for. When amnesia broke, through its gate marched every person I ever hurt, one after another, and I broke down one afternoon in a little diner on La Cienega Boulevard, sobbing into my cheeseburger while the other patrons hastily paid up their tabs and bolted, as though fleeing the spectacle of an epileptic fit. I cried from the diner to the parking lot, I cried from that afternoon to that night, all the way home and into the next day. I cried for Viv, I cried for Sally, I cried for the women I hurt before Viv and after Sally, I cried because my father was dead, I cried because someday my mother would be dead, I cried for my conscience and my faith. I cried for my dreams. I was quite a basket case that day, when amnesia broke and I remembered again; I cried for all my failures, and for that moment's failure in particular: the failure to transcend memory.

Sally called last night. Viv was over at my place in a foul mood, wondering why none of her film work was bringing her any real money—and if she wasn't making money, then what was the point, and why wasn't she doing what she really wanted to do, like building her Memoryscope? In the midst of this serious discussion the telephone rang, I answered, and it was Sally. Of course Viv knew immediately. Later she accused me of "practically cooing," though I know from the sound in Sally's voice that to her I seemed as cold as ice; it's funny that two women can hear exactly the same thing at the same time and hear not entirely different words or meanings, which one might expect, but entirely different heartbeats and temperatures. Sally was more right than Viv. I was colder than I was cooing. We hadn't spoken since she got married. Typically, she was in town for only one night and calling at the last minute to say that Polly was with her, and wondering if I wanted to have breakfast with the two of them in the morning. I answered that it wasn't possible. She asked how I was and I answered that I couldn't talk. She rushed to hang up, either right before or after I began to add, "Let me know if—"

Let me know, I began to say, if you ever come back to L.A. Viv, already in the furious throes of a full moon, was on her way out the door before I stopped her. I knew that later she'd regret going, and that I'd regret letting her go. "She couldn't care less whether you see Polly," Viv answered bitterly. Viv thinks the worst of Sally partly because she needs to, because she feels that Sally stole something that was Viv's before Viv and I ever knew each other existed, and because she believes she's worthier of it than Sally ever was. As to whether Sally truly cares or not that I see Polly, I don't know. I believe she does, but it doesn't matter; what matters is that over the weeks and months and years, I haven't been able to get Polly out of my mind. I was a father to her even as I was never the father she wanted. I was the one who bathed and fed and read her stories and put her to bed when her father was off strumming his guitar and listening to people tell him he was a genius and basking in little Polly's distant adoration, and the knowledge that besides being a genius he was the world's best-loved father. And then one day I disappeared. I cut her off as I cut off her mother, as I cut myself off from the past and from my memories one by one, because I wasn't brave or strong or big enough to rise or at least sidestep the pain long enough to see a little four-year-old kid for an hour or two now and then. My pain was pretty petty compared to the confusion she must have felt; and it was my choice, after all, because she was four years old after all, so it couldn't very well have been her choice. Later I told myself I did it because my continued presence in her already con-fused life could only compound the confusion; and I knew *that* was a lie as soon as I tried to convince myself I believed it.

Polly isn't all the guilt I have left, just one of the biggest parts of it. It bobs in the arctic stream of my memories like the shard of ice from a much larger block in the far distance, along with smaller receding shards. There is the guilt about my marriage. There is the guilt about Viv and the pain of our first year. There is the guilt about Christina, a low-rider in a black beat-up T-Bird and a lazy Cheshire smile and a beauty mark over one eyelid, who I knew after Sally and whose time and faith and warmth I cava-lierly used up and wasted; I came to feel a great affection for her even after our passion was over, at a time when I could not yet pinpoint any capacity for love I might still have, and even now I still miss that affection. Little pieces floating in the cold current: a string of bedded women who claimed they expected nothing when I knew they expected everything, but I accepted their dis-claimers anyway so I could have their bodies for a moment and release into them all the pain that can be released but none of the pain that can't. Farther back is the guilt about my father's death, as banal as it is universal, over things unsaid and gestures unmade: "If you have anything to tell him, tell him soon," my mother, crying, warned me two weeks before he went. Left to my own devices, I can *drown* in guilt. I wake in the night to a wave of it suspended high above me in the dark. Part of me has been hoping for it; sometimes I wonder if it is less a barometer of my morality than another expression of my ego—vanity disguised as evidence that I still have a conscience. Then I turn on the light. I think about Sally and the wave vanishes, because about Sally of course there is little guilt, which is why she's been such a luxury to me for so long, and why I was so reluctant for so long to give her up. The pain of Sally is cleaner, and there hasn't been that much pain in my life recently in which I could pretend to be so pure. But then Sally calls and I hear her voice full of sadness and trepidation, and the pain isn't quite so clean anymore; and then I remember Polly, and everything else is remembered again too.

Here, in the Last City of the Last Millennium, I have meant to defeat guilt and memory once and for all, though I know the effort is doomed. It isn't an amnesia of the mind I pursue, or an amnesia of the heart; it is rather an amnesia of the psyche that sets me free. I've been working on my stutter. I almost lost it for a while but I've gotten it back, better than ever. I open my window and lean out into the street and stutter at the world, frightening animals and alarming somnambulists and causing cars to swerve. Every word ricochets in the back of my throat until I achieve true senselessness, until not a line of communication with anyone else is left, until every exchange is irrevocably rude. Standing in the shadows of street corners I open my mouth and let go at the passersby. It's more than a hesitancy, it's more than a slight tension in the larynx, it's a full assault. In the movies the stutterer is always the one unhinged, the one so pathetically weak he winds up hanging himself, once he has fulfilled his function of giving the audience a good belly laugh. My stutter is different. Mine is a stutter, refined by the day, perfected by the minute, that will drive everyone else to hang themselves. People clear a path at my approach; they hear it coming, like a siren or an alarm. Every memory I have left tangles on the inane bursts from my lips like the words tangling on my tongue. The only sound I don't stammer is the moan of my orgasm. But I'm working on it.

In the Stutter was born the Dream. I don't remember my first word, I don't remember my first stutter, but I'm told they were not the same, that my first word was stammer-free; thus, the moment of my truest eloquence was the moment of my earliest communication, back before the beginning of memory. Did I best know myself then, before the stutter, or have I come to know myself best since, when who I am has been defined by the stutter? I don't have an answer. The stutterer is both the person I really am, and someone I am not. He is the intermediary through which I've been forced, by the impairment of my speech, to reveal myself to the world. But whatever passed through my mind the first time I stuttered, at the age of four or five, whatever awful virgin humiliation was breached, only to be compounded over the years, then the decades, through childhood and adolescence into youthful manhood to the shores of middle age, I've forgotten. I've wiped it away. Everything about me has felt fundamentally flawed since, in the way I suppose everyone feels a fundamental flaw. But my flaw is only a secret from everyone else as long as I keep my mouth shut. Beginning with the simplest introduction—"My name is ..." —my secret is revealed, since my own name has always been one of the most impossible words to express fluidly.

Here are the rules: I can talk about this, you can't. The most casual reference to it by another person still humiliates me. That I might make it a matter of public record does not mean I'm open to discussion on the subject. I will fool you from time to time; sometimes I won't do it at all. Some years back, giving a reading in a book store, I was asked about it afterward. "But you haven't stuttered once," someone piped up from the crowd of listeners, expecting I'd find the observation reassuring. "Oh," I said, "you wanted the stuttering version? I didn't know that. I only do that when I want to amuse people. No, this was the Top Forty version—the stuttering version is the dance mix. Less melody and more percussion, and it goes on all night...." No one ingratiates him or herself, no one worms his or her way into my confidence, by initiating a discussion on stuttering. I remember a counselor, later in life, long after the Stutter School, advising that a stutterer "must face his stuttering," as though the stutterer is not confronted by his stuttering every moment. As though every moment of the most perfunctory social intercourse does not involve the choice to speak or not, does not involve a hundred rapid-fire decisions having to do with word selection, phrasing, the mad dash or the clandestine tiptoe across the minefield of semantic bombs, verbal spasms, rhetorical tics waiting to detonate on the end of one's tongue. And between the utterance of the sound, and the act of violation by which the stutterer listens to himself, the minefield is crossed back, the return journey made to some private painful assessment by which he concludes: "It didn't sound so bad, did it? It was almost *sonorous*, wouldn't you say?" It may be that the stuttering of the past wasn't as bad as I remember, but only in the same way the stuttering of the present is always worse than I hear it, until I play my voice back, on a tape perhaps, to my own appalled realization.

Listen. I don't know another way of talking about it that doesn't skirt some sordid spectacle of self-pity, self-absorption, self-loathing. And rather than risk any of those, I'd as soon take everything back, and forget about it, and pretend, as I've always pretended, that the man who writes these words on paper is the true one, rather than the one who spits them out fitfully. I come from a long line of stoics: Scandinavian, Celt, American Indian. Blabbermouths these people are not. It's possible that if I'd never stuttered, I never would have become a writer, though we'll never know. But whatever imagination I was born to proved to be, from the beginning, the only safe haven when the stuttering began; and whatever grand vanity I might have begun to form was cut off at the knees or, more precisely, the throat. In the interior of my imagination, my words always belonged to me, I did not belong to them. In this interior as well, only I could know my own integrity when I was seven years old and the teacher called my mother to complain I must have plagiarized the short story we were assigned to write, since my strangled speech offered no convincing evidence I could even read, let alone write. It was ten years before anyone was truly convinced. By then, if teachers and principles were ready to concede I *could* indeed write the things I claimed to have written, they argued nonetheless that these were not the sort of things I *should* be writing. It was too late. Having asserted my imagination and won my voice, I would not give them back.

Well, I couldn't give them back, could I? What of me would have been left? A stutter or silence. I had been a little seven-year-old kid, after all, with everything I was and everything I dreamed of being shrouded by the static of my own mouth; until I broke through. And then I had gone too far to surrender the word, and the more forbidden it was, the more irrevocable was my claim to it. Much later, buried under all the unpublished manuscripts and all the years piling up right behind them, I might very well have surrendered the word if it would have left me anything but faceless, voiceless, beingless. By the end of those fifteen years that stretched from twenty to thirty-five, when I had so futilely tried to become a published novelist, I had long since crossed the terrain of dejection to despair: but in the Stutter was born the Dream, and it pushed me from one effort to another across so much defeat that when the breakthrough finally came, modest as it was, it commanded that I destroy everything that had come before, including the pile of unpublished manuscripts. And because that small breakthrough had seemed so elusive, such a monstrous mountain to scale, I had this idea that once having scaled it, everything else about the Dream would finally lie at my fingertips. Having caught the tip of the Dream, I assumed the rest of it was simply to be taken. I don't know why, five novels later, it didn't happen. Any conjecture would only sound graceless, bitter, self-justifying. I've seriously considered the most obvious answer, that I was never as good as I hoped or wanted to believe. That the Dream was fantastic relative to what my talent really was. Looking back I can't help seeing the worst: my insights as trite, my imagination as second-rate, my facility for words only as glib as I always wished my talk could be. More than that, I see my faith in myself as most counterfeit of all. Looking back, I'm not sure now I ever believed the Dream was really possible. Because if in the Stutter was born the Dream, in the Doubt was born the Stutter, and so the Dream was always infected by Doubt. I've thrust myself forward not out of faith or even will but the sort of primal force of habit that moves an animal to the place that nature commands it, to graze or mate or die; and somewhere past the rubicon of inspiration's replenishment, where I was emptying myself more than I was refilling, and even though I didn't really believe the harshest words of my harshest review, which suggested, like the second-grade teacher, that I was really nothing more than a glorified plagiarist, the Doubt could not help but still assume it was one more thing I was guilty of.

And then I was exhausted. Now, like a once devout man who comes to doubt God, I have no more vision, no more ideas, no more nerve. In the name of growing older, growing wiser, I find myself pulled toward the vortex of a capitulation that, as a younger man, I despised in others. It confuses me. I want to be wise—and then I wonder, in that desire, whether wisdom is the enemy of passion, or whether believing that wisdom is the enemy of passion is only the sign that I'm neither wise nor passionate. I only hope that I'm left with more than rage or the cheap cynicism of everyone who fails his or her dream, and can only therefore scorn the dreams of others; God knows the world is full enough of such people. My ever-growing inconsequentiality seeps in beneath the door of one room after another, the public and then the literary, the private and finally the secret. I got a call the other day from the head of a stutterer's "support group," if you can believe such a thing, wondering if I would be a part of it: "But what is it you *do* in this group anyway?" I wanted to know. "Spend all night just trying to get through the minutes of the last meeting? Do you protest stuttering comedians, movies that laugh at us? Do you make the world *sensitive* to our plight? Are you going to make my stuttering *inconsequential*, is that the idea? Are you going to collectivize my stutter, so it's not my burden alone to bear? You st-st-stay away from my stutter," and I slammed the phone down, and was struck by the silence around me.

One night, a few months ago, I woke in a fit of absurd inspiration. I got out of bed and went into the other room, and pulled from the shelves the books I'd written, and began tearing them apart, ripping them down their spines and casting away the covers, spreading all the pages on the floor around me. This went on all night until I looked up not only to see dawn but Ventura in my doorway. He had been up early to work, had gone down to the corner café to get some coffee, came back and saw the light beneath my door and knocked; and when I didn't answer, and all he heard inside was the ripping of pages, he came in. Now he stood looking at me surrounded by a thousand disembodied pages on the floor. Excitedly I explained to him my brainstorm. I told him I was going to rewrite all my books into one huge book except *with the stutter*—from beginning to end one colossal, sprawling, staggering epic of manic stammering, stunned gasping, throttled gulping and violent hiccuping that would sum up all of our lives, the times in which we live, the age behind us and the one to come. After this, not only would no one ever write another book, no one would want to, all eloquence exposed for the bankrupt rhetorical currency it is. By the time I finished Ventura had turned the oddest pallor I've ever seen, gray around the eyes and white at the edges of his hair. He looked at me as though he was uncertain whether to lock me in the room and take all the sharp objects on his way out, or say and do nothing, with blind faith that my seizure would pass and I would return to normal. He chose the latter, nodding silently and backing slowly out into the hallway. When he was gone I just sat there for a while and, just as silently as he had gone, got myself a forty-pound trash bag and scooped up the pages and filled the bag up. Then I lowered the window shades, turned off the telephone and went back to bed.

Christ, I wanted to be a hero once. I wanted to be something so much larger than I am that I might be out of earshot of my own voice. I wanted to save someone or something, to redeem some ideal, to find and live in that moment between utter desperation and the exhilaration of desperation, when the only recourse left is to burst free of oneself. Now I've forgotten that as well. Now my stutter is all that's left of that attempt, and it survives only because it's ridiculous enough to survive and to remind me, every time I open my mouth, that the only courage left is to try and forget the unforgettable.

ᢙᢏ

I wake up in Viv's bed, but when I reach for her I find my wrists are bound to the bedposts. I can't help giving my arms a good tug to see if they come free, to make sure I haven't just tangled myself up in the sheets. For a while I lie there staring up into the blackness of whatever is across my eyes, and for what seems like a long time nothing happens at all. In the night air I'm a little cold, since I don't have anything covering me: "I'm cold," I finally break down; there's no response. After a minute or so I'm suddenly certain Viv isn't in bed at all. After another minute I'm certain Viv isn't even in the apartment. Then I remember, dimly echoing out of the last moments of whatever dream I was having before I woke, the sound of a door opening and closing. I cannot be sure, there in the dark, whether I'm actually afraid. In my mind I begin to see, more vividly than I've ever seen before, Viv's loft, all her mannequins and steel sculptures, the towers and obelisks and pyramids with their exotic feathers and little windows that peer in at pods and pearls. Naked and bound to Viv's bed I see them surrounding me in the dark; and as more time passes I become more acutely aware of the waves of the ocean in the distance, the muffled wet whir of helicopters in the fog overhead and, far away, gunshots.

It begins to rain.

After a while I lose sense of time. I'm not sure if I've laid there thirty minutes or an hour, or three. Then I hear steps outside the door, and the door opens, and then I hear steps coming up the stairs of the overhanging platform, and it doesn't take long to figure out they are the steps of more than one person. I can't tell if she has turned on the light. The only thing I'm certain of is that someone is with her, and for some time there's no sound at all, as though they are standing by the bed looking down at me. Nothing is said. After a few moments they go back downstairs and there is the clinking of glasses and the sound of something poured, and then I hear them walking around below. Whoever is with her expresses no surprise at the situation. Flashing through my mind is the morning out on Pacific Coast Highway in my car with Sahara from the Cathode Flower, and Viv declaring they would have their revenge; but I really have no idea whether it's Sahara. It could be anyone. It could be Sahara or one of Viv's friends or a woman she just picked up in a bar: "Hello, my name is Viv and I have a naked man at home tied to my bed." I'm still trying to decide if I'm afraid, when the warm mouth I feel almost makes me jump out of my skin, because I hadn't heard them come back up to the bed. I assume it's Viv's mouth but I can't be sure. It takes in so much of me it alarms me. My erection feels like a betrayal, a sign of how easily my psyche will sell me out for a rush. And then I feel both of them and there's no knowing which is Viv, who I still trust, and which is the other one, who I have no reason to trust, and what is the alchemic confusion of both of them intertwined, least trustworthy of all. I'm vaguely aware of being inside one and then maybe the other, or maybe it's the same, each of them climbing on top of me and having their turn, and then one of them putting me inside her and the other straddling my face and putting herself in my mouth. I think I recognize the taste of Viv; I'm almost sure it's Viv's hand stroking me when I come. She knows what it's like for me to come this way, not inside her but out in the open, with her watching, except now there is someone else watching too, a stranger I will never know, or someone I may know but who will always have been a stranger to me in this moment. At the moment of orgasm Viv knows I want to hide; but there's nowhere to hide now, with my wrists and ankles bound. My exposure is excruciating.

"Everything you are," someone whispers in my ear, "is in my head." Someone else kisses my mouth, and then the other one kisses my mouth, and I think to myself, They're both Viv: there are two of her now. I fall back to sleep.

When I wake, I'm untied. The blindfold is gone. The gray light of either morning or afternoon, I'm not sure which, fills Viv's loft; it's still raining. Viv is not next to me in bed but naked on the couch downstairs. No one else is there, but two half-drunk glasses of wine sit on the cabinet next to the refrigerator. My legs and my cock are streaked with lipstick; I go into the bathroom and wash, and then, still wet, kneel by the couch and kiss Viv the way she kissed me hours ago. She clutches my hair in her sleep.

⚮

Not far from the newspaper's office you can grab a boat down the sunken subway. The city keeps trying to board up the old Metro entrances, but people just come along and rip the boards down. Ever since the tunnels flooded years back after the subway was first built, sidewalks have rumbled like they would to a train, except it's the sound of the underground canals rushing from the Valley through Laurel Canyon to the Fairfax Corridor, then branching east to Hollywood and Silverlake beyond that, or south to Baldwin Hills. There the tunnels fork again: one winds toward the ghost marina and the other picks up the L.A. River and continues on toward San Pedro and the harbor. Sailing down the southward canals from any of the makeshift docks that riddle the underground, you pass transients living in catacombs and old abandoned subway cars floating in the grottos. Siamese-twin lizards skitter across the tunnel ceiling, and the deep white bleached roots of the trees that line Crescent Heights and Sixth Street crack through the subway walls. If you take the boat all the way out to Santa Monica the subterranean river deposits you out into the steaming bay, where a cobalt sky explodes above you and the city looms up in back, wreathed by a mane of smoke. Over the years, through the millions of fractures in the walls that line the sunken tunnels, canal water has seeped into the ground until the whole city stands in a big black lagoon of quicksand....

Viv tells me about a dream she had. In this dream her father has been murdered; in retaliation she sets the killer on fire in the middle of her loft. As he burns, with the light of the fire washing the walls until they run like the colors of a painting, the killer turns into me, though it's not at all clear whether I was thekiller in the first place. Viv is very disturbed by this dream; I think I'm most surprised that she feels compelled to tell me about it, as though it's a confession, or something I'm obligated to explain or account for. "But it was a very pretty fire," she assures me.

We decided to leave L.A. for a few days. We drove out of the rain that began falling the night I was tied to her bed, and left it behind us in the Cajon Pass, hitting Las Vegas that evening where we got a room high in one of the casino towers. From the back seat of the car Viv declared she had no interest in gambling whatsoever, but two days and a couple of dozen Bombay Sapphires later I had to pry loose her death-grip on a slot machine finger by finger. Nights we spent at an old strip joint in Downtown called the Golden Garter; the girls weren't bad, not emaciated California blondes but dark Nevadan Rubenesques. I was not lured by any strange women into the casino swimming pool, and we were not buried under the rubble of an earthquake; but I did have a bizarre dream of my own one night, if not as incendiary as Viv's. I dreamed I was trapped in a long dark room. Making my way to the end of the room I was desperately trying to open a door which was outlined by light from the other side, when I heard someone call me. Over and over someone called as I pounded on the door, until the sound of my name became so persistent that I woke up. Barely conscious, I realized I was standing at the window of our room and Viv was talking to me. She had gotten up to go to the bathroom and then in the bathroom heard sounds in the front room and rushed out to find I was standing at the window pounding on it, trying to get out. Since our room was eleven floors up, it was just as well I didn't. Befuddled, like an old man losing his mind, I just stood there in the dark until Viv took me by the hand and coaxed me back to bed. . . .

When we drove back to Los Angeles, the same rain was still falling. It was the kind of rain L.A. never has, one storm after another sweeping up from Mexico and in from the sea, dousing all the backfires. Now the whole city bulged, pocked by footprints full of water and rumbling with the sound of surging canals below; between storms the air filled with a hiss from the steam rising off the rings, and when the sun broke, a shroud of golden light hovered over the city. The houses on the distant hillsides above the steam looked like small white villages floating in the sky, and then the hillsides gave way from the rain and slid to earth, and the floating villages vanished into the air. The rain was a lucky break for Viv, who found the moat of fire surrounding Jasper's house conveniently extinguished just in time for the erection of her Memoryscope, which she brought to the outskirts of the city by truck and hired hands. Jasper was nowhere to be seen, but her stepfather watched from the house tower; he shook his fist at her, yelling something that couldn't be heard. The Memoryscope stands ten yards from the house and ten yards above the ground, pointed east to a morning sun that never shines anymore, waiting to reveal its first memory in the rip of a sunlit dawn. Almost immediately after putting up her Memoryscope, Viv developed a burning in the pit of her, above the belly and below the rib cage—not far, I suppose, from her heart. It was as though, in a dream, she had set the center of herself on fire.

There's no getting away from a sense of things breaking down. . . . Around the same time Viv started getting sick I woke one morning to find that not only was L.A. raining but the Hotel Hamblin as well. The entryway in my suite was leaking and the woman next door was virtually washed out, her mattress floating around her apartment like a soggy raft. Of course there was nothing to do about this, since anarchy now reigned in the building along with the rain, what with Abdul hiding from the posse of women that stalked the premises searching for him— not that Abdul was in charge anymore anyway, nor that it ever mattered when he was. "It's raining in the hotel," I informed Ventura in his doorway, which answered with a pronounced drip on the top of my head. Ventura was sitting in the same chair he always sat in, in the same hat and cowboy boots; it was clear he couldn't care less about the rain. In a minute he would explain how the aberrational proximity of Antarctica to one of the moons of Jupiter had tossed the hemisphere's whole weather system off kilter, and we could expect relentless, Biblical rain for seven years. But he didn't go into all that; he had a couple of more important announcements. The first and least interesting was that he was dying.

He's made a number of declarations of this sort in the time I've known him; I think he's barely escaped death on thirty or forty occasions. If it's not creeping stomach rot or a cancer nobody's heard of, it's his heart beating in an unduly eccentric fashion. I've come to take news of Ventura's pending demise metaphorically: one of his most famous pieces for the newspaper began on the front page in big black letters, YOU, NO MATTER HOW HEALTHY OR RICH OR SMART OR BEAUTIFUL, ARE GOING TO DIE, followed by a six- or seven-thousand-word elaboration for whatever local narcissists were still under the illusion they were immortal. This isn't to say I don't take dying seriously myself. It isn't to say I don't think about it all the time, or that a day has passed since I was about eight when it hasn't crossed my mind. At this particular moment, for instance, I was trying to decide if drowning in my own apartment was, as deaths go, more ridiculous than it was exotic, or more exotic than it was ridiculous, with the drip drip drip on my head in Ventura's doorway persuasively making the case for ridiculous. I could tell, though, that Ventura didn't think he was going to drown in his apartment; he was contemplating the prospect of going sooner than that. It was the blood this time. The doctor, Ventura explained, had informed him he had blood "the consistency of cream." He said this again, and noticeably brightened; the writer in him couldn't resist the poetry of it. "Blood the consistency of cream," he said for the third time, lowering his cowboy boots to the floor. He was smiling now. He was *happy*. The romantic *doom* of it. He was a walking cholesterol time bomb, a ticking butterball; he started working it over in his mind, pacing the room, giving it a little extra Sicilian flourish each time. "Blood the consistency of cream." He loved it! His face was a grimace of ecstasy.

He was less ecstatic about the second bit of news, and that was what worried me. It is when things are breaking down in the abstract that Ventura is most sanguine, so when he said without any real joy in his voice that something was up at the newspaper, I had a bad feeling this wasn't just one of Ventura's run-of-the-mill apocalypses. Ventura couldn't quite put his finger on it, but Freud N. Johnson appeared to be agitating himself into a final psychotic assault on Shale's job, eyes peeled and fingers twitching for the hair-trigger excuse. "This would *not* be a good time for me to have to quit," was all I could say, contemplating my state of affairs at the moment. "Doesn't Johnson know what would happen if he fired Shale?"

"He's moved way beyond that kind of rationality," Ventura answered. "Firing Shale has become an impulse he has to satisfy, like the impulse to walk into a post office and start shooting people. If anything, he's convinced himself that *nothing* will happen, that writers threaten to quit all the time in these situations and then never do. Which of course he's right about." I couldn't say I knew for sure what Ventura would do if Shale were fired; I'm not even sure he knew, and that was what was really throwing him. For Ventura, quitting the newspaper might be a kind of death altogether more serious and real than blood the consistency of cream. Soon he was trying to talk himself out of his pessimism—"Well, nothing's probably going to happen for a while"—which was so out of character as to be *really* ominous.

A sense of general crisis approached on the horizon. Over the next couple of days I realized I was inhaling without fully exhaling, and in the meantime the rain didn't stop. It was raining in the halls of the Hamblin, the stairs became creeks; driving across the city I skidded and swerved around one disaster after another: flooded intersections, broken water mains, cresting sewers, streets buried under mud slides, springs bubbling up from the subway rivers underground. One afternoon during a brief lull I was heading home, passing Sunset and Laurel not far from where Scott Fitzgerald lived when he wrote for the movies, past the Chateau Marmont and the Cathode Flower and, standing on the northern side of the boulevard, the little Princess of Coins. I guess she was trying to drum up business while there was a break in the weather. She was typically fetching in a little black skirt and tight silver sweater, gazing eagerly up and down the Strip.

I was just gliding by when, first like a small leak the earth had sprung, and then in a stream, the base of the hillside behind her suddenly exploded in a torrent of water and mud. The underground Laurel Canyon subway channel had broken through, and in seconds the Princess was completely washed away, like she was never there at all; horrified, I still couldn't help bursting out laughing. Mud splattered my windshield and the water that crashed out into the street carried my car a few feet before I got some traction back—and then, not three feet beyond my headlights, her head bobbed up out of the water in the middle of Sunset Boulevard, the look on her face completely dazed, too shocked to really register what had happened. I opened the car door and grabbed her by anything I could get my hands on, her arms, her sweater, her hair. Along the Strip in the windows of shops and small office buildings, people watched amazed. The surge of the water slowed but my car still felt like it was trying to float away, and as I pulled her into the car the Princess, a tangle of wet hair and clothes, was spitting up brown water, gasping and coughing. For all I knew she was drowning. As soon as I had her in the car all I wanted to do was get off the Strip and down the hill to where I lived, just hoping that if she was going to choke to death she would at least do it before we got to the Hamblin so I could dump her by the side of the road.

But she wasn't dead when I parked the car in the garage. For several seconds I sat in the driver's seat trying to get my bearings, while in the back seat she continued gasping and sputtering and blowing water out her nose. Between hysteria and asphyxiation, she was regaining her breath before her senses. After ten minutes of listening to her coughs and sobs and wheezes and curses I got her out of the car, where she went hysterical again at the sight of all the water in the flooded garage from the backed-up drain pipes. I got her up to my place where she barely had the presence of mind to know she needed to go to the bathroom; she was in the bathroom a long time. After a while I knocked on the door. When she didn't answer, and I had knocked again and she still didn't answer, I finally said, "You have to tell me you're all right so I don't break the door down."

"I'm all right," I heard her voice from the other side. Finally she came out. She was still wet and her hair was still a tangle, and she was still coughing and trying to get water out of her lungs. She had taken off her wet clothes and wrapped herself in a towel. I got her my bathrobe. She took it and went back into the bathroom and came back out with the robe on. She stood lost in my gray bathrobe in the middle of the apartment. "Do you want to lie down?" I said.

She nodded.

"Well you can go in there," I said, pointing to the bedroom. Without looking at me, she went back into the bedroom. "You can close the door if you like," I called after her; she didn't close the door so, a while later when I heard her sleeping, I closed it myself. I gathered up her wet clothes from the bathroom floor and took them to the cleaners down at the end of the street, and when I returned the bedroom door was still closed. A few hours later, when it was beginning to get dark, she emerged long enough to go to the bathroom again and into the kitchen to get a glass of water, and then disappeared back into the bedroom; around midnight I pulled some blankets out of the closet and made myself a place to sleep on the floor in the front room.

I called Viv. She was tired, in more pain from the burning in her stomach, and I made a mistake: I didn't tell her about the

Princess. "You sound funny," she concluded, and as we continued talking about nothing particularly important except how she was feeling, I don't think I stopped sounding funny. In the middle of the night, in my sleep, I thought I heard the telephone; but when I woke the ringing was gone, and I wasn't sure whether it had been a dream or not, and looking out the tall windows at the night and the clouds and the moon overhead I thought for a moment that I was back in the Seacastle, right after the Quake. I sat up to look for a small feral blonde in the doorway who I would come to know as Viv, before I realized I was on the floor of my apartment. It took a second to remember what I was doing there. It was a while before I went back to sleep; the next time I woke it was early morning and the Princess was sitting in my big black chair, still wearing my gray bathrobe, staring out the windows.

I sat up from the floor. "Are you all right?" I said. She stared fearfully out the windows at the clouds, as though dreading a downpour that seemed only moments away. Finally she acknowledged me with a quick look, pulling the bathrobe tighter to her before returning her gaze to the sky. "I wish it would stop," she said, though not really to me; she glanced over at the entryway, which certainly hadn't stopped dripping, and where I had covered the wet carpet with rags and a couple of buckets. I got up off the floor and pulled on my clothes, and gathered up the sheets and blankets where I had slept. "Do you want anything?" I asked.

After a moment she said, "I had some cereal."

"What's your name?"

"Why?" she blurted. She fully intended to sound hostile. Instead she couldn't help sounding afraid and confused, as though the experience of the previous afternoon was not only still sinking in but had so fundamentally rattled her she wasn't sure how to answer the question even if she wanted to. Exactly which name did I mean? Her working name? The name she would take when she became a movie star? Her real name, assuming she could remember it? I took a shower and dressed and washed the dishes, emptied the buckets and changed the rags in the entryway, all while she sat in the chair looking out the window. "I'm going down to the cleaners to get your clothes," I told her, to no answer, and headed out so I could get back before the rain started, walking down the street and picking up her skirt and sweater and stockings and underwear. I was now eagerly anticipating getting the Princess out of my apartment. When I got back twenty minutes later, she was not in the black chair anymore or the bathroom; I was a little dismayed to find her back in bed, lying on her side staring at the walls. She very much appeared as though she had no plans to go anywhere any time soon. I stood at the side of the bed looking down at her with her clothes in my arms. "I don't like the dripping," she said.

I cleared my throat. "Your clothes are clean now. I can take you anywhere you need to go."

"I don't need to go anywhere," she answered, staring at the wall.

Reluctantly I hung the clothes in the closet. "There's a telephone," I pointed at what was pretty obviously a telephone sitting on a low glass shelf right next to the bed, "if you need to call anyone to come get you."

"There's no one to call," she said. She looked up at me for really the first time. She brushed her hair from her face and, slowly and casually, moved the sheets of the bed off of her. She was naked. She looked impossibly young. "You can, if you want," she said.

"It's all right," I shook my head.

"Are you a fag?"

"No."

"Don't you like me?"

"Yes."

"Don't you think I'm pretty?"

"Yes, I think you're pretty."

"Then why not?"

"It's all right, I said."

"But why not?" She said, "I'm not sick, if that's what you're afraid of. I don't have anything."

"That's not it." I was getting angry.

"So why not?"

I was getting angry and I wasn't even sure why. "Because," I sputtered, "it's all right for a guy to treat you decently every once in a while without you having to fuck him for it." She appeared completely confounded by this. "Do you want to sleep some more?" I sighed.

"I just want to lie here," she answered, pulling the sheets back over her. For the rest of the day she didn't come out of the bedroom. Later that night, finally showing signs of life, sitting at the table inhaling some scrambled eggs and a plate of toast, she began to talk a little, though it was the usual talk I had no use for—about a brother in jail, a sister hooked on junk. . . . The last thing I wanted to hear about was her young depressing life. Studying her, I couldn't tell if she was sixteen or twenty-two or anywhere in between. "Don't you work or anything?" she said between toast, as though wondering what the hell I was hanging around all the time for. "I'll have a Coke."

I got her a Coke from the refrigerator. "I work for a newspaper."

"Doing what?"

"I'm a writer."

"What do you write about?"

"Movies, mostly."

"You write about movies?" she said.

"Yes."

"I'm going to be in the movies someday."

"No kidding."

"What do you write about the movies?"

"I write about whether I like them."

Her fork was poised in mid-air, and she peered up at me through her blonde hair. *"You write about whether you like them? You mean, you go to movies, and then you write about whether you like them."*

"Yes."

She started to say something but stopped, certain she couldn't have possibly heard right.

I took the bull by the horns. "Tomorrow we'll take you wherever you need to go."

"I don't need to go anywhere," she said.

"There must be somebody worrying about you."

"There's nobody worrying about me."

"Where do you live?"

"I don't live anywhere."

"Where do you stay?"

"I stay wherever I am." She brushed her hair from her face. "Whoever I'm with."

"We can take you to a counseling center or something. Where they can help you with your problems."

"I don't have any problems."

"There might be someone who can make some arrangements for you, so you don't have to do this."

"Do what?" Narrowing her eyes she said, "What do you mean, so I don't have to do this? What's wrong with what I do? You know," she managed her most insinuating tone, "I'll bet you've driven by my corner before, haven't you? I'll bet you've driven by a lot, checking me out. As a matter of fact, didn't I do you in the car a couple of months ago?"

"You see," I explained, "I'm a lot older than you, so you can spare me the shocking streetwise philosophy. I'm not talking about whether it's wrong in general, I'm talking about whether it's wrong for you. And you never did me in the car. The only thing you ever did in my car was get your little ass pulled out of the water yesterday when you were about to wash down Sunset Boulevard."

"I already said thanks," she muttered petulantly, though she hadn't said any such thing. She got up from the table, standing in the kitchen. "I don't have anywhere to go," she said, suddenly sounding like she could get loony again, like when she first got here. "I stay with a guy until he's done with me and then he pays me so I can get a room somewhere, in a motel or something, if I don't get another john right away. There's no point having my own place because I'd never sleep there anyway."

I didn't want her to get loony again. "OK."

"I don't have any money—I've lost two days' work being here."

"Oh, well, gee, I'm really sorry about the lost work."

"If you gave me the money for two days' work, maybe I could go."

"How much?"

"Five hundred dollars."

"*What?*"

"All right, all right," she said. "It's not my fault you won't fuck me for it."

"I thought that was for saving your life, and letting you stay here."

She looked down and started picking at the ends of her hair. "It was," she said in a little voice. She looked up and stared bleakly out the window. "I can't leave yet."

"When can you?" I snapped.

"*When it stops raining,*" she wailed. And there it was: she was the rain's hostage and I was hers. I let her stand there in the kitchen crying a good half-minute before I got up from the table and handed her a napkin to wipe her face. Let's talk about it tomorrow, I told her as gently as possible. I kept thinking maybe the rain would break and then she would want to leave. As she headed off to the bedroom and I once again hauled the sheets and blankets out onto the floor of the front room, she looked at them once before disappearing and said, "It's not my fault you sleep on the floor."

The next day it was raining harder than ever. The Princess, however, wasn't paying quite as much attention to the rain anymore. She wasn't regarding it with quite the same wide-eyed terror. Thumbing nonchalantly through one magazine after another, she seemed to have almost forgotten about the rain, which I took to mean she felt securely enough ensconced under my roof that the rain rather bored her now. The day passed: she slept, she ate, she read magazines, she took a bath, she read more magazines, she slept some more. She brushed her hair, she did her nails while draped across my big black chair, she turned the radio up one end of the dial and down the other and over and over to whatever station happened to suit her, which none ever did for more than five minutes. She soon seemed quite comfortable with the whole set-up, and the more at home she got, the farther my gray bathrobe slipped from her body until, by the end of the second day, she was casually walking around wearing nothing at all.

On the phone, meanwhile, Viv sounded worse. Her stomach was on fire as doctors subjected her to a battery of tests and found nothing. "Viv is sick," I told Ventura, back in his dripping doorway. "She's dying," he answered, not looking up. "I'm dying, you're dying." He was sitting at the table in his apartment intently sorting out old papers and letters; he actually had off both his hat and boots, taking care of his final affairs in his socks. Along with the papers and letters the table, which was usually piled with books and articles, was now covered with lettuce and carrots and tomatoes and zero-fat salad dressing, as well as a baguette from the corner bakery. Sitting among the roughage was a very legal looking document; it was his will, which he had already begun to write. "Are you leaving me anything?" I asked.

"Why should I leave you anything?" he answered. "You're the guy who gets rid of everything. By the time *you* die, you won't have anything left to leave anybody. You've already made up your mind you're not leaving anyone a single fucking thing."

"Some of your movies, perhaps. The hysterical ones. *The Naked Spur. The Strange Love of Martha Ivers.*"

Now he looked up. "That's what you want?" he said indignantly. "Out of all this"—he swept his arm splendidly over the disarray of his apartment—"you want *The Naked Spur* and *The Strange Love of Martha Ivers?*"

"I have a problem. I mean, besides the fact that I'm dying."

"You don't understand," Ventura said, pointing his finger at me. "It obviously hasn't sunk in with you yet. Besides the fact that you're dying, you don't have *any* problems."

"Do you want to hear my story or not?"

"Oh why not. Let's hear your story." So I told him about the Princess. "You mean," he said, ripping open a lettuce bag and shoving a leaf into his mouth, "this girl's been here the last two days?"

"In my apartment."

"Where have you been sleeping all this time?"

"On the floor."

"Does Viv know this?"

"No."

"Oh, Viv *doesn't* know this. Oh," he said with relish, "I *like* this story. Can I ask why she doesn't know?"

"Because I haven't told her."

"Can I ask why you haven't told her?"

"Well, she's been sick, and.... Look, obviously I should have told her. I haven't done anything to feel guilty about, but by not telling her I've acted guilty, so now if I do tell her.... She said the other night I sounded funny. If I tell her now, it will confirm her suspicions. Guys don't sound funny for nothing."

"No," Ventura agreed, "guys usually sound funny for something, and usually it's something women don't think is very funny."

"But if she finds out later," I went on, "even though I haven't done anything, I still tried to hide it from her, even though there was nothing to hide—"

"My God, and you think I'm more fucked up about women

than you are? A man who's a bad liar even when he's telling the truth." He shook his head. "Why don't you just kick the little hooker out?"

"She has nowhere to go. And she's afraid of the rain."

"Yeah, well, you know how long that would stop me. If she was in *this* apartment, which she never would have been in the first place, she'd have a New York minute to find somewhere to go before I threw her undoubtedly adorable, undoubtedly profitable little ass right out in the street, rain or no rain."

"Yes!" I cried. "That's it! *You* could do it, you're much more of a bastard than I am—"

"Forget it," he shook his head, shrugging off the compliment and gesturing at the vegetables and papers and will. "I have matters to attend to. I don't need some pretty child following me around like a lovesick puppy."

"She won't follow you around like a lovesick puppy. I know you find this hard to believe, but she'll sit in a chair reading a magazine like you don't exist."

"Fat chance."

"Well then, even better if she's following you around like a lovesick puppy. It will make it all the easier for you to kick her out." Ventura ripped off part of a baguette and bit into a tomato, thinking. "She won't leave until it stops raining," I said, despondent.

"It's going to be raining a long time," he pointed out. "It's a big change in the weather pattern. All those volcanoes going off in the northwest last year. Where does she live?"

"She doesn't live anywhere. She has nowhere to go. She has no one to call, and nowhere she needs to be. She has no problems. Get this: I asked her where she stays, and she said, *I stay wherever I am.*"

His mouth fell open. "She said that?" He took out his little notebook and wrote it down. "What's this existentialist's name?"

"I don't know. I call her the Princess."

He abruptly stopped writing. "The Princess?"

"Can't you take her for just one—"

"Wait a minute, wait a minute. *The Princess?*" He closed his notebook, set down the tomato he had been eating and wiped his mouth with his hand. Then he threw his head back and laughed for five minutes. When he stopped laughing, his eyes had become lit by a deranged, nasty glint; I could practically hear the knuckles of his mind cracking. "Oh, *well* then," he sneered, "in that case, *by all means.* Bring the *little Princess* right over." Unwittingly I had put the situation to Ventura in the only terms he would have ever found irresistible. The Sicilian anarchist in him had been waiting his whole life for a princess to stray across his trained sights, or anyone so unlucky as to think of herself as any kind of princess, whether a local beauty queen or sorority row belle or Sunset Boulevard strumpet; and now, with his life practically passing before his eyes, he wasn't going to let slip away one last opportunity to deflower her bourgeois pretensions. "I think," he snarled happily, drawing out every syllable and small spittles of foam forming at the corners of his mouth, "everyone should, just once, have a princess living in his apartment. I mean, if I should expire tonight in my sleep, who better to clean up the *blood* and *bile* and *muck* and *shit* but a princess?"

"I'll be right back!" I cried. I rushed back to my suite to get her. If I hadn't been so elated I might have almost felt sorry for her, except that I knew, of course, it was Ventura who really didn't stand a chance. The Princess knew it too. She was long past being impressed by me or Ventura or any man; the only thing that intimidated her now was the wet two-hundred-foot journey from my corner of the hotel to his. "I like it *here*," she said matter-of-factly in the doorway of my apartment, staring down a dark hallway that had become as drizzly as a rain forest, before I made it clear that her only two choices were Ventura or the street. She dressed for the occasion. In her high heels and black skirt and tight silver sweater she slipped right past him into his apartment like he wasn't even there, and I thought I actually saw a flicker of doubt cross his eyes, like maybe now he was no longer the only person in the universe who didn't know that he didn't stand a chance. The rest of the day I hid behind lock and key, begging the sky to stop the rain before Ventura would be prying my door off its hinges with a crowbar and tossing her little body back into my flooded entryway.

Time passed. The rain fell. The ceiling in the hallways appeared to sag. Small brown rivulets ran down from where my walls met the roof, and I could barely keep up anymore with emptying the buckets and mopping up the carpet. Sure enough, thirty-six hours later Ventura hadn't gotten rid of the Princess either. "After all," he tried to insist, most unconvincingly, "it's tempting fate or karma or whatever you want to believe in to just kick someone out on the street when you're dying. A little too close to the hour of judgment—right under God's nose, so to speak." As to whether he was sleeping with her, "well," he allowed, "of course she acts like she isn't interested in me at all, but I know better. I can't get mixed up in that, though. Besides," he added bitterly, "you didn't happen to mention to me that *thing* you told her."

"What thing?"

"That business about being treated decently for a change, or whatever it was. She told me about that, you know."

"I didn't think she had the faintest idea what I was talking about."

"That was a *terrible* thing to say. Now even if I wanted to sleep with her I couldn't, because you went and said this *thing*. Now if I sleep with her, I'm a heartless old fuck while you're some kind of . . . paragon."

He was getting me back with that last part, of course; he knew how I felt about paragons these days. More time passed. The rain kept falling. I crossed the storms and the city to the Bunker, where Viv spent longer and longer periods in her loft lying flat on her back in bed; the burning came and went like the weather, durations of pain growing longer as the durations of relief grew shorter. In the twilight of his life Ventura had taken up again with his Sufi goddess, so now and then the Princess was returned to my suite: he and I tossed her back and forth like a live grenade. By this time she didn't give the rain outside a passing glance; rather she directed her attention to what she considered the growing deficiencies of her stay at the Hotel Hamblin. Eating her way through my refrigerator, she offered an increasingly sardonic commentary on the culinary selection. Considering the sheets and towels something less than mountain-spring fresh, she deposited them in a pile in the entryway, soaking up the rain water and waiting for me to launder them. For someone who had nowhere to go and no one to call the first twenty-four hours, she now talked on the telephone all the time, in conversations that were either interminable or unsettlingly businesslike, at peculiar hours of the day or night. One afternoon, another girl showed up. She had cropped black hair and wore thigh-high pink boots and a pink lace minidress with nothing underneath. When I answered the door she didn't say a word, slipping past me into the apartment like I was the doorman. She and the Princess had a touching reunion. The two sat around all afternoon eating cashews and crackers and calling out to the manservant for Diet Cokes, catching up on old times and, I suppose, old tricks. I was about to ask why the Princess didn't stay with this other girl, where they could reminisce about the glory days of Hollywood prostitution at greater length, when it occurred to me with horror that the other girl might also be one of these Nietzschean I-stay-wherever-I-am streetwalkers, and Ventura and I could wind up stuck with both of them. I breathed a sigh of relief several hours later when the girl in the pink boots and pink lace dress finally left—at the very moment Dory happened to be coming up the stairs. Dory looked at her and looked at me and looked back at her, while catching a glimpse of the other nearly naked girl in my doorway.

After that, the women in the building began to take more note of the nymph who didn't wear very much and constantly crossed back and forth the length of the hallway from Ventura's place to mine. My mind became bombarded by epic, ever-maniacal fantasies of johns showing up in the middle of the night and crazed vengeful pimps banging on my door and vice squads crashing in through the windows on ropes. Desperate, Ventura and I cooked up a scheme to try and foist the Princess onto Dr. Billy. We took him out to dinner at a fancy restaurant with high chandeliers and roaring fireplaces and waiters who wore capes, where we kept buying him snifters of imported Armagnac which he happily consumed while waiting for the other shoe to drop. Naturally it turned out to be a waste of time; we had counted too much on a nature that wasn't nearly as debased as he liked to profess it was. "Let's pretend first of all," he said, savoring his Armagnac, "that

I'm not married. You remember Jane, the woman I married? Even if I wasn't married, as I understand it, you," by which he meant me, "went and said a *thing* to her. Isn't that right?" he asked Ventura.

"He definitely said a thing," Ventura confirmed.

"It was a slip of the tongue," I replied miserably.

"You can't go around making outbursts like that," Dr. Billy argued, "without ramifications. By saying this *thing* you've tied all our hands, if you see what I mean. Even if I wasn't married, there's nothing I could do now with this girl anyhow, after you've gone and said this thing, without me being some sort of vile asshole."

"She's used to vile assholes," I assured him.

"Let me ask you something," he went on, drinking faster now. "What do you suppose will happen when word of your little arrangement gets out? What will Viv think? What will your girlfriend think," he said to Ventura, "whoever she happens to be at the moment? What about the women living in your hotel, or the ones at the newspaper? If they think there's a Cabal now, wait till they find out you're passing a hooker back and forth between you."

"It's not an arrangement. We're not doing anything with her."

"May I have another Armagnac please?" Dr. Billy called to the waiter. "You know as well as I that no one will believe that," he said, turning back to us. "No, it's obvious you guys are sitting on dynamite, and you just want me to climb on with you."

"It's absurd," Ventura growled. "We've got a hooker we're not having sex with who we have to keep secret because no one would believe we're not having sex with her."

"Worse than that," I said, "we have to keep her secret because no one would believe that we kept her secret in the first place because no one would believe us."

"I hate to tell you this," Ventura declared to me with enormous satisfaction, like he didn't hate it at all, "but this is your fault."

"What made you bring a hooker home anyway?" Dr. Billy asked.

"I explained that," I said.

"Oh right," Dr. Billy replied, "I remember now. You were saving her life or something. It was a humanitarian mission. You were a regular . . . what was the word?" he said to Ventura.

"Paragon."

"You were a paragon."

"He felt sorry for her," Ventura snorted.

"The guy who keeps telling us he's not a romantic anymore," Dr. Billy guffawed. Ventura guffawed back, although I don't know what the hell *he* was laughing at, slumped over his desk at night and snoring in his spinach leaves while the Princess slept in his bed. At any rate, the only thing Dr. Billy was going to help us do was empty our wallets while he drank everything put in front of him, so Ventura and I went back to taking the Princess off each other's hands whenever we could, while waiting for the rain to stop. Instead it just came down like a drumbeat for the approaching moment when the whole thing would blow up in our faces. The women in the Hamblin were giving us dirtier and dirtier looks every morning the Princess strolled down the hall from Ventura's place to mine, in her heels and tight little black shirt; and on the phone with Viv I was sounding more funny, not less.

One night I took the Princess with me to a movie I had to

review. In a screening room up on the Strip, not far from where I had first bailed her out of the water that fateful afternoon, a ponderous Czech film engaged her attention ten or fifteen minutes before she began squirming in her seat. "This movie's boring," she finally complained at a clearly audible volume; I ignored her. "This movie's really stupid," she insisted a few minutes later, to which I leaned over and whispered "Be quiet" as the other people in the screening room began looking at us. "I hate this!" she cried after another minute, and in the seat behind us the long-time film critic of the city's big daily paper leaned forward and warned, "If you can't be quiet, I'll have you removed."

"Fuck you," the Princess answered.

At that moment a plan hatched in my head by which I figured if she could just get herself kicked out of the screening, in our brief but significant separation that followed I could duck through the other exit at the front of the room, make a beeline for the car before she got there, and drive away with her running tearfully after me waving her arms. The problem with this plan was that when the publicist finally came along to eject the Princess, the Princess refused to leave without me, and so in short order I was being ejected too. I protested, of course. The big-shot critic in back, becoming more and more outraged with every bit of commotion, finally exploded, "Get out and take your little whore with you!" to which the Princess, rather than flying into the scornful fury I might have predicted and suggesting within earshot of everyone that she had "done" him a couple of weeks before in the back seat of a car down at the corner of Sunset and La Brea, instead began to sob pitifully. "Call her that again," I managed to answer before I felt the hands of the security guard on my back, "and you're going home with your eyeballs pinned to your lapels," but the next thing I knew the Princess and I were outside, and I was sprawled on the sidewalk in the rain.

"Are you all right?" she said in her little voice, standing over me a few seconds before scurrying back under an awning, where she watched the rain fall on me for a while. I picked myself up off the sidewalk. We drove home in seething silence. Even though she had never particularly cared before about having a conversation, I could tell now she would be happier if I said something, so I didn't, because I didn't want her to be happier. When we stopped at a traffic light I turned to look at her and she recoiled, not as if the look in my eyes was something she had never seen before, but as if she had seen it plenty of times, all too often. I was about to reach over, open the passenger door and give her a good shove when the light turned and the car behind me honked. I was still thinking about it as we drove down Fountain Avenue picking up speed—ten, twenty miles an hour, thirty, forty. . . . In the garage we sat for a while, the dark quiet of the car welling up around us.

"I'm sorry I cause you so much trouble," she finally murmured, picking at the ends of her hair. "I know you've been nice to me."

Just as Ventura and I were at our wits' end, the episode with the Princess resolved itself rather ironically. For days we had been waiting for the rain to stop so she would leave, but instead it just kept coming down, harder than ever; and then the morning after the incident at the screening, when Ventura was at one end of the hallway and I was at the other, and the Princess was walking from me to him or him to me—I had long since lost track of who was transferring her to whom—suddenly the ceiling gave way and a hundred gallons of rain collapsed into the Hamblin. Like the day I picked her up out of the rapids of the Sunset Strip, it nearly washed her down the stairs; she only barely side-stepped the deluge in time. She began screaming like a banshee. Still screaming, water flooding the hallway around her, she fled down the stairs and out the front of the building, and down Jacob Hamblin Road where we could hear her all the way to Santa Monica Boulevard. Ventura and I ran down to the hotel lobby behind her, where we locked and bolted the doors and silently thanked the rain, which had condemned us to her in the first place, for now delivering us from her.

～✕～

The day she erected the Memoryscope, Viv had lunch in the Glow Loft District with a guy she had known since art school. He had been married for a long time, with a couple of children, and worked for one of the few studios that were still left in L.A. He wasn't someone with whom Viv had an especially close friendship, but they got along well enough that, once beyond the cordialities, he felt free to tell her the story of a woman he had loved very much, since around the time his marriage had gone bad. He never had an affair with this woman but thought of her as his best friend and confidante, and dreamed that once his children were grown he would spend the rest of his life with her. One day, only a few months before, the woman had been killed in a car accident with her husband; their child, a little girl, had been in the back seat and emerged miraculously unscathed. Another couple driving by when the accident took place pulled their car over and held the little girl until the police and ambulance arrived, praying with the child and protecting her from the sight of her dead parents. Now the studio executive could only live with the realization he would never have the time with this woman he had longed for and dreamed of.

For days and weeks Viv was haunted by this story. She was terribly shaken by the chance he had had to be happy, and how that chance was now gone forever because he had never taken it. It was after hearing this story that she began to feel the pain in her stomach, below her heart. Doctors couldn't tell her what was wrong; a few suggested nothing was wrong. But I knew something was wrong. If anything, Viv was the kind to try and minimize something, ignore it, so that even when she called in the middle of the night in agony, she couldn't quite bring herself to ask me to come. One night I was shocked to find her doubled up on her bed, her face as yellow as her hair and both streaked with sweat; the pain had spread from her stomach to her back, where the muscles had convulsed so long she couldn't stand it anymore. She hurt so much that when she cried she hardly made a sound. I put some of her things into a bag and took her down to the car, and drove her back to the Hamblin slumped and dazed in the seat next to me; and as I kept trying to tell myself I had had no idea she was so sick, she kept murmuring over and over, under her breath so that I could barely make it out, "I guess you're not such a bad guy after all." It didn't make me feel any better.

After a day or two in my apartment, I realized she was starving. She couldn't eat anything; anything the least bit solid seemed to cut right through her. I concocted one gruel after another that she wouldn't eat because it hurt too much, and no amount of badgering on my part could force her. When she wasn't sleeping she was bent in pain, a terrified look in her eyes, and when she did finally fall asleep, the pain woke her up. "What's wrong with me?" she cried. For days this went on, and I got it into my head that one last No from those first days at the Seacastle, one last No that had been hiding up inside her that she had never released, was devouring her from the inside out. . . .

Finally, though, after time, the general sense of crisis began to pass. Finally the rains stopped as unequivocally as they had begun; down the hall Ventura appeared to survive, at least for the time being, the creamy blood frothing in his veins. Perhaps there was nothing left of Viv for the No to consume, and so it was the No that starved, wasting away; perhaps a predatory doubt inside her had evolved into a winged resolution that was suddenly poised to take flight. After a week of my pabulum she slowly graduated to hot cereal, mashed potatoes, rice and bread and ice cream. Still exhausted she slept all day and night, and in the new sunlight through the window she looked about six or seven years old. Viv always hated it when people told her she sometimes looked like a little girl; but sitting in the corner of my bedroom watching her sleep, I was surprised by a momentary desire to have a daughter someday, if only she would look just like Viv. Then one afternoon she sat right up in my bed from out of her sleep, as if from out of a dream. "I have to go to Holland," she announced. It was the first fully coherent sentence she had said in a week.

"Holland?" I stood by the bed looking down at her, and put my hands in my pockets, not sure what else to do with them. If I were to have put them on her, it might have been mistaken as an attempt to restrain or suppress something. My heart sagged like a ceiling full of rain.

"To build the other Memoryscope," she explained.

"Why Holland?"

"Because that's where the one here is pointed."

"How do you know?"

"I dreamed it," she said. I nodded. We could pull out a map and check; but what was the point? I had no doubt that any map would say Holland as certainly as her dream did. "So I have to go to Holland," she said, "to build another one, pointing back."

I sat down on the bed beside her.

"Come with me," she said.

"I can't."

"Why?"

"I don't know."

"It seems," she said, "like you should know."

"Yes, it does."

"But you don't. So you can't."

"Not yet, anyway. Something's not finished here for me."

"What?"

"Well," I tried to smile, "that's what I don't know."

"So how long do you have to stay here before it's finished?" and then, irritated, she answered herself, "I know, you don't know that either. You don't know anything."

"I don't want to lose you," was all I could think to say.

She asked, "Do you believe, after all your disastrous romances, that you're capable of loving deeply?"

"Yes. Maybe more," I answered, though I didn't want to have to explain that, because I wasn't sure I could.

She seemed unconvinced. "I need your undying passion, like you had for Sally and Lauren."

"You make me happy."

"That's not the same as undying passion," she said, and I couldn't think fast enough to explain that while my passion for Sally or Lauren might have been undying, the man who felt those particular passions had died, and that while I bore him a resemblance, I was different, and that the passion I felt for Viv was a new kind of undying passion, of a new man, and that it was better because she was better, because I trusted her in a way I could never trust anyone else. I remembered a night she had come to me, long ago, in our early days when I was at my most mute and we weren't really getting along; it was late one night, and early in the morning Viv had to catch a train out of town—a business trip or family visit, I don't remember, or maybe one of those little Viv impulses that was going to take her wherever she happened to wind up, Butte or Madagascar or Holland. On this night I had one of my headaches, and she sat in the dark stroking my brow till I fell asleep. There are a few things I know I'll remember at the end of my life. Some of them may be things I would as soon forget, things so small they should have been forgotten a long time ago, but so sharp they can't be; others are things like Viv exhausted, sitting in the dark for hours on end stroking my brow until I fell asleep. She probably doesn't think twice about it now. She's probably forgotten it completely. But I think about it all the time, every time my head feels like it's splitting down the middle: it is the soothing touch of trust and forgiveness; and if any other woman has ever touched me like that, and in retrospect I can imagine one or two might have, I was neither smart nor old nor unselfish enough to recognize it. Thinking back on it, it makes me ashamed to have ever suggested that a woman wouldn't die for love.

Right before Viv left for Holland came K's most recent correspondence. Now, you understand I don't necessarily cop to everything K has to say; she has only seen the secret room, after all, and the literary one I suppose, so her perspective must be considered accordingly. But after copping to everything else, I don't have much reason to conceal anything anymore: "S, I fell into a river of thought about you this morning, and this is the current I fell into. . . . Your sense of love is overwhelming and imprisoning. You contrive both release and relief from it, which then makes you feel guilty. Then you suffer for your guilt, but it's preferable to the suffering of a great love. You are powerless in the throes of a great love so you're compelled to assert yourself in various ways, eventually gaining your freedom. The price of freedom is guilt. The price of love is guilt. The pain of separation is preferable to the stress of obsession. You're possessed and obsessed until you break away—so, from feeling powerless and resentful, you gain a sense of mastery and control through domination and bondage. But conversely it's her love that dominates and binds you. Love courses through you with such intensity (you may laugh) that you rebel against it, and against the feeling of being controlled by something or someone else. In one way or another you are going to free yourself, in order to feel that you're not powerless. So you'll force yourself on her and derive satisfaction from it, and when you try to subdue her, you're trying to subdue that which subdues you; but *you* are really the one you're subduing. . . . Pretty good for a Saturday morning, don't you think?"

God, I can't stand it.

I can't stand that she had to go. After she told me she was going, she was angry, I think; I was not; and she was angry, I think, *because* I was not, not to mention that I wasn't going with her and couldn't offer a good reason why, even as I could have offered a hundred good reasons why I should. We didn't talk about it after that. We didn't talk about anything. In the void of our talk I thought furiously, to formulate a reason that we could talk about, but I couldn't think of any that counted. Over the next couple of weeks, as she prepared to go, the sun hurtled toward L.A., to fill the hole in the sky where the rain used to be. The city became a swamp. Buildings buckled and roads turned to glue. Fauna grew from the Hamblin floors and walls; toadstools erupted from the cracks of my baseboards and lichen layered the ceiling. A radiant red moss covered my windowsills and strange mounds rose beneath my carpet. I weeded the kitchen and pruned the bathroom, and hacked my way to the refrigerator with a knife. Sometime during the night before she left, I finally got angry but I didn't know at what; I had been getting angry a lot lately without knowing why. Nothing had broken the silence between Viv and me through all the recent weeks, or through the night before her departure; and even after I got angry it could not break through the silence of the drive to Union Station to catch her train to St. Louis, where she would then catch a plane to Europe. Even walking to the train there was nothing I could think to say that was worth breaking the silence for: the small talk in my head only felt like it would trivialize everything we felt and everything we held back. I kept wishing she would tell me again I wasn't such a bad guy after all. On the train we found her compartment and I helped her with the luggage; she was still a bit weak. And then, all I could finally say was, "God, I can't stand it," and she looked at me with the hope there was more. And there *was* more, and I wanted to tell her, but I couldn't just now, just yet.

She threw her arms around my neck. She pulled her face to mine, and put her little mouth to my ear. "I'm still so hungry for you," was the last thing she whispered, before she disappeared like a ghost of the Seacastle, who had stepped from the shadows just long enough to show me not who I was but who I could be, before she stepped back.

∾⧑⧍∾

The day after Viv left, Shale called with the news that Freud N. Johnson had finally fired him.

He was quite calm about it, which is not quite to say passive. As usual, he seemed most concerned about how to prepare the staff for the news; he had already told both Dr. Billy and Ventura, and asked that I not say anything to anyone else for twenty-four hours, until the firing became effective. "I know," he concluded, "that this doesn't come at an easy time for you. I don't want you to do anything stupid. There's absolutely nothing you have to prove to me." Of course, I muttered. I hung up the phone and typed up my resignation. I waited for Ventura to call, which he did, and then Dr. Billy; both asked what I was going to do, just to make sure, I guess.

I didn't presume anything of anyone else. I was close to broke, but my circumstances were no more dire than others': Dr. Billy's dead millionaire money ran out some time ago, and he hadn't been able to get his latest documentary about sex addicts in Anchorage off the ground. No one had more at stake than Ventura, who confided he was deeply in debt. As Ventura suspected might happen, Freud N. Johnson did offer him the editorship of the newspaper; thus he was confronted with a choice between destitution and not only security but something that I think had always represented to him a secret dream, to run the paper he had started. I don't think Ventura had ever given up on that dream. He always thought it was really his newspaper and, in a way, he had always been right. Now the tone of his voice was both funereal and charged, or whatever pitch suits the man who has to decide between having everything and having nothing, and finds for vague, almost inexplicably moral reasons that what should be the easiest decision in the world is the hardest.

By that evening the rumors were rampant. Around midnight the noir blonde from the advertising department called almost giddy with excitement; I finally hung up on her, because she was just enjoying the whole thing too damn much. The next morning it became official, and I got ready to head down to the newspaper. More than just wanting to get it over with, I also didn't want anyone to think I had wavered, and I suppose it's possible, though I honestly don't think so, that I didn't want to waver on my own account either. The Hamblin was in full bloom this morning, the sun blasting in through the hole in the hallway ceiling where the rain had collapsed; exotic vines wound up out of the elevator shaft. Ventura was strolling up and down the hallway lost in thought, his hands in his pockets. I told him I was heading down to the newspaper. It wasn't until then I was completely sure what his decision was; he said Dr. Billy was on his way over and I should wait and they would go with me. Billy had phoned this morning, Ventura said, "wanting to know if we would be quitting if you weren't." Obviously I didn't have an answer for that. Half an hour later Dr. Billy showed up, and for a while we stood around looking at each other in the hallway before Ventura said, "Let's go."

The newspaper office was in a tizzy by the time we got there. The official word was now definitely out. I didn't feel like talking to a lot of people about it, holding their hands and repeating ad nauseam my little speech about how everyone had to make his or her own decision. I certainly wasn't going to try and rouse the rabble. I wanted to get in and get out. The three of us confronted Freud N. Johnson in his office with our resignations. His face went a distinctly sick shade of pale when we walked in. He sat behind a huge gleaming black desk that appeared to have been chosen both to assert his importance and protect him from moments just like this one, and on top of this mammoth desk was absolutely nothing but a digital clock and a video entitled *How to Fire People*. After a while he couldn't bear sitting any longer, so he stood up. We didn't beat about the bush. I had no illusions about the impact of my own leaving; of the three of us I knew I'd be the least missed. Dr. Billy was a much bigger blow, to both the paper and the staff, not only because of his popularity but because his departure dramatically contradicted what some might have misperceived as a survivalist's amorality about office politics. It was Ventura's loss, however, that the paper would find especially devastating, not to mention extremely inconvenient for Freud N. Johnson to try and explain, since the paper was not only losing a prospective editor but its most famous and mythic figure. So now Johnson was too shocked to say much, and while it surprised me at the time, in retrospect it's entirely predictable that his main concern was not trying to talk us out of quitting, or making sure others didn't quit, but preempting whatever bad publicity might come out of the whole thing. He tried a bit of strong-arm-ing that was frankly beyond him. If there was any trouble about all this, he warned, he would put out any number of stories about Shale: embezzlement perhaps—his mind was whirring like a little wheel with a rodent inside, racing in place—or harassing female employees.

"You try that," Dr. Billy said, stepping up to Johnson around the desk and pressing his nose inches from the other man's, "and I will come back, and find you, and get you."

"Wh-Wh-What?" Johnson croaked.

"I said," Dr. Billy repeated very calmly, "that if you try that, I will *get you.*" I don't know exactly what he meant, and I'd bet almost anything Dr. Billy didn't know either. But that didn't mat-ter. None of us had ever seen Dr. Billy do anything like this, and it was a little frightening, every bit of his affability falling away to reveal a livid core—to which the color of Freud N. Johnson's face went from ill to cadaverous. If I had tried to threaten Johnson in this way, it wasn't likely anyone would have taken it very seriously, including Johnson, and if Ventura had done it, well, Ventura was crazy enough that while everyone would have taken it seriously, no one would have been shocked by it. More-over, Ventura was taller than Johnson, and I was taller yet, and it would have been different for Johnson to be threatened by a taller man: it might have allowed him the luxury of seeing him-self as a sympathetic figure, being bullied. But Dr. Billy was looking right into Johnson's eyes and Johnson was looking right into his, and in this moment Johnson was having one of the few true epiphanies of his life, one of the few true moments of clar-ity where he actually understood something profound, which was that Dr. Billy O'Forte could be a foot shorter and he would always be a big man, and Freud N. Johnson could be a foot taller and he would always be a little man. And that realization was almost too much for him; I wouldn't have been surprised at that moment if he'd run howling from his office out into the street and thrown himself in front of a truck, if only he had the self-respect to do it. Instead he cowered and fell back into his chair, far below Dr. Billy's gaze, at a height that suited him all the better, and said, "I want you to know I respect you for feeling that way. I want to thank you for telling me that, and I want you to know how much I respect that you said it." The next day he would call Dr. Billy again, just to make sure Dr. Billy understood how much Freud N. Johnson respected Dr. Billy for having told him that he would come and get him.

To their credit, in the next twenty-four hours two other writers quit as well. They included an English woman who had just passed up a couple of other job offers the previous month, including a teaching position and a big-time gig at a newspaper in Chicago; and a guy who had just closed out his house with his wife and packed everything they owned off to Washington, D.C., contingent on an arrangement with the newspaper that he would continue to write from the East Coast as a staff writer. Without thinking about it ten seconds he quit anyway, he and his wife last seen driving off into uncertainty, neither prospects nor steady income anywhere in sight. I suppose in these situations you can always figure there will be people who, with the least leeway possible, will take a principled position anyway. Back at the suite, the messages came in on my phone machine over the next forty-eight hours. There was one from the noir blonde, apologizing for the conversation the night before, and as the news filtered out—like I've said, people three thousand miles away find out what's going on in L.A. before anyone here does—writers and journalists from other newspapers and magazines called to get the story. Those were the tedious messages, which I nonetheless returned. Much better were the outbursts from others on the paper's staff, a rare few of which were mature and consoling and regretful, most of which were frantic and resentful. "You've abandoned us," angrily sobbed one woman. Seethed another, "You're so *lucky* you could quit." There apparently seemed to be a general feeling among the staff that those of us who quit didn't really need these jobs, but worked at the paper as some sort of hobby. Over the coming days my machine recorded many more wails of woe about how terrible it was to have to still work at the paper, as well as expressions of alarm when it came to light that Shale had actually saved the jobs of a number of people that office gossip had it he was trying to get fired. I have to admit I had quite a good time with all these messages. I drove around the city playing them over and over on my car stereo, a long symphony of collective sniveling so rapturously shameless it verged on the transcendent. There was a genius about it, really, the way the kids had managed to turn themselves into the martyrs and still collect their paychecks. It seemed rather dim of Ventura and Dr. Billy and me that we hadn't thought of it.

According to Ventura, the universe doesn't know from random. "Happens all the time," he used to say confidently to the most peculiar instances of synchronicity. So there might well have been meaning—though I'm not claiming one—in the coincidence of the letter I received right after turning in my resignation. It was from the Committee of the First and Only Annual Craters of the Moon Film Festival, inviting me as a guest to the festival's opening night, where there would premiere the long lost but rediscovered and restored silent masterpiece *The Death of Marat.* The festival was also pleased to announce that the film's director, Adolphe Sarre, would himself attend. My first reaction, particularly given the timing, was that the joke had been taken rather too far. But then I remembered that I was, after all, the one who had taken it there.

❧✦❧

From the summit of Laurel Canyon, the second light to be seen in the northern hills on the other side of the Valley—if you move your gaze westward—is my mother. She lives there where she's lived my whole life, in a two-bedroom flat above a little theater she used to run. From the summit of Laurel Canyon it used to be twenty minutes by freeway to reach this light; now it's a little under an hour by surface streets. Now the only ones who live in the Valley are the ghosts of the Indians who lived here to begin with, until the Spanish monks came and built the mission, and the keepers of the lights in the hillsides, of which I count no more than six or seven most nights, and on some nights not that. If her eastern neighbor, whoever he might be, leaves his house dark, then my mother becomes the first light rather than the second, and I have to backtrack.

My mother is in her late sixties. As one is supposed to do but rarely does, she seems to have gotten better at life as she's gotten older. With my father gone she hasn't had much choice, unless she was going to give it up altogether; and though in that first year following his death she may believe she came close to such an option, no one else who knows her is likely to think so. Give me the rest of my own life and I'll see if I can remember my mother ever giving up on anything. I worry about her being alone, of course—I still wince at how easily, just months after my father died, I almost left L.A. with Sally—though sometimes I think she worries about my solitude more than I do hers. For a woman of such strong ideas about things, it must have taken all of her will to resolve, sometime after I left home around eighteen, not to tell me how to live my life; but she hasn't, even if once in a while she hints gently. Driving out tonight I already know she isn't going to be happy with my two bits of news: that I've quit my job; and that Viv has left. Quitting a job on principle is the kind of grand-standing self-congratulatory gesture I've been making my whole life, so she'll probably get used to that one, but as for Viv, my mother is more partial to her than to anyone I've ever been with. The two of them have the same edge, as well as a nearly genetic hostility to ambiguity, however much wisdom may have taught them how much life is ambiguous. "If you ever let Viv go," my mother laughed not all that long ago, "I'm afraid I'd have to kill you." She was only half kidding when she said it. She had drunk only enough wine to inspire her to say the truth, rather than so much as to say what she didn't really mean. She fears and dreads, I think, what she senses is my true nature: to go it alone in the end. But recently I've come to suspect it's only part of my nature; just how big a part is what I've been trying to figure out for a while now, along with everyone else who blindly, haphazardly wanders across the firing range of my life.

My mother cooks dinner and we discuss movies, the empty theater beneath our feet and the days when it wasn't empty, and politics and the country. We disagree a lot about politics, except that as time passes each of us moves toward what the other views as an evolving reasonableness. We usually have a good time in these discussions, though lately, as things in the country have gone the way they've gone, I guess I don't enjoy it quite as much. "Your father couldn't talk about these things without getting angry," she remembers correctly. We don't talk that much about my father; perhaps both of us sometimes wonder if we should, though it doesn't feel like there's something significant that's being avoided or left unsaid. When he died we didn't have a funeral or a memorial, since the one thing we all shared, my father most of all, was an abhorrence of ritualizing death. He was privately cremated and his ashes cast at sea, as I would want to be. Still, there are times I wonder fleetingly if maybe we should have done something after all. I don't know. I suspect not doing something seemed stranger to other people than it did to us. Having married the man when she was eighteen and spent over forty years with him until his death, my mother was baffled and a little annoyed with herself when, a year after he died, she wasn't over it yet. She may be the kind of person who couldn't function in her indomitable fashion if she allowed herself to believe that, in fact, she would never really be over it. Being the sort of person I am, I accepted that from the beginning, and that somehow made it easier.

Now when we speak of my father it's a fond reference, like to him getting pissed off about politics. I'm sure I've thought about my father at least once every day since he died. It's in the most casual way, not with grief but rather as an aside: I'll say something to him as though he's there, something that would make him smile or laugh. In one way, as I imagine it is with all children, I've not accepted his death at all: his absence hasn't sunk in, the way it must sink in all the time for my mother. When I think about him I don't think of him as unhappy, the way I used to. My mother finally, gently corrected an earlier misimpression on my part that my father hadn't been all that content with his life; and as I've gotten older I've come to see she's probably right, because I've come to see how one makes his peace with the passing of his dreams, or how those dreams are displaced by ones at once less grand and more full, at once more ordinary but no less profound. I was too haunted, after he died, by a confession he made fifteen years before, when I was about to leave for Europe and no one, including myself, had any idea when I would be back; and in the early morning hours before my plane flight, my father asked that I forgive his "feet of clay." I hadn't the faintest idea what he was talking about. I had never thought his feet were anything but stone, because what I admired about him wasn't the fulfillment of any big ambitions but the small moments that few people witnessed, like at his brother's funeral, for instance, when he stood up to all the assembled aunts and cousins to comfort my dead uncle's ostracized, grief-stricken ex-wife. Now I suppose if there's anything I do regret not saying to him before he died it's how much I admired that moment.

Either that, or I'd have tried to tell him it never really mattered to me that he couldn't read my books. I assume this bothered him a lot more than it did me. He just didn't know what the hell I was talking about, any more than I knew what the hell that feet-of-clay stuff was, not to mention that I wasn't always all that sure myself what I was talking about in my books. I never thought it was all that important that I completely understand what I was saying, I knew the books came from some place more real to me than any literal understanding; and if my father could have read them that way, well, then I guess he wouldn't have been the person my father was. For him to have confronted that would have been to further confront, as he must have already done, the most mind-boggling part of being a parent, which is that even the child who comes from you is not ever wholly *of* you, that there's always a part of the child that is always beyond the genes or shared soul of any father and mother. What my father did understand was that this was my dream, to write these books, and that I had held on to that dream long past the point any sensible person would have. He may have also envied my plain dumb luck that I always knew what my dream was, when I don't think he was ever sure what his was, until those last fifteen years when he realized it was the life he had had, the wife, the son, and that no other dream was ever likely to have been better. Maybe he suspected that, in knowing my dream, I also knew something else, something he didn't. What I know now is that he knew something I didn't, and haven't yet found the wisdom for.

They seem so slight now, so insignificant, my very specific dreams compared to his vague ones. One writes first to find himself, then one writes to find the universe. One writes for wisdom: the writing is the road and the wisdom is the place to where the road is going. This remains true until later when, over the course of much writing bad or good, inconsequential or important, one has constructed a literary persona, the purpose of which then becomes its own self-perpetuation. Then you begin to suspect that only the persona is the place to where the road has been going—which means you have not been on the road to wisdom after all. You begin to suspect you've only been processing wisdom, as you've processed all your experience, as you've processed and used all the material of your life in order to prop up an identity, a shabby romantic image of yourself; and in the process you've missed everything. A few years ago I realized that while I had always written on my own terms, I had come to evaluate the worth of that work, and therefore my own worth, on the terms of others, and that not only was this corrupt, it was the very kind of contradiction from which insanity, the insanity of true lostness, is born. Faced with such a realization I was either going to, out of genius or courage, persist—or, out of genius or courage, desist altogether, disappearing like Rimbaud with nothing to say, although if *that* isn't a load of self-romanticizing horseshit, I don't what is. Fresh out of genius and running a tad low on courage, I've neither persisted nor desisted, which, whatever the dangling participle of life's sentence this has turned me into, has at least left me wondering; and brought me back to my father.

I wait for wisdom; and still wait. It may be a while. I live in the shadow of my own life. Having developed a literary persona, the writer inevitably reaches the point where the only real remaining test of integrity is whether he or she is willing to smash that persona and see what's left when the dust settles—with the terrifying possibility that nothing will be left. Now I tire of never being old, never being young, never being either child or man. I tire of a perpetual adolescence, without either childhood's purity and wonder—not to be confused with innocence, since children are the least innocent of creatures—or adulthood's weight and power. I was an old man in my youth and I feel adolescent in my aging, old before my time and immature after it. Even as I imagine death always hovering, I still haven't reached the moment when I can really imagine my own dying, which is what I've always assumed the moment of true wisdom to be, even as it might also be the moment of true madness, or even as it might be a leap of imagination beyond even a madman's ability to leap. I've been caught between the certain knowledge that my dark impulses are destructive, and the certain dread that it's a collapse into a premature kind of death not to sometimes follow those impulses into sensual experience. I wait for wisdom and the moment when my life is revealed to have ballast, and in the waiting I'm left believing, fifty-one days out of a hundred, that God exists—or at least that life exists on the level of Mystery—but also just suspicious enough, just faithless enough that, in my suspicion and faithlessness, I'm bound to proceed through the remaining forty-nine on the awful, nearly unspeakable assumption that there is no mystery at all, only molecules.

In the passenger seat next to me, though, on the long drive back across the Valley, my father makes the case for mystery. On the long drive back through the wind-washed night, he doesn't have to say a thing, he only has to be there in the seat next to me: it isn't the first time. He's been there before, on other nights. I've dreamed of him often; in all but the first dream, I never had any doubt they were anything but dreams, dreams in which we were together again, back before he died. But in that first dream, not long after he died, I was quite aware he was dead, and we argued a long time about whether it was a dream at all. My father won the argument, the way the ghosts of Indians on the road back to Hollywood win their argument, making the case for their own mystery, before they scatter.

❦

Then the ghosts of my beautiful dead city scattered. One morning Abdul's apartment was empty, except for the trash strewn across the hardwood floors he was so proud of; he and his pregnant golden Indiana girlfriend cleared out in the middle of the night, beneath the wrathful surveillance of the Hamblin's female tenants and under cover of a darkness that peers through the still unrepaired gash in the hallway ceiling. Veroneek sold Network Vs. and took off for Oregon, along with Joe the wolf who is possessed by the soul of a man. Shale moved his family back to Boston by way of New York, or New York by way of Boston, and Dr. Billy got a position at a university in Iowa teaching a course on Sex Addicts in American Literature, where to his dread everyone will feel compelled to call him doctor. His wife Jane is writing a novel.

I think Dr. Billy, and I know Shale and Ventura, had a fleeting hope the situation at the newspaper would become so galvanized one way or another that something radical would happen, a palace coup or a general uprising on behalf of justice. All of them are too smart to have placed much stock in such a scenario, but they couldn't help hoping anyway. I still get messages on my phone machine from people on the staff. A lot of the calls that come in are hang-ups, the line disconnected long seconds after the machine begins recording, some mysterious presence hanging in the air wondering what to say or whether I'm really not there. Word has it that the mood of the paper is ghastly, and that Freud N. Johnson walks around the Egyptian Theater like a dead man. I'd be a liar if I said I didn't find this satisfying, but beyond that I can't say I give the whole thing much thought at all. It almost never crosses my mind. It's pretty clear that, for me anyway, something is over.

Ventura has decided to go back to Texas, and there apparently isn't anything I can or should do to dissuade him, any more than I could dissuade Viv from going to Holland. He is planning to take a circuitous route there, the exact course of which is known only to the universe or the moons of Jupiter or the tides of Bora Bora, which he trusts will be divulged to him when the universe is good and ready. Ventura might be audacious enough to take on the Twentieth Century, but not the universe. He wants to tour the secret volcanoes of America and stand at their rims long past the dusk, staring into the craters. God help us when he divines their lava, deciphers their embers; he'll be damned impossible to live with. I worry about him. Of all of us his courage in quitting the paper was perhaps greatest, and now he is at the loosest of its consequences' ends. I want to shake him out of it; but Ventura does his own shaking. When the day comes for him to leave, we share a shot of tequila and, when I can't stand the tears in his eyes, I turn away, and pretend that when I turn back he won't be gone.

The sun has stopped hurtling toward Los Angeles, having come as close as it wants to get. The city swelters. The Santa Ana winds whip through and everything is as crisp as the kiss of a fallen live wire. The distant trees beyond my windows blow slow and soundless as though to a gust from the center of the earth, so primordial that its roar still rattles around the deepest passages of the planet. The sky is a heat-shimmered blue, unviolated by smoke as it hasn't been in a decade, none of the rings having burned since before the rain. After the rains passed, everything was soaked for weeks and then everything bloomed, grass grew, and then everything went very dry, so that one errant flicker of fire feels like it could set ten miles blazing in seconds. From billboard to billboard I see the Red Angel of L.A. peeling away in long strips that curl and hang, until all that's left of her are the vertical remains, as though behind the bars of a jail cell; all the billboards of the city taken together might add up to one whole Justine. All the time zones have subdivided into smaller and smaller time zones, until everyone is his or her own time zone and the city is alive with time, a maelstrom of a million uncoordinated clocks all set at different hours and minutes. Out of the dark, after the sun falls, through the hole in the roof of the hotel hallway, the movies come at me one after another on mysterious airwaves, never stopping until I'm the one who's hysterical: *Touch of Evil, Johnny Guitar, Sweet Smell of Success, Point Blank, Pretty Poison, Mondo Topless, Cutter's Way, Lifeforce, Nightdreams, Wax, Twin Peaks Fire Walk With Me, The Last Temptation of Christ.* . . .

Their images fill a life that has apparently begun to vanish. I got two interesting letters just the other day. The first was a confession from K in Virginia. She's been alluding to this approaching confession for some time now, it's been on the tip of her tongue in the midst of a long fragmented story she's been telling me about a love affair she's having with a prison guard. Since I somehow seem to have missed the beginning of this story, I'm not clear whether the prison is real or metaphorical. It may not matter because, as K puts it, "it could be that nothing I tell you is true," though I don't know whether that's part of the confession or a preemptive denial, undoing the confession before it's made. For a while I thought the confession was going to be that she's not beautiful; and indeed when she hints at this—"It's ironic, you wouldn't look at me 2X"—I'm ashamed that she believes this matters to me, that I've somehow made her believe it matters and my shallowness is so transparent. But that isn't the confession either. The confession is this: "I'm a fraud," she writes. "Not in things I've said necessarily, but in how I first got your attention. I had been given, as a gift, a letter you once wrote to someone else ten or fifteen years ago. In this letter you listed several areas of concern that seemed to be on your mind. So I decided to address those same concerns, one by one, and in the same order, so that, in effect, you were receiving a letter from yourself. This was the password into the secret room. When you received my first card, you thought you had found someone on your wavelength. You had, and it was you."

Along with this confession from K, the second piece of mail I received was a package from Shale (a New York postmark). It accompanied an article that ran in a magazine back east about what had happened at the newspaper. "A good piece," Shale wrote, "the writer got most everything right; but there's something I should tell you ..." and then, as delicately as possible, went on to explain that the piece mentioned—and quoted—every writer who quit except me. It was curious. Well, no, it wasn't just curious: it was breathtaking, how irrelevant I actually was in the scheme of things, so uniquely insignificant that my resignation alone among all the others was not worth noting. And then I could only wonder: was it moral vanity on my part after all, to have quit? Was the point of my gesture simply to catch someone's attention? Perhaps I had really begun to vanish long ago, like the lights blinking out on me in Central Park, without knowing it, my solipsism too consuming to notice my own vanishing until I was now presented with this incontrovertible evidence, the void of my name. Perhaps it was that, after I distanced myself from memory, memory now distanced itself from me. I began pulling out old newspapers. I began pulling out all the issues where my reviews had run, to reassure myself of something I had probably never been assured of in the first place: and that was when I saw it, or, more accurately, saw what there was not to see. I couldn't find a single review I had written. "I'm sure I had something in *this* issue," I was babbling to myself, the front room frantically strewn with newspaper: but there was nothing in any of them. Nor an entry in any table of contents. I checked the staff box; I wasn't listed there either. Had they inadvertently omitted me some time ago, and I just hadn't realized? There was no indication at all I had ever written for the newspaper, with a single exception; and I don't have to tell you, do I, which particular piece *that* was.

I called Viv. She was living in a suburb of Amsterdam, searching the Dutch marshes for the exact coordinates where to erect her Memoryscope pointing at Los Angeles. It was midnight; she answered sleepily, eight o'clock in the morning on her side. We talked from the opposite sides of consciousness, hers the side of waking, mine the side of somnambulism. I think I called to prove to myself I was still here, but talking to Viv just proved to me she was there, and made me crave her all the more, tormented both by how close she sounded and how far away. So everything I did and everywhere I went for the next few days all I could think of was Viv, in the market and at the café down the street, walking along the Strip and staring at the old St. James Club outside my window. It was Viv I was thinking of the afternoon at the car wash, when I was watching the two Mexican guys dry my car, wiping down the fenders and tires; in the distant hills to the east was the first fire I had seen since back before Christmas. I couldn't quite place which ring was burning, it looked farther than Silverlake, over around the empty high-rises of Downtown northwest of the Glow Lofts; and I even said to another guy standing there waiting for his car too: I guess they're burning again—and he said no, rumor had it this was not an *official* fire but rather accident or arson, what with everything so dry; and I was watching the smoke, my mind following its circles up into the sky, when it occurred to me, I'm not sure exactly when, that only one of the two Mexican guys was actually drying the car, the other wasn't doing anything but walking around looking at it, and that he was quite well dressed for a car-wash attendant. In fact I was thinking he was probably the best dressed car-wash attendant I had ever seen, when he blithely got into the car. The first attendant looked at him blankly, with no real alarm; and it was just about the time the well dressed guy in the driver's seat was turning the key in the ignition that I finally got out of my chair and began walking toward him, a message now having finally, lazily blurted across my brain: *This guy who's starting your car right now does not work for the car wash.* I was at a dead sprint by the time he was pulling my car out the driveway, and I was running alongside pounding on the roof as he hit the gas up Hollywood Boulevard. He was already flipping the ashtrays, raising and lowering the power windows, fine-tuning the bass and treble on the stereo and generally enjoying all the snazzy accessories of his brand new *clean* car, adjusting the rearview mirror for a particularly good view of me running helplessly after him.

In retrospect it wasn't such a big thing. People get their cars stolen in L.A. all the time, and worse. My running alongside the car as he was driving off, trying to get the door open and my murderous hands on him, wasn't the smartest thing I've ever done; for all I know he might have pulled out a gun and shot me. Far more serious to me was that, as it happened, I had a lot of personal effects in the car, clothes and tapes and books and papers, though I don't really remember why. It was as though I had consolidated my whole life in one place just for the taking. At any rate, I plummeted. Whereas in any other circumstances the theft of the car would have been just a colossal drag, now it took on an unbearable weight after everything else—Viv leaving, quitting the paper, the dispersion of the Cabal. And then all the other things. The other things that had been there all along, the slow vanishing of my life one thing at a time, one person at a time, one moment at a time and one dream at a time. I lay at home in bed watching the fauna and spores grow out of my walls and ceiling, feeling at the same end I felt in that dream when suicide was not so much a radical emotional act as a sensible one, one that would get me in sync with the true status of my life. That's all the theft of my car was, the last straw; in another frame of mind I would have absorbed it or taken it as a sign of something. But I wasn't in any frame of mind to take anything as a sign of anything, so I lay on the bed listening to hang-ups on my phone machine, silences so long and ominous that even the machine couldn't stand them, and began hanging up first.

The day after my car was stolen I was lying there on the bed—from time to time I think I must have been vaguely aware I could smell smoke, from somewhere out the window far away—when, with the fall of darkness, the phone machine clicked on again, once again to no voice on the other end; and I grabbed it. I'd had enough. It was time to let the world know who it was dealing with: a man who had had his car stolen from a car wash. But when I answered, right before I heard her voice, I was thrown back in memory by the sound of her breathing; I was in Berlin again, answering the phone in my hotel room in Savignyplatz. And then she said, in her slight German accent, "Can you smell the smoke?"

"What?"

"Can you smell the smoke?"

"Who is this?" I said, but I knew who it was.

"You know who it is."

"Yes, I can smell it."

"Do you know what it's from?"

"It's from the fire."

"Of course. But do you know what the *fire* is from. . . ."

"Are you all right?"

"It depends," said Jasper, "what you mean by all right." Her voice sounded hollow and strange. "In a way, I'm all right. In a way, I'm better than ever, I'm free. But in another way, you know, I guess it's not all right."

"What are you talking about?"

"I guess it's not really all right . . . you know. I mean, considering."

"Considering what?"

"Considering what I've done."

"What have you done?" I said. But I didn't have to travel very far around the dark side of my imagination to guess. I could see him standing on the stairs looking down at us in the dark, the night that Jasper, Viv and I were at her house.

"Help me," she said.

"Are you at your house?"

"Yes."

"Is your father . . . is your stepfather there?"

"Well . . . it depends what you mean. In a way, yes, he's here. Could you please come now?"

"No, I can't. I don't have a car. It was stolen yesterday. From a car wash," I added.

"I need you to come," she just said, in the same tone of voice.

"For me. It's not for him. There's nothing to do for him anymore. But before whatever happens next, it just seemed right that I should call you, of all people."

"Jasper—" I said, and she hung up. I put down the phone, picked it up again to call the police, but replaced the phone before I did. I checked the cash I had on hand which, with a little bartering with the cab driver, might be enough to get me to her house; how I would get back I'd worry about later. As I left the Hamblin the Santa Anas were blowing more fiercely than ever. Maybe it was just the hour but the city had never seemed so debased and deserted; I had the feeling the only ones left were Jasper and me and the cab driver, and maybe the asshole who stole my car, assuming he wasn't already half way up the coast with it. The Korean cab driver seemed agitated the minute I got in the taxi, and grew more so as we crossed town. The whole noisy night had turned itself inside out, the usual cacophony of alarms and helicopters blotted up into emptiness and only the wind coming through the taxi window and the sounds of running footsteps and cries in the dark that sounded neither human nor animal. Through the branches of the trees stripped by the Santa Anas I could see shutters banging and windows being closed to keep the night out; through the windshield ahead of us the sky was red from fire. Are they burning tonight? I asked the driver, but all he answered—he must have repeated it five times between Hollywood and the switching yard east of Downtown—was "Strange city tonight, strange city," and the way he said it I couldn't be sure if it was a coded message or just broken English. Half a mile from Jasper's house he refused to go further, glancing fearfully at the ravine of flames. I walked the rest of the way, crawling over railroad tracks and crossing the plain that surrounded the house, the dark form of which I could now see in the distance, a wood and steel stalagmite jutting up out of the wasteland, the dark form of Viv's Memoryscope just beyond that. At the time, the fire in the hills seemed far away.

The door to the car tunnel was open. I went in and every few feet called out. The front door of the house was open but there was no light on beyond it, and I kept calling Jasper's name. I went up the stairs to the second level, my legs so wobbly I could barely climb. Jasper was waiting in the large circular room lined with windows, seated in the black chair in the room's center. No lights were on but I could see her clearly in the light from the fire in the hills that had seemed far away just minutes before. Just beyond the windows, the long tank pool was dark. She was wearing the same simple dress she had worn at the filming of *White Whisper*; the room was hot and with one hand she kept pulling her hair up on top of her head to cool the back of her neck, while the other hand held a cigarette. She didn't appear crazy at all. She was very calm. She didn't even glance at me as I came in.

I was looking around. Whatever I expected, there was no sign of anything amiss. I wasn't sure if I was relieved or angry. "What's going on?" I said.

"Thank you for coming," she said calmly from the chair.

"What's happened?" I kept looking around me.

"What do you think has happened?" she flirted. I was paralyzed by this feeling of wanting to strangle her and wanting just to get out. Her face changed at this, and she said, "Don't leave. You can't leave." She added, "Please help me."

"You have to tell me what's happened," I snapped. I kept looking for him. "Where's your father?"

"Please help me," she kept saying. She stood up and walked

210

toward me in the dark, through the red light of the fire through the window. "Right now you can help me most by not asking too many questions. There will be lots of questions later. Right now what I need most is someone who won't ask lots of questions, who will just be here with me awhile before everything changes." I crossed the room to the windows. Outside, Viv's Memoryscope was silhouetted in the flames, which seemed to become less distant by the moment. "I could smell the smoke this morning," she said, coming up behind me, "the minute I woke. I could smell it with the break of day. It's Viv's smoke."

I turned back to her, away from the window. "What?"

"Did I show you my scrapbook?" she said. "That night you were here? Yes."

"You showed Viv."

"I showed Viv." There was the whistle of a train; but it sounded like a shriek. "I don't think Viv liked my scrapbook."

"I don't want to stay here," I said. "If something has happened, you need to call the police, and if you want I'll stay with you until they come. But otherwise I don't want to stay."

"It was you in Berlin."

"No," I said.

"Yes," she insisted evenly, "it was." The train shrieked again. I turned from her and went outside onto the patio where the pool was. I peered over the wall.

I was astounded to see the train rumbling in from the north toward the switching yard. It wasn't moving especially fast or slow, but its whistle was increasingly shrill and strangled. The caboose was on fire, and the fire was moving up the train very fast, car by car; like a snake on fire the blazing train coiled across the dry field where the bloom of the rains had already turned to kindle. Everything behind the train went up in flames, and it appeared to be heading straight toward us when it jumped the track and skidded for the Memoryscope. Stopping just yards from the sculpture, it toppled onto its side in a blinding white din, and the field exploded as though soaked in gasoline.

Embers sailed toward us over the wall. They caught on the tower of the house and in their light I almost thought I saw a motionless human form stuck on the tower's pinnacle. One part of the house after another was burning, and I don't remember whose idea the bathysphere was; since I was becoming more and more panicked it might have actually been Jasper's, which seems remarkably cool-headed on her part. But it was obviously the only place we had any chance before we were overwhelmed by fire, and now it bobbed in the water as though having been placed there all along for just this moment and purpose. Without saying anything she stepped briskly around the flickering black water of the pool; and when I had clambered down into the module behind her, groping in the dark, she pulled the hatch closed. It was pitch black inside. In the dark the faint outline of the dials and meters looked like ancient etchings on the wall of a cave. Through the sphere's glass porthole we could see the red sky above as we sank to the bottom of the pool; a huge red bubble floated up from beneath us. For a second it enveloped us, and then disappeared toward the surface.

In the windows and glass hatch the water shimmered bright red, and I could see the flames sweeping overhead. The question was whether, escaping incineration, we were just going to cook to death. Even with the air cranked to maximum, the heat from the water of the pool came through, and without a thought Jasper ripped off her dress. In the fiery red glow her body was as absurdly fecund as ever, like a seed about to burst. Soon I peeled off my own clothes. We'd been lying there several minutes on opposite sides of the small compartment, faint from the rising heat and the dwindling oxygen, when she said, not long before I passed out, "Tell me. . . ."

"What?" I murmured.

"I know it was you on the telephone in Berlin," I heard her say from the other side of the bathysphere. "But . . . that night . . . it *was* you who came to the hotel, wasn't it?"

"Why?"

"The last time you were here, you said——"

"Forget it," I whispered.

"You said . . . what did you say? You said, how did I know it was the same man. How did I know the man in the hotel room was the same as the man who was on the telephone."

"We shouldn't talk," I croaked.

"But just tell me," she said. "I mean, why did you say that? It *was* you who came. It was. Right?"

"Yes, it was," I said. Maybe she knew it was a lie and maybe she didn't. Lying to a woman isn't easy; she knows when you sound funny. And it would have been too much to explain, there under the flames, that between the phone call and the rendezvous in the hotel I had died in Berlin, though not for the last time, and perhaps not even for the first time. Each time you die, the old skin falling away to reveal someone else, it's not such an easy question to answer, how much remains of the man who once was. So even if I had made it to our rendezvous, it still isn't so certain that the man in the hotel room would have been the same as the man who was on the telephone. But I wasn't going to explain all that now, even if I was naked with her in a bathysphere at the bottom of an old tanker full of water, everything above us burning. I wasn't going to use up the last bit of the air we shared to tell her all that. It wouldn't have mattered, and it wouldn't have been what she wanted to know anyway.

Right before I passed out, I suddenly understood what she had meant about the smoke. Slumped across the bottom of the bathysphere, staring up through the glass hatch, I suddenly realized what she meant when she said she had smelled it with the first break of day. Whether she was crazy with her demons or crazy with the truth that night, or crazy with both, I don't know; so I can't be sure that it was really the Memoryscope that started the fire. I can't be sure it was the first ray of dawn, coming over the eastern hills, that cracked the mirrored length of the Memoryscope and ignited the fire at its cross hairs, in the hills of the distant ravine at the flashpoint where memory meets amnesia. But right before I passed out, staring up through the glass hatch, I saw streak across the sky not the light of fire, not the light of electricity, not the light of combustion, but the light of the last memory Viv's sculpture ever broadcast; and naturally it was the memory that explained everything. It was a memory from so far back in my life as to have been seemingly beyond remembering; but there it was, through the glass hatch of the bathysphere in the red sky above me: the first word I ever stuttered. When I saw it, just before my eyes closed, I murmured, "Of course," and I'm almost sure I heard Jasper whisper back, "G-G-Goodbye."

But when I opened my eyes, the memory had vanished again. I don't know how long I was unconscious; it was certainly a while, because when I regained consciousness the bathysphere was floating back on the surface of the water and the hatch was open, and the sky was not black or red but the pale gray of morning. I could still smell the smoke from the smoldering house and the fire that had moved south. The fireman and paramedic who revived me gave me a blanket to wrap around myself, and I was as wobbly climbing out of the bathysphere as I had been climbing the steps of the house when I arrived the night before. Up above, a cop was waiting for me; the charred house was crawling with cops and firemen. If there had been a human form in the tower the night before, there wasn't anymore; there wasn't a tower anymore, just a black stubble. Wouldn't you know that the Memoryscope came through it all, though it didn't exactly have the same shiny luster, scorched black as it was. I was led by the cops through the house and down the stairs, and out the car tunnel to a van where they let me put my clothes on, and then to an unmarked squad car that waited among half a dozen cop cars and several fire engines and ambulances. One squad car was pulling away, and I thought in the back seat I briefly saw Jasper. But I couldn't be sure, and she was nowhere else to be seen, and I didn't see her again.

◌◦◦◦◌

I was down at police headquarters several hours, almost all of it waiting for something to happen. Then a couple of detectives came around and asked some questions. They asked what I was doing at the house and what I had seen there, and how I knew Jasper. I told them exactly what had happened, from the phone call on, summarizing the gist of it while leaving out my own suspicions. They asked if I had an intimate relationship with Jasper and I said no; I wasn't sure exactly what they meant by intimate, and decided to take a chance and leave Berlin out of it. They pointed out that the two of us had been naked in the bathysphere: "It was hot," I explained. I was surprised they didn't press me on it. As I look back, they must have known everything they wanted to know, and nothing I was telling them contradicted anything. At the end, when they said I was free to leave, the investigating detective in charge added, "By the way. Did you report a car stolen a day or two ago?"

"From a car wash," I said abjectly.

Five or ten minutes later when they finished laughing, the guy in charge said, "Well, we have it." They had found it on Cahuenga between Sunset and Hollywood, a mile and a half from where it had been stolen. It was still warm when the police got there, apparently abandoned only moments before by whoever had been driving; inside had been a knife and a streak of blood. They gave me a ride over to where the car was impounded, and after signing for it I was led through a maze of several hundred other cars. The car was pretty well trashed, just this side of undriveable. The side was caved in, the right front fender dented so that it barely obstructed the wheel. Driving it off the lot, I was sorry the detective had told me about the knife and the blood. I actually thought about taking it to a car wash, but that seemed to be tempting fate.

Instead I just drove with all the windows down, to blow the evil spirits out. Everything that had been in the car was gone, of course, the clothes and books and papers probably pitched into a side alley somewhere, and all my tapes discarded too; the musical taste of someone dippy enough to get his car stolen right before his eyes at a car wash was probably a little too quaint for guys who drive around all night knifing people. In the stereo was the only tape the thieves apparently found too fascinating to toss: my cassette of the phone messages I received after quitting the paper. So I drove on listening to the messages over and over, heading for Downtown and passing the seared ruins of Jasper's house and Viv's Memoryscope, and then on down the highway toward San Bernardino, all the way to Fontana before turning north into the Cajon Pass. An hour later I was in Victorville and an hour after that Barstow. In a phone booth in Barstow I called a woman in Texas whose number Ventura had given me in case I needed to leave him a message. I told her to let him know the next time he checked in that I was heading for Vegas, and when I got there I would call her back for any message he wanted to leave me. I could stand to see him.

I don't know how many of the evil spirits I lost in the Mojave, but it wasn't enough of them. An hour and a half after Barstow I crossed the state line, and a little less than an hour after that I was in Downtown Vegas, off the Strip, where I checked into one of the casinos there. Even in seedy Downtown Vegas, the casino valet did not look very impressed with my bashed-up car. I telephoned the woman in Texas again, who confirmed that Ventura had indeed called from somewhere in Monument Valley, got my message and was heading for Vegas, where he had a reservation at another hotel nearby. He would meet me the next night at the Golden Garter. I drew every cent I still had out of an automated teller and went and bought myself some underwear and a new shirt and toiletries, since I had nothing like that with me, and then wandered around Downtown the rest of the night playing blackjack and winning just enough to keep playing and wandering and drinking. On a corner some guy handed me one of those flyers that has pictures of beautiful naked women with phone numbers, so you can call them up and have them come to your room and if they bear the remotest resemblance to the picture you can pay them a hundred dollars to get naked for you and perhaps fuck you for several hundred dollars more. I called one and when she said hello, I hung up.

The next night I waited at the Golden Garter. While watching the strippers I got into a fragmented conversation with a guy I thought was about sixty years old until I saw him better in the light, which revealed that beneath his white hair he was probably closer to my age. He was a nice enough guy, kind of sweet in the purely unvarnished way of someone who has a screw loose. Soon I was waiting for Ventura to show up just to extricate me from the situation; but instead another guy came along who looked like he stepped out of one of those old Fifties or Sixties mob or private eye movies, very dapper—the last guy I knew this dapper, before the one who stole my car that is, was Abdul. Everything about him was sharp from his tailored clothes to his shoes, in striking contrast to the dimwit with the white hair, who it became clear was the older brother that the younger one looked out for. After that a couple of other guys walked in who looked like they were about to shoot up the joint. I was beginning to think I should get out.

"You should get out," the well dressed private-eye said.

"I'm waiting for someone," I explained uneasily.

"Oh. He's not coming."

"What?"

"Guy named Ventura? He's not coming."

Amazed, I finally managed to sputter, "You know Ventura?"

"Let's say we cross paths now and then, whenever he's in Vegas. Anyhow I have a message for you: he's not coming." He went on, "His car blew up on the Arizona highway, somewhere in the desert."

I was flabbergasted. "Is he all right?"

"Yeah, he's all right."

"But is he *all right*? He's *very* attached to that car."

"Now that you mention it, he sounded oddly serene when I talked to him." He said it like the sort of guy who didn't say the word *serene* more than once or twice in a lifetime, not to even mention the word *oddly*. "Anyway," he looked over his shoulder at the other two guys near the doorway, "you really should get out of here now."

So I got out. I went back to the hotel room and called the woman in Texas, getting no answer, and then tried to call Viv in Amsterdam, also getting no answer. I knew then I was going to do one of two things, which was call the girl in the flyer I had hung up on earlier, or slip out of the hotel without paying my tab and get in the car and keep going up the same highway I had come in on. I don't know how long it was before I crossed the corner of Arizona that leads up to Utah. I was well into my tape of phone messages for the umpteenth time before I impulsively ejected it from the tape player and threw it out the same window all my other tapes had gone out, five or six hundred miles back in Los Angeles. At some point I pulled over to the side of the road and slept a bit; I woke to the sun coming up over what I presumed was the distant southern tail of the Rockies, the rocks of Utah glimmering an iridescent rust. I drove on.

Somewhere north of St. George, in the middle of nowhere, I was chased for a while by two maniacs in a black sportscar. They pulled up inches behind me and stayed with me for thirty miles; at one point I suddenly swerved to the side of the road and stopped, and then took off again as fast as I could when they stopped too, a couple of hundred yards ahead. I kept trying to shake them like this until they finally drew up alongside me, looked me over very carefully and, apparently determining I wasn't whoever they had thought I was, shook their heads and then sped on, leaving me in their dust. An hour outside Salt Lake City I got a speeding ticket. I was sure the cop was mistaken when he said I had been going ninety-five miles an hour; surveying the damage of my car, however, only seemed to confirm his suspicions. I tried to tell him about the psychos stalking me in the black sportscar; he couldn't have been less impressed. An hour later I was stopped for speeding again: "I just got a ticket!" I almost sobbed to the second cop, who looked at me like I was a mental case. Nearing the border of Idaho I finally checked into the last motel room in a little town where every other motel had a No Vacancy sign in front. The motel room reeked of the sweet smell of insecticide and before I crossed the street to the local steak house, where I had a filet and salad and three straight vodkas, I opened the window to air the room out. When I came back after dinner I found the room swarming with bugs. A cloud of gnats had blown in through the open window, attracted to the bathroom light, and a strange sense of hysteria welled up inside me as I closed the door of the bathroom trying to shut the bugs off from the bedroom. I took off my clothes and got into bed, and lying there in the dark I felt gnats covering my entire body.

I knew I wasn't actually covered with gnats. But it didn't matter that I knew it, I could feel them anyway; I could feel them from my feet to my chest, crawling all over me. I kept telling myself I wasn't really covered with gnats but it didn't matter how often I said it, I didn't believe it. That was when a black wave of fear came over me, because I knew at this particular moment I was losing my mind. It was the most peculiar and terrifying thing, to hear the arguments of my rational mind and know they were true and still reject them, to bear cool, almost analytical witness to my own breakdown. My psyche simply did not believe my brain. I was seized with an almost overpowering impulse to get out of bed, dress, jump in the car and speed down the highway in exhaustion, as I had been speeding ever since Vegas, piling up speeding tickets because I could not make myself slow down. And I knew—there wasn't a doubt in my head—that if I succumbed to this impulse I would run the car straight into the side of a mountain. I knew without any doubt whatsoever that I was moments across the line from sanity and moments this side of killing myself; and yet it was everything I could do to resist the impulse anyway. There in the dark, crawling with gnats I knew were not really there, everything came rushing back to me, the onslaught of memory and all my failures; and for the first time in my life I felt something that was unique to me: a loneliness to which I had vainly prided myself as being untouchable. I didn't have any doubt I was moments away from this being the last night of my life.

I turned on the light. I threw back the sheet and looked at my naked body for a long time, pointing out to myself over and over again that it was not covered with gnats. After an hour I finally began to believe myself; and finally I pulled the sheet back up, turned off the light, and went to sleep.

The next morning I got back in the car and continued on up the highway. That afternoon I got another speeding ticket, which I accepted as jauntily as the cop delivered it, since this was a particularly ridiculous ticket; this time I was quite certain I hadn't been going a mile over eighty. I was on a small road out in the Idaho countryside, because the map said it was the only road to where I was going, and just before dusk I reached Craters of the Moon, and the line of cars backed up for the festival.

I waited in the line for a little over an hour before I finally reached the entrance booth, only to realize I hadn't brought with me the letter of invitation that I received the day I quit the paper. But the guard had my name on a list and let me pass anyway, and I cruised through the black craters and rolling charred valleys where everyone was waiting for the film to start, a lunar drive-in of a thousand cars stretched before me. People were sitting on their hoods facing a huge white sail that had been hoisted from a mast in the earth. I parked my car and got out. Darkness fell.

The film was projected onto the white sail. Now and then the film would fill with a wind blowing from Canada through the craters; we were a black ghost ship called *Marat* sailing the Idaho plains. There was no sound from either the film or the audience until the end, which was greeted with a rising, sustained roar. I was relieved the movie was nothing like I imagined it. Somewhere between my review and this moment it had become its own thing. Afterward a tiny old man stepped in front of the blank white sail and, in the lights, merely waved; and as the people and cars were leaving I wandered toward the screen, drifting against the tide of the exiting migration. Just as I was beginning to think I was wasting my time, I saw him, surrounded by a crowd of festival officials and photographers flashing their cameras, and I stood there a while watching, ten feet away, only because I wanted to get a look at him.

God, he had to have been a hundred. But he seemed as sharp in spirit as he was feeble in body, basking in all the attention even as he looked like he had been around a little too long to take it all too seriously. And then in all the hubbub, there in the dark where

I wouldn't have thought he could possibly see me, he saw me. He turned, looked right at me and smiled expectantly, as though he was waiting for me to say something. I came closer and one of the officials stepped up to keep me back, but the old man signaled to let me through. People stopped for a moment, thinking he was about to say something and wanting to hear it; but I was the one who spoke. "Everything is gone from my life," I told him. "Everyone has left. And I don't know what I'm supposed to do anymore. And I've driven all the way from Los Angeles just so you could tell me."

For a moment I thought he didn't hear me. For a moment he turned back to all the other people trying to talk to him; but then he raised his hand and—

And Adolphe Sarre turns back to me with the same smile, no longer expectant but fulfilled, and at a volume I should not be able to hear but which I can make out perfectly, all he says is: "Embarrass yourself." And we look at each other for one more moment before the crowd swallows him up.

I return to the car, get in and, at the first sane speed I've driven in three days and a thousand miles, head back the direction I came, the perfect Stuttering Fool of the American Tarot.

∽✠∾

I cross the Idaho–Utah line and I don't stop, because even if I had the money for a motel room, I'm not stopping anyway. Out of utter fatigue I pull over just shy of Nevada and sleep an hour, and then continue, passing Vegas a little before noon. A little after noon I'm back in California, Station 3 just beginning to filter in at the far end of the radio, and in a daze I take myself on into Los Angeles, nearly seventeen hours after leaving Craters of the Moon. Far past exhaustion, far past adrenaline, without a reason for being back, without a single reason to take me across one black ring after another into the bull's-eye of Hollywood and then through the Black Passages on the other side, through Beverly Hills and out along the border of Black Clock Park into the Palisades, I pull my car off Sunset Boulevard and drive up to the same bluff where I went the morning after Viv and I kidnapped Sahara from the Cathode Flower, just in time to see the sun fall into the sea.

⌖

From the bluff I have the same view of the whole bay, the smoking ruins of Malibu to the north and, to the south, the paramilitary outposts of Palos Verdes. At sea the hundreds of Chinese junks that sail out this time each month depart with their mystery cargo.

Listen. I'm going to try one more time. I don't promise anything will come of it, or that I won't try to put it off for as long as possible, or that in the meantime I may not have to do something sensible first, like find Viv for instance. I don't promise that the deep fault line that runs from my psyche through my brain out my front door and down the street won't run all the way from L.A. to America and beyond, all the way from memory to the moment and back, splitting me up the middle and leaving half of me on one side and half of me on the other. Not far from this very bluff where I am now is the beach where I once told a

224

woman about talking to myself; actually I can almost see the very place, right down there. Now, just for a while, we're going to pretend that I'm talking to myself again, like I used to. Now, just for a while, we're going to pretend—don't take this personally—that you're not here at all. Most of the best things I've ever said, the most fluid, stutterless, *sonorous* things, were to myself, and now I'm going to try one more time to say everything I can find in me that might be worth saying, and hope that whatever I find in me to say is only the road, and not the place to where the road is going. And then when I'm finished, perhaps I'll be finished for good. There's always the off-chance that, from another bluff, I'll actually be able to see the place to where the road is going and that, having seen it, I'll find that nothing else needs to be said. But there's also the chance that, having seen it, I'll find something entirely new that needs to be said, something I never knew before that I could say. And then, having tried one last time, perhaps I will try once more.